My Life on a Plate

My Life on a Plate

India Knight

A Mariner Book

HOUGHTON MIFFLIN COMPANY

BOSTON • NEW YORK

First Mariner Books edition 2001

First published in England by Penguin Books Ltd.

For information about permission to reproduce selections
from this book, write to Permissions, Houghton Mifflin Company,
215 Park Avenue South, New York, New York 10003.

Visit our Web site: www.houghtonmifflinbooks.com.

Library of Congress Cataloging-in-Publication Data
Knight, India, date.
My life on a plate / India Knight
p.   cm.
ISBN 0-618-09397-4
ISBN 0-618-15444-2 (pbk.)
1. Married women—Fiction. 2. Mothers and sons—
Fiction. 3. London (England)—Fiction. I. Title.
PR6061.N525 M9 2000
823'.82—dc21   00-061320

Printed in the United States of America

Book design by Robert Overholtzer

QUM 10 9 8 7 6 5 4 3

The author is grateful for permission to quote from
"Comment," copyright 1926, copyright © renewed 1954
by Dorothy Parker, from *The Portable Dorothy Parker.*
Used by permission of Viking Penguin, a division
of Penguin Putnam Inc.

FOR MY MOTHER

Oh life is a glorious cycle of song,
A medley of extemporanea;
And love is a thing that can never go wrong;
And I am Marie of Romania.

—DOROTHY PARKER

one

WHAT SHOULD HAPPEN IS, I should somehow catch my reflection in a mirror, or a shop window, fifty or so pages in, and describe myself to you that way. Seems a bit contrived to me, that method, besides which, if I catch my reflection in shop windows, I tend to scream with horror, rather than tip my head to one side and make measured, composed observations. Also, I always want to know what people look like right at the start, don't you? You'd feel pretty peeved if you discovered, much later on, that I was a psychopathic two-ton Tessie with flat feet and a moustache, or—worse—some hateful, eating-disordery twig that wafts around in Prada smelling of sick.

So let's get things straight. I don't smell of sick. (That's my friend Amber, whom you'll meet later. Her hobbies are bulimia and self-help books. My hobby is being compassionate.) And I don't weigh two tons, although, as a ripe size 16, I'm hardly what you'd call frail and reedy either. What else? Five nine, dark hair, green eyes—oh look, I'm sounding all sexy, which isn't quite right. Let's see. If you asked Kate, my mother, she would shake her head very sadly, as if I were an especially precious kitten that had died in tragic circumstances, and tell you I've 'let myself go *disgustingly*'. And I suppose she would be right. I mean, I've got the man, the house, the children: why not celebrate by tucking into a doughnut or two of a morning? Or an apricot Danish, or indeed a whole tube of Pringles . . . As a consequence, I favour elasticated waists and loose tops, although I have a sneaky liking for vulgar shoes and organza (which I try to curb, as nobody wants to look like White Trash Slut Mum at the PTA meetings). The best way I can think of describing myself is: we're not talking control pants yet, but we're not going to pretend that they haven't struck us as being a pretty damned handy kind of a garment either.

My name is Clara, which is quite pretty, and my surname is Hutt, which isn't, although it enables me to think of myself as Jabba the Hutt in my more self-loathing moments. This is useful. I have two children, Charlie, who is six, and Jack, who is three. I have a husband, Robert, who is a mystery (does anybody actually *know* what goes on in their husband's head, or is it just me?) but quite attractive. I have a part-time job as a magazine writer, a big house and nice clothes, and friends that don't smell of sick as well as some that do. I am thirty-three. And some days I wake up with the sneaky feeling that my life isn't all it should be.

In the current climate, you probably want to know how I Got My Man. I do feel quite pleased with myself, sometimes, actually. I look at my friend Tamsin, thirty-four, single and desperate, and feel a warm glow of intense smuggery. Sometimes, though, I am so overwhelmed with jealousy — I can't remember the last time I was out all night, drinking martinis and flirting with strangers — that I feel compelled to initiate lectures, masquerading as conversations, about all the things that might go wrong if one were — perfectly hypothetically, of course — trying to have a child past the age of thirty-five. This is because, despite external appearances, I am a) on the childish side and b) not very nice.

Getting my man: why, the trick is to be young and attractive. No, not really. The trick is not to look. Robert and I were twenty-five when we got married, which is comparatively young these days, and I weighed three stone less and was a bit of a minx, which helped. I can say it, now that I am an Old Married Lady, with my minxdom very much behind me—rather like my cellulite. I don't know quite what happened. We met, we fell in love, we got married. It helps not to be desperate, as I'm so fond of telling Tamsin in my meaner moments.

Anyway, eight years! Isn't that amazing? And I haven't strayed. Well, I haven't got naked. I kissed someone I used to go out with, at a party, two years ago, but I don't think that counts. Does it? It was only a peck, though it was pecking with intent. I try not to think about it too often. Married women pecking exes with intent is like opening a tiny window and letting in a shaft of light. People in my position really oughtn't to do it. Or think about why they might have wanted to.

My mother is on the phone. It's Robert's birthday next week and, she says, we 'need' to make a plan. What I would like to do is have dinner, in a restaurant, alone with my husband. Life is, sadly, not quite that simple. Mine is the kind of family that likes to involve itself intimately in all aspects of each other's lives. So on Robert's birthday we'll all be having dinner together: me, Robert, my mother, Kate, my half-sisters, Evie and Flo, their boyfriends and my stepbrother, Tom. We don't actually get on with each other terribly well—my sisters excepted—but, coming from the kind of family we do—'fragmented' is an adjective that springs to mind, as does 'dysfunctional'—we like the idea of these get-togethers, in theory if not in practice, and no one more so than my mother, the über-matriarch. The dinners often end in screaming rows, and someone always weeps. One of the things I like about

3

Robert is his composure in these situations, which he seems to find amusing rather than exhausting.

Anyway, heeeeeeere's Mummy:

'Clara?'

'Yes, Kate.'

'Don't sound so *resigned,* Clara. I am your mother.'

'I know, Kate. You are. Isn't it bliss?' I can't help myself with my mother. I just can't help it.

'It's bloody *discourteous* to put on that bored voice and be sarcastic.' Kate is getting agitated now. Kate is revving up.

'I'm not putting on any voice, Kate. Anyway, you are bliss.' And it's true. She is, sometimes. But not today.

'Christ, Clara. You're so sly and rude. Just like That Bloody Man. Your genes are coming out.' This is a reference to my father. Kate and he were married for six months. He was followed by two more husbands, and we're bracing ourselves for number four, who's bound to occur sometime soon. My genes are always coming out, apparently. Peepo!

'Kate. Robert's birthday. Dinner. Where shall we go? Have you spoken to Evie? Flo?'

There is a pause, during which Kate splutters.

'Do you think I have nothing better to do with my time than chase all of you all over London? *Do you think?* I have a very busy life. Very busy. The busiest, Clara. I can't be expected to be your social secretary.'

'I know, Kate. I am busy too—the boys. . .'

'The boys! Those poor children. Don't drag them into it.' My children are always 'poor' when Kate mentions them, presumably because they have me as a mother and not Kate. Many men Kate knows are 'poor' also, because they have the misfortune not to be married to her.

'Kate, it was your idea, the dinner. But fine. I'll round everyone up. Since you are so very busy, and since my life is one enormous vacuum.'

'Hola!' Kate suddenly shouts in my ear. 'Hola! Up here! In

the drawing room! Did you bring the Chanel pale pink? El pinky? Para los fingers? Clara, darling, Conchita's here for my manicure. Which reminds me. Your fingernails are a *disgrace*. I shudder to think of them. I practically *retch*. Call me later.' And she hangs up.

two

I THINK INCREASINGLY about Robert in the bathroom, where his mysteriousness is most apparent. Because my husband defecates in secret, like a very shy cat.

In eight years of marriage, I have never been aware of his going to the bathroom for evacuation purposes. I'm not complaining as such, obviously—I don't go a bundle on the whole companionable his 'n' hers windfest that some of our friends seem to enjoy ('Better out than in! Hahaha'). And I really wouldn't be at *all* happy if Robert decided to have a comfy dump while I was in the bath. It's not like I long to go into the bathroom and be hit by clouds of air freshener either.

But I still think it's odd, the felineness of the, ah, motions. I mean, *eight years*. Of course, this assumes he has motions— I wouldn't actually know. Perhaps he never poos. Perhaps he is biologically unique and I should point out his existence to the British Medical Association, and they could send men in white coats round to give him anal probes.

Sweeeeeeerve. See? Now I'm going to crash the car and we're all going to die. I mustn't think about anal probes at school-run time. If I crashed the car, children's lives would be lost for the sake of one bottom-thought. Not even a sweet, motherly bottom-thought involving, say, Pampers or nappy rash or Sudocrem. A *probe* thought: a bad thought.

Sometimes I feel completely isolated, going through the motions (as it were) behind glass. I don't know my husband at all, I suddenly realize, not for the first time, and the silent bathrooming is a symptom of my lack of knowledge. And while we're at it, why is my life like this? This morning I ran out of time, again, and am driving the car in my pyjama bottoms, again, with a sweater of Robert's on top, again. I have no make-up on (speaking of which, surely I'm too old for a shiny nose at 8.42 A.M. — I'm thirty-three, not fourteen). But here we are outside school and everybody else seems to be perfectly groomed. Again. There's Carmel — too much foundation, but at least she's matt. There's Jane, looking pristine in her snappy little suit and sexy-but-demure heels. She's lost so much weight she is beginning to look like a lesbian from the 1930s.

I'm going to have to get out of the car in my pyjamas any second.

There is Naomi, looking fresh-faced, though I know that no one looks like that first thing in the morning without the help of expertly applied *maquillage*.

'Muuuuuuummmeee!'

'Not now, darling, I'm parking.'

'Mummmmeeeeee!'

'I am parking.'

'MUUUUMM . . .'

'Stop it, Charlie. I am *parking*. Don't make me want to break your legs.'

See, that's another thing that's not quite right. I don't speak to my children like the mummies in books. I mean, Charlie is six and his language is already atrocious; not swearing so much as his vast panoply of hideous, faintly disturbing terms of abuse. 'You tiresome retard,' he says to his brother. 'The devil is going to come and spike your bottom with an enormous fork.' Or, to some hapless toddler who's come to play for the afternoon, 'GOD, you exasperating creature. WHAT IS IT? TALK, for God's sake. God GOD bloody GOD.' I have only myself to blame. I started off with the noble intention of not wanting to be one of those women who made stupid noises at their children. But now I keep forgetting that my children are small, and even I am appalled by the vigour of their language.

I park the car.

'What was it, Charlie?'

'I think I've got nits,' Charlie says. 'My head is all itchy.' He looks up at me imploringly, with his huge blue eyes. I don't know where my children's colouring—fair hair, light eyes—comes from. I feel like their ayah sometimes, or like a swarthy South American nanny.

Jack drops his teddy with excitement. 'With legs?' he asks. 'Nits with heads and legs and 'normous TEETH and tiiiiiny weeeeny willies?'

'Shut up, Jack,' Charlie says. 'You moronic toddler. You are a Barbie.'

'You are a *Sindy*,' Jack bats back without missing a beat. 'Nits! They will poo on your head!' He is beside himself with delight. 'They will plop all day. Urgh! Stinky.'

I feel so tired sometimes, after the school run, even though it's only 9 A.M.

This morning, with the hideous inevitability of Greek tragedy, is the morning Naomi chooses to corner me. She suggests we go for a coffee. Naomi has dropped off her three children—all of them immaculate in matching duffel coats, shiny shoes, beautifully ironed chinos (I once had to physically throw myself on top of Charlie, landing on his mouth, as he was telling Linus, Naomi's eldest, 'My mummy told my daddy you're dressed like a poof'). Naomi is examining her French manicure by the gate, waiting for me. Knowing her—and I do, too well—she is secretly doing her pelvic-floor exercises. Hup-two-three-four, and hooooold. She has had a terror of postpartum incontinence ever since a woman at her NCT class explained that sometimes she leaked when she laughed or sneezed. As a result, Naomi herself always looks slightly uncomfortable when she laughs, because she is so busy fretting about 'accidents'.

'Clara! Darling! Don't you look *fun!* Pyjamas again, eh? What's that on your leg?'

'Jam. We were late,' I mutter ungraciously, cursing my mother for her absurd dawn-chorus phone calls, and then cursing myself for pretending we'd be at all organized even if she hadn't called.

'We nearly were too,' Naomi says, not, I suspect, remotely truthfully. 'I made waffles for breakfast and we got a little bit delayed.'

Naomi's breakfasts are legendary: home-baked rolls, waffles, pancakes, three kinds of freshly squeezed juice . . . No treasure of hers is going to school on lumpy Ready Brek and chocolate milk. I know about Naomi and the breakfasts—laid at the table, properly, not grabbed on the hoof—just like I know about Naomi and the facials and the bikini waxes, and the permanent diet and the highlights every fortnight, and I shouldn't really mind, but this morning I do. How can I be friends with a woman who snacks on kiwis, for God's sake?

'Does Richard poo?'

Naomi's subtly but effectively made-up eyes—three shades of brown expertly blended for that natural look—widen perceptibly.

'Clara! What do you *mean,* does Richard "poo"?'

'I mean, Nomes, does he do Number Twos?'

'I don't see . . .'

'I need to know. It's a perfectly simple question. Does Richard do Number Twos, darling? Does he dump? Does he Make Biggies?'

'Of course he . . . goes to the loo.' Naomi is mortified, and faintly cross. 'What are you on about, Clara?'

'And you have physical evidence of this? Sounds? Odours?' (A very Naomi word, 'odours'.)

'Don't be vulgar, Clara. Stop interviewing me. I was going to ask you for coffee, but you're being so odd this morning . . . I don't know.'

'Oh, God. I'm sorry.' And I really am. I should be much nicer to my friends and not tease them. I wish I hadn't tormented Naomi—partly because she is looking red and flushed, really uncomfortable, but also because I suddenly have an unshiftable picture of Richard's vast arse perched atop a toilet. 'I don't know what's wrong with me,' I add by way of an explanation. 'Come on, let's go. For coffee, and you can tell me all about the dinner party. And then I have to go home and organize Robert's birthday.'

And off we drive, in convoy, mothers both, surrounded by other mothers, in other cars, going to have other coffees. I feel like an ant. I feel like jumping out of the car and running. Whenever this happens, I Count My Blessings, like this:

1. I am A MARRIED WOMAN. Everybody wants to be married. Don't they?
2. I have divine children, even though they make a habit of getting right on my nerves 90 per cent of the time.
3. I have regular sex. Ish.
4. I have a large, complicated, but ultimately supportive family. It's very charming, really—sort of fashionably Irish. What are a few drug problems and the odd instance of kleptomania between (step)siblings?
5. Everybody gets bored sometimes. Better to be bored with a partner than bored by oneself. No?

My Blessings reassure me less and less these days, especially Blessing Number 5. I must think up some new ones.

three

ROBERT'S BIRTHDAY is organized: twelve of us at Oliver Peyton's newest restaurant, 8 P.M. next Tuesday. He comes home from work and I inform him of this joyful fact, and he appears to be pleased.

Robert's working hours are ludicrous. He edits a women's glossy magazine and is forever hanging out at the printers', or having drinks with advertisers, or going to ghastly shop openings where C-list semi-celebrities drink bad champagne and show too much cantilevered cleavage.

I used to go with him, years ago, in the mistaken belief that these events were somehow residually glamorous, but I wised up. Also, I discovered that celebrities, C-list or otherwise, tend to be unfeasibly short. Kate Moss: minuscule. The Spice Girls: micro-beings. Tom Cruise: your actual, real-life dwarf. Bless them, and everything, and I know it's not their fault, but there's nothing like a really short person to make one feel gigantic, a huge, clumsy, lumpen oaf of a creature. Of course, Robert isn't terribly tall either. If I wear heels, I tower over him. Robert, in fact, has a smaller waist than me; better cheekbones, too. I will, I accept, never be one of those women in ads who look all Sunday-morningish and sexy in their husband's loose 501s and white shirts. I could wear Robert's

501s as legwarmers, if I unstitched the crotch, but that's about it. The sweaters he thinks of as 'baggy' are the ones I wear skin-tight, 1950s-starlet style. I can't help sometimes wondering what it would be like to be with some strapping six-foot-three-er.

Robert parks his briefcase on the sofa, kicks off his shoes, pecks me perfunctorily, but not unaffectionately, on the nose and asks what's for dinner. It's 9 P.M. and the children are in bed. I was drinking white wine before Robert arrived, with so much enthusiasm that I forgot to tidy up the kitchen, although I did manage to bung a chicken in the oven. The kitchen floor, though, is strewn with Play-Doh and odd bits of Lego; the dishwasher sits unemptied; plates are piled up in the sink; this morning's papers are scattered all over the table.

'Clara, it's a tip in here,' Robert states unemotionally (please assume that everything my husband says is stated unemotionally unless I indicate otherwise). 'What were you doing all day?'

As I keep saying, we've been married eight years. In that time, I have trained Robert to desist from yawning like a woman (by emitting a high-pitched scream at the end of the yawn), from baring his teeth to check for plaque when looking in the mirror, from blowing his nose in the most disgusting, probing, exploratory way, from wearing really ugly underpants with piping. But I haven't yet managed to convince him that I don't lie around all day eating grapes, being massaged by oiled Nubians. So my voice is a little bit terse, with just a hint of sourness, when I say, 'Oh, you know. Picking fluff out of my belly-button. Trying on shoes. Eating crisps. What do you *think*, Robert? Taking the boys to school and nursery. Organizing your birthday. Hoovering. Making beds. Buying a present for Charlie's friend Alex, who's having a party on Saturday. Collecting your dry-cleaning. Answering the phone every thirty seconds. Mopping. Collecting the children from school. Making their tea . . .

'All right,' Robert says, smiling, but I haven't finished. I can't help but notice that, as well as smiling, he is looking distinctly bored by my litany.

'. . . Playing Killer Penguins for an hour, giving them their bath, practising Charlie's reading—he's really getting quite good—reading them stories, running up and down the stairs for a bit because they wouldn't settle, cooking your bloody chicken . . .'

'Chicken?' says Robert, yawning. 'I had some for lunch. I had lunch with Richard, did I tell you?'

'And then, and *then*, I sit down for a nanosecond with a glass of wine, for the first time all day, and you ask me what I've been up to?' I am really pretty annoyed, not least because this is tiresomely familiar territory.

'He's having an affair.'

'Who?'

'Richard. He's having an affair.'

'Who with?'

'Acne Girl.'

'No!'

'YES!'

This is what I love about Robert: he is the world's best gossip, almost feminine in his relish of detail, horrendously bitchy. Acne Girl is Richard's PA and, as you might expect, she has bad skin. I have a thing about bad skin: it makes me feel sick. Acne Girl is what my mother might call a slattern. She always looks like she's just had sex, possibly because she just has—especially with this exciting new development to consider. Her clothes are the kind that inevitably look slept-in. Her hair is tousled. She is undeniably sexy, in a dirty way. But she does have appalling skin for a twenty-three-year-old.

More to the point, Richard is Naomi's husband. I am longing to hear about why Richard has decided to have an affair at this late stage, but I feel sick thinking about Naomi. I know she's ridiculous, but her heart is kind and she tries so hard, with her Shaker kitchen and polished wooden floors and her incessant stew-making and her children who look like they've been picked out of a catalogue.

'Her pelvic floor!' I cry. 'It's too poignant.' And it is. Who will notice its marvellous resilient elasticity now?

'He's doing it for sex, apparently,' Robert says, lighting a cigarette and settling into an armchair.

'But so is she! She doesn't want to pee when she comes! She wishes not to *leak,* Robert, and who can blame her?'

'Who indeed? Apparently,' Robert continues, 'sex with Naomi is like going to the gym. It's very much doing it by numbers.'

'What about me?' I cry.

'Clara, I can't keep up. What about you? I thought we were talking about Richard.'

'Is it like numbers with me?' Unattractively neurotic, I know, but there you go.

'Sex with you? No, it's not like numbers.' Robert is sort of smirking. I hope very much that he is remembering some hot and heavy action, and possibly even getting a stiffy at the unbearably erotic recollection. There is an opaque sort of silence while Robert stares at me, still smirking. 'It's the opposite of by numbers, I'd say,' he opines languidly. 'It's messy. Like you, darling. Like the kitchen floor.'

'Is it hot?'

'The floor?'

Why is he being deliberately obtuse? Why?

'No, the sex. With me.' I need to know. I mean, it seems absurd to me to spend so much of one's life having sex with the same person without ever really talking about what it is like, past the first flush of passion. I suddenly sit bolt upright, having had the most terrible thought: maybe sex with me is disastrous, catastrophic, vomit-making.

'Hot?' says Robert. 'Sometimes. It can be. Shall we eat?'

four

I'VE WOKEN UP FAT. But of course. It's Robert's birthday, after all, and his birthday party is tonight, and it might have been nice to look a little bit glamorous. But no, I've woken up fat. Worse, I've woken up fat for absolutely no reason at all. Did I stuff my face at dinner last night? No, I did not. Did I help the children demolish that tea-time packet of Jaffa Cakes? Nope. I controlled myself, because I didn't want to wake up fat. And I did anyway. I can't believe it. I can't believe that today, of all days, I have woken up with the face of a pig.

I stagger into the bathroom, fatly, on my trotters, and peer at my face in the mirror. I could oink with disappointment. The face is about twice the size it was yesterday; not to mention suspiciously shiny. And—oh, treat of treats—I have two spots lurking near my hairline. What *is* going on? I am closer to the menopause than I am to puberty. Surely acne and sudden nocturnal weight gain ought to be behind me now? Poor Robert, earlier on, being given a birthday snog by his shiny-faced, pustulant porker of a wife. No wonder he didn't have time for a quickie. I remember when every spare minute was devoted to quickies, or at least I think I do. It seems improbable somehow, and sometimes I think I suffer from an exceptionally acute case of False Memory Syndrome.

That's put the kibosh on the natural look, then. My newly obese face calls for extreme measures, for panstick and concealer and all the trickery I can muster up. But really, what is the point of a shelf full of inordinately expensive creams and unguents if I'm going to wake up looking like a bloated teenager? After staring at myself, sighing loudly, for ten minutes, I resolve to let my face be for the time being. It needs to breathe. It needs to *settle*. It might benefit from some fresh air. I might go for a walk later and blast the old pores for a while. (This is a very unappealing thought. Walking, to me, constitutes exercise, and I'm not big on exercise. I am the kind of person who has longed for a Stannah stairlift since I was sixteen.)

Meanwhile, I splash my face with cold water and tie my hair back. I hate doing this. It always becomes painfully apparent that I am not naturally a raving beauty. Devoid of make-up, hair bunched weirdly on top of my head, I look like a cross between an old potato and a slightly corpulent man: a terrifyingly bad look, I think you'll agree. I don't know anyone who looks as hideous as I do in the morning. Robert wakes up looking like a skincare ad from *GQ*, which I find unsupportive. No wonder I spend so much of my life in a furious bad mood.

The problem with waking up fat is that a small part of you always thinks, Ah, sod it—I've woken up fat, so I might as well spend the day eating. I am trying very hard to keep a grip here, but I managed to do a big Sainsbury's shop yesterday and the fridge is groaning with deliciousness. I don't think one smallish bacon and egg sandwich would hurt much, do you? And I'm going for that walk later. I'll just walk a bit longer and get rid of it.

Scouring through the papers, a gentle dribble of mayo-drenched bacon juice winding its way down my chin, I feel utterly content. I even start looking forward to dinner. It'll be nice to see Flo and Evie, and I haven't seen Tom for a couple of months, so there'll be lots to catch up on. My mother adores Robert, so she'll be on her best behaviour. It looks like it might be a fun evening. Except, of course — and here I drop my bacon sarnie in horror — that the dress I want to wear, a dry-clean-only little black number, cleverly cut to hide excess stomach, is *dirty*. I must, must, must remember to take it to the two-hour dry-cleaners as soon as I've finished breakfast. Speaking of which, the children have left a couple of half-eaten muffins behind . . .

It's 7.30 P.M. The boys are murdering each other. I forgot the dry-cleaners, inevitably, and so am squeezing myself into an old, but forgiving, stretchy black number. I only had time to shave my legs from the knee down, which gives a kind of goaty, centaur effect (to match my star sign), but who cares — it's hardly as if anyone is going to be examining my legs. I spent an hour doing my make-up — I bribed the children with chocolate, which was successful, unless you count the fact that half of it is smeared over the sofa — and I look okay. Less fat-faced than this morning, though hardly sculpted of cheekbone. I can't find any clean knickers. Charlie and Jack keep stealing them to give to the hamster 'for nests'. I stole them back a couple of times, only to have to run to the loo in public places to whip them off, suddenly disgusted at the idea that a rodent, albeit a sweet-looking one, had nestled in my gusset.

Robert is ready to go, in his impeccably tailored, classic-with-a-twist Richard James suit, pink-shirted, wearing a groovy tie. He looks handsome. He says, 'I thought you were wearing the black see-through number,' with a tiny moue of disappointment. I feel a little kick of indignation. Surely 'You look hot, baby' would be a more morale-boosting comment. But Robert, I realize with a stab of something approaching sadness, has never called me 'baby'. He has never called me anything sexy. 'Clara' and 'darling' is as affectionate as he gets.

'Why don't you ever call me sexy things?' I ask, cramming my feet into my only pair of Manolos while slipping my arm into my trusty grey coat. (I really must buy a new coat next winter—this one is years old and beginning to show it. Five years ago, it wouldn't have occurred to me to put on something so desperately unfashionable—I'd have rather frozen to death. Five years more and I'll no doubt be pioneering the return of the shell suit as part of my ongoing Comfort At All Costs, Even If It Makes You Look Really Plain campaign.)

'Clara, what are you banging on about now?' Robert says, checking his reflection before peering distractedly at his watch. 'What do you mean, sexy things? Like what?'

'Like, like, like, oh, "tigerbum",' I say rashly, not really having thought very hard about it.

'Tigerbum? Tigerbum? Are you seriously suggesting you would like me to call you "tigerbum"?' Robert is grimacing, and I can tell he is trying not to laugh.

'Well, no—not necessarily "tigerbum", which sounds a bit like I have a stripy behind because I don't, you know, understand how to wipe myself . . .'

'Clara!' Robert practically shouts, the smile wiped off his face. 'You say the most grossly unattractive things.' He wrinkles his nose up at my verbal bad smell and looks around him fastidiously, as if I were about to reveal my excrement-smeared posterior at any moment. Sometimes Robert gets right on my nerves.

'Well, it's true, isn't it? I don't want to be a stripe-bot. No, I meant things like "baby" or "sweetheart" or "sugar". Sweet names. For sweet me.'

Robert sighs. He looks perplexed. 'Sour-sweet,' he mutters to himself, adding, 'We have to go,' and tossing me my pashmina. (See what I mean? I am Last Season Woman.) 'We're going to be late. Come on. Snookums. Fluffkins. Sweet One.'

I didn't mean the names people called Kylie give their teddies, I want to say, and why does he have to sound so sarcastic? Never mind. I cheer myself up with a last glance in the hall mirror and thank Monsieur St Laurent for the world's best concealer. I look quite attractive, in a dishevelled kind of way. In my head, I say to myself, 'Heyyyyy—lookin' good.' I don't know why I say this, since I am not the Fonz, but there you go. The prospect of an evening *en famille* does strange things to me.

five

MY FAMILY are very well dressed. Prada shifts and Jimmy Choo shoes and Ozwald Boateng suits with Technicolor linings: they're a well-groomed lot. Their hair is sleek. They do that thing of always looking perfectly finished: no snagged tights or chipped nail varnish or flecks of spinach on the front teeth for them. Their skins are taut and polished, their dentistry impeccable. They look expensive, all of them. Except me. They always make me feel like a cheerful, simple-minded wench, skirt tucked up into my knickers, arms weighed down with ales.

I don't know why this should be, although it is definitely bosom-related in part. If you have largish bosoms, which I do, they often form a robust sort of shelf half-way up your torso. This shelf, helpfully, acts as a receptacle for any stray debris resulting from a meal: crumbs, drips of sauce, even the head of a prawn once, which made me scream. The other women in my family are relatively flat-chested, and their clothes hang properly. They'd no more find a giant prawn perching on their décolletage, staring at their face in a sinisterly intense black-eyed way, than they would wear American Tan tights with a reinforced gusset.

I brush my dress down self-consciously; as usual, I've managed to get toothpaste on myself, and the damp stain still shows. I can see Flo, in her wispy little Tocca slip. I can see Evie, tossing her lowlights and looking edible in a Dolce & Gabbana number that shows her Wonderbra. And I can see Kate. Kate is regal in navy Prada ('so simple'). She is already berating the waiter over something or other — probably the bad feng shui of the room. I sigh. I gulp. I take deep breaths.

'Clara!' A friendly hand snakes itself around my waist. It belongs to Tom, my thirty-six-year-old stepbrother, who 'works' as a fashion photographer, although he only ever seems to take actual pictures once in a blue moon. 'You look gorgeous,' he says sweetly. 'Have you met Tarka?'

He points to an absurdly emaciated beanpole standing reverently a few paces behind him. Another model, obviously, and American by the sounds of it. She looks like a sexy insect.

I say, 'Hello, Tarka. Otterly delighted to meet you.'

Tarka looks blank and says to Tom, 'I didn't know Clara was Irish.'

Tom winks at me and says to Tarka, 'Actually, hon, she's Japanese.'

Tarka says, 'Wow! That's, like, so cool. I do a lot of work in Tokyo. Your English is so good!'

I bow solemnly, less geisha than sumo champion.

'Another record-breaking simpleton . . . Where do you find them?' I hiss at Tom, not unaffectionately. I couldn't look less Japanese if I tried. It's like mistaking an African tribal chief for Benny from ABBA.

Tom shrugs. 'Dunno,' he retorts. 'Can't remember. She's a crap cook' — Tom is obsessed with food, which is paradoxical since he seems to favour women who appear not to need any — 'but she, er, has other qualities.' We snigger companionably. I wouldn't call Tom nice, exactly, but he does make me laugh.

*

Kate is tapping the side of her glass with her knife. 'I'd like to say a few words,' she says, 'on this happy occasion.' She beams at Robert, who is deep in conversation with Flo. 'Florence!' she shouts. 'Stop talking to Robert. You can't *possibly* be saying anything interesting and he is bored of looking polite.'

Flo, who is used to this brand of motherly chat, raises her eyes to heaven. Robert smiles at her reassuringly. Kate clears her throat.

'The marvellous thing,' she begins, fixing the horizon and smiling beatifically, 'the marvellous thing is that we're all here. And that we all love each other. Despite the fact that most of your fathers are frankly *unspeakable* human beings with terrible emotional problems . . .'

'Not to mention physical,' sniggers Flo, remembering Maurice, husband number three, whom Kate refused to sleep with on the grounds that she hadn't been able to see what he looked like throughout their courtship—she was too vain to wear her glasses and suffers from myopia. The poor man was eventually driven into the comforting arms of his therapist. Kate has, ever since, insisted on the fact that the therapist is blind. 'The poor blind thing,' Kate says at parties. 'So brave, without her stick. Of course, at home it's tippety-tap, all day long.'

Kate is continuing. 'We are all here and we all love each other. We support each other. And it is in the spirit of supportiveness that I would urge you all to keep the bread rolls away from Clara, who is in serious danger of turning into . . . well, a sort of pudding on legs, really.' Kate looks pensive. 'Or perhaps a hippopotamus. Which, I think we all agree, would be a terrible shame for such a pretty girl.' She turns to me, radiating motherly love. 'You're so beautiful, darling. Don't become obese. For all our sakes.'

You're probably thinking this is quite mean—and, indeed, it is—but I am used to Kate and her funny little ways, so I mutter, 'Go away,' at her, not unaffectionately, and grab a roll off a passing waiter. Robert winks at me across the table. Tom says, 'You look great, Clara.' Tarka, helpfully, says, 'Yeah, big is beautiful.' Still, Kate is nothing if not democratic. We are asked to raise our glasses to celebrate the fact that Evie hasn't gone off to the loo to be sick yet; as well as to toast Robert.

After a few minutes, we all begin to settle into what seems to be developing into a relatively peaceful occasion. We've barely tucked into our starters — my bruschetta look particularly appetizing — when Kate taps her glass again, awkwardly, with her right hand. Unusually for her, she is looking disconcerted.

We put our forks down again, but Kate does not immediately fill the expectant silence. She clears her throat. Amazed by this less than gung-ho display — Kate is giving every impression of looking *nervous* and nerves are not normally part of her repertoire — Robert and I catch each other's eye.

Tom's eyebrow is lifted quizzically. 'Spit it out, Kate. Dinner's getting cold,' he says, for which he would usually be rebuked (Kate wouldn't care for being linked with *saliva*). But there is no rebuke forthcoming, and suddenly the whole table is silent.

'There's something else,' Kate says, and then pauses again. The moment is filmic. The seconds turn into a good minute and a half, during which there is a pin-drop silence. Kate seems to be struggling.

'Oh no,' Tarka suddenly yells. 'It's like the bit in *Who Will Love My Children?* when the matey — the matrey — the mom gets real sick. She's, like, gonna die. So she gets all her kids round and she's, like, crying. Because, you know, who will love them?'

This impertinence seems to snap Kate out of her reverie. And how.

'Oh *really*,' she says, eyeing Tarka with a basilisk stare that has the immediate effect of reducing the latter to a serious bout of lip-wobbling. 'For God's sake, you *cretinous* young woman. It is nothing of the sort.' She sighs to herself. 'I can't believe that my stepson has a girlfriend named after a variety of lentil. I mean,' she adds, raising her voice, 'my daughter may be fat'—and here she points at me languidly, so that half the restaurant cranes around for a good look—'but at least *she has a brain*. Of course, she wastes it terribly . . .' There is a pause here, then: 'Christ! Anyway. I, um. I, er. I . . . Well, darlings, I've met someone. Someone very special. A soulmate, you might say. An exceptional human being. And . . .'

'Please,' I say, meaning it. 'Please don't marry him. Please say you're not going to marry him.'

But it's too late. Kate, flushed and beaming, has slowly lifted her left hand for us all to see, and there, sparkling quietly, is a giant, square-cut emerald. 'He's a wonderful, wonderful man,' she is saying, as though in slow motion. 'He's a seer.'

'Is a seer, like, a lord?' asks Evie, who, though lovely, is not necessarily the brightest little pixie in the forest.

'No, Evie, that's a *peer*,' I explain kindly.

'One who pees,' says Flo, purely to confuse her.

'A lord who pees?' blinks Evie, thoroughly muddled. 'Gross. So what's a seer, Kate?'

'One who sees, darling,' Kate replies. 'One who sees. He is a mystic. He has an ancient soul. As do I, apparently . . . He has looked deep within my soul and chosen me.'

Fancying this seer-ing lark myself, I look around the table. I may not be able to look deep within the assorted souls— and I may not want to—but I notice that Tom's just ordered a double whisky and Evie has hit the bread rolls, always a sign that she's in the mood for a spot of inter-course regurgitation. Flo is staring at Kate, her mouth hanging slightly open, blinking fast. I'm smoking, wishing my mouth were wider so that I could fit in more fags. Even Robert has his head in his hands.

'Isn't it heaven?' Kate is asking, somewhat rhetorically. 'He is *the* most special man.' And she proceeds to tell Robert all about this paragon—his name, apparently, is Max and he is American—for the rest of dinner.

six

I CAN'T SIT AND THINK about my family all day. It's all very well mournfully considering the nightmare at hand, but some of us have work to do (although of course some of us have trust funds instead, as I am reminded every time one of my stepsisters goes shopping and returns trip-trapping like a Billy Goat Gruff on new Patrick Cox heels, swinging Gucci carriers). Which is why Thursday morning finds me in the kitchen, gulping down vile Nescafé—I always think coffee tastes faintly of halitosis, though not as much as lager does—in full panic mode.

Still, we're hardly talking anoother deh slaving down t' pit. The kitchen's scrubbed refectory table is strewn with newspaper and magazine cuttings. A tape machine and a six-pack of Duracell AAs squat patiently by the side, mingling with this morning's leftover bowls of Sugar Puffs, a dog-eared copy of *Toddlers Love Learning!* (synonyms of 'poo', yes, rudimentary division, no, in my experience), a forsaken-looking Jar Jar Binks toy (deemed very last season by fickle Charlie) and some pink and blue Elvis knickers sent to me by Amber in this morning's post. I love Amber. She makes me feel like I still have fun. *And* she cares about my underwear. In fact, since we make sporadic attempts at going swimming together (whenever I manage to overcome the distressing impression that I look like an egg in my cozzie), she's the only other person who ever sees it, apart from me.

Cuttings, batteries, panic: yup, it's interview time. And what with Robert's birthday and Kate's news, I'd forgotten all about it until the phone call from Araminta, editrix of *Panache,* the glossy weekly for which I write, came last night. Hence the somewhat rushed 'research'. Normally I'd give myself more than half an hour to get the measure of my interviewee.

Mug in one hand, exceptionally delicious (ergo third) croissant in the other, I can't help but notice from the magazines littering the table that today's candidate is pretty easy on the eye. He is a dancer, one of a new breed that, according to a clipping by Ismene Brown of the *Daily Telegraph,* is revolutionizing the contemporary dance scene. I haven't time to find out quite how this is achieved (apart from the fact that my interviewee clearly doesn't shave his chest—is this modern, I wonder?). Unfortunately my knowledge of ballet comes, in its entirety, from a slim tome entitled *Angelina Ballerina,* a book about a gifted young mouse that was most popular with Jack until he recently decided that ballet was 'for girls' and abandoned it in favour of *Know Your Stegosaurus.*

Still, our Mr Dunphy here—Christ, he's Irish! I do hope he isn't another clippy-cloppy Lord of the Dance, 'I Am Celtic Culture' type—looks pleasant enough. He looks very pleasant indeed, actually, if you like that dark 'n' brooding kind of thing. I'm sure we'll have a nice chat about . . . oh, I don't know, tutus or U2 or something.

More pressingly, there's a distinctly high whiff emanating from the hamsters' cage, and I reluctantly tear myself away from Sam Dunphy's suspiciously blue eyes (contact lenses, doubtless, but I must say that black-haired, blue-eyed combo is not uneffective). I scrumple him up, in fact, and shred him in the Magimix, razor-blade cheekbones and all. Nobody nice is that cartoonishly good-looking and he'll make lovely fresh bedding for Binky and George Roid (the Hammy Roids, named, I'm afraid, by mature me). After which there's just time for a quick application of powder—I must change the light bulb by the sink; it's almost impossible to see in there—and blusher, and away we go. No point in lipstick, since he's clearly a Ballet Poof, besides which I've only got until 3 P.M., since I need to get to school. Dunphy had better not have too much to say.

Well, that was fun. Not. I thought the Irish were supposed to be friendly. Turned out that our Mr Dunphy is something of a serious young man—more James Joyce than Yootha unfortunately, given my distinctly lowbrow approach. Granted, I should have remembered his faxed biography, and going straight in with the chest-hair question—'Did you stop shaving because it was all sort of *itchy?*'—was perhaps not as intellectually challenging as an opener should have been, but I thought it would at least break the ice. And then that look he shot me—'Me Man, You Infant'—when I said, isn't it too funny about your compatriot, The Edge from U2. 'What about him?' said Dunphy icily. Well, I said, isn't it too funny that he *exists?* The man's forty-two and has a spastic name, and as jokes go it's surely a very good one? Dunphy fixed me with his gimlet, azure stare (definitely lenses, and eyeliner too, I would hazard), not saying anything, unsmiling.

No wonder I needed a drink. And then another, and then a third, quite forgetting that drink accentuates my irritating trait of unconsciously mimicking people's accents. I've noticed that some people don't suffer from this affliction. They can talk to an American from the Deep South without sounding like the love-child of Tennessee Williams and Dolly Parton—if such a thing were imaginable—or to an Antipodean without turning into Dame Kiri. Alas, I am not of their number.

And after the second Black Velvet—I thought Guinness and champagne would be, you know, sympathetic, but he seemed to prefer mineral water—I suddenly found myself coming over all Andrea Corr. Which is when Sam Dunphy leaned over and said, 'Are you taking the piss?' I said, thinking aloud, 'The mick, surely?' and it all went downhill from there.

Back at the kitchen table—my mouth is dry and I have the beginnings of a headache coming on, brought on, I think, by shame—I dejectedly flick on the tape machine. We're talking cringe-o-rama. I go scarlet, then puce, breaking into one pre-menopausal hot flush after another as I listen again to the last bit of our brief 'conversation'.

Me (sounding, frankly, pissed): 'So, I've heard ballet dancers all sleep with each other, all day long.'

Him (terse): 'I'm not a ballet dancer.'

Me (inexplicably aggressive, facetious): 'Really? How odd. What kind of dancing then? Ballroom? *Morris?*'

Him (terser): 'Contemporary. I choreograph too. Did my agent not send you my biography? I trained at ballet school, of course . . .'

Me (interrupting, giggling): 'Did you wear those girlie tights? And do tippy-toes?'

He (gobsmacked): 'Tippy-toes? Do you, ah, mean points? Christ. I'm not a woman.'

Me: 'And tight tights?'

He: 'I'm ignoring you. Anyway, I was at the Dublin Academy of Dance from 1987 to . . .'

Me: 'Go on, you can tell me. Girlie tights?'

Him: 'Jesus. Why don't we take a break? Have a coffee. Have some water . . .'

Me: 'No thanks, I'm not thirsty. So then, dancing. Are we talking shag-frenzy or are we not? Because the reader demands the truth.'

Him: 'I'm not even going to answer that.'

Me (gently, like Claire Rayner talking to someone handicapped): 'Because it must be a comfort, a great comfort—I mean, so many of you, all ostracized for years and suddenly it's quite normal . . .'

It's his turn to interrupt me. 'How do you mean exactly, "ostracized"?'

This is when I pointed out that it can't have been easy being a gay Catholic, er, ballerina boy. It is also where he stopped the interview and walked out. Idiotically, because I was drunk and embarrassed, I put on my best mincy voice and shouted, 'Oooooh! Temper!' after him. That was some mean look he gave me as he walked out. Some mean comment too: 'Do your homework, little girl.' Rude bastard, in his tatty white T-shirt that was at least two sizes too small. And grubby-looking too, frankly. Slept-in-looking.

I suppose I'd better call Araminta at the magazine and explain. She said last night that she was relying on the interview for a cover—not possible now, of course, although there should just be time to shoot a new one. But Araminta, when I get through, is pretty annoyed. Araminta is, not to put too fine a point on it, raging. Words like 'unprofessional', 'lax' and 'fuck-up' fall from her impeccably glossed lips. I try to explain—about my mother's engagement and how it's disengaged me, about my mix-up over dates, about getting pissed by mistake, about the hamsters eating into my research time—but Araminta's having none of it. The cover's been shot, apparently. Not only this, but every magazine in the country's after an interview with Dunphy, who is, she says, 'about to go mega'. We were, it seems, amazingly lucky to get him. And I blew it. There's nothing for it, she says. I am going to have to ring him up and apologize. Personally. It's an order. She dictates the phone number and makes me swear ('on your life, Clara') to call him forthwith.

Yes, well. It's all going to have to wait, because it's time for the boys' tea, and then Robert and I are going to dinner at Tamsin's. Tamsin is my oldest friend, along with Amber—

we've all known each other since school. One of my missions in life is to pair her up with someone, if only to stop her whingeing. Her mission in life is a) to marry and b) to mate, though, increasingly, not necessarily in that order. Tamsin is, according to herself, the *ne plus ultra* of Old Maidhood: an unloved, shrivelled shelf-dweller whose genitalia are cob-webbed through lack of use. She has panic attacks when she gets drunk, during which she witters on about how she'll never have a baby, and if, by a miracle, she does, how said baby is bound to have 'at least a harelip. I mean, I'm thirty-four — it's *geriatric,* Clara, for a first child. And I don't think I could cope with Down's.' And then she cries. And I feel much better.

To my shame — well, my slight shame — I like hearing her talk like this. It makes me feel superior. (I told you I wasn't very nice.) It makes me think that I am very, very lucky to have Robert and the boys. (The luck of having the boys is never in any doubt — I'm not *that* bad — although I must con-fess to a certain sneaking longing for spontaneous weekends away, say, or a quick two days' shopping in Paris with a girl-friend on the spur of the moment . . . pastimes which are as dead to me as the rah-rah skirt or the stripy legwarmer.) Lis-tening to Tamsin drone on about being lonely, and all men being bastards, is superlatively good news for morale: the oral equivalent of a family-sized pack of jam doughnuts with a side dish of vanilla custard (to dunk).

I tell Robert about Dunphy in the car on the way over to Belsize Park. Single girls, I reflect, can afford to live in Lon-don's green oases (in a box, in Tamsin's case, but a very pretty one). When you're reasonably well paid and fending only for yourself, a hefty mortgage is not the albatross it becomes for women like me, with families to feed and clothe, school fees to pay, cars to run — which is why London's most unfashion-able reaches are slowly being colonized by young families. We live in the East End, among an odd mixture of crack dens, the dispossessed and People Like Us. I love it, actually. But there's no denying I also love Belsize Park, with its trees and wide streets and pavement cafés. Our nearest café is inside Tesco's, and they do Sunday lunch for £2.99; Tamsin's is by her front door and does lattes and frappuccinos and all-day breakfast with organic bacon.

'Araminta does have a point,' Robert says, manoeuvring our ancient Volvo through the streets of London with his cool effortlessness. He is the most composed man I have ever met. 'It isn't exactly professional to get pissed and insult the star.'

'I didn't say it was, Robert. I didn't suggest I should adopt it as a *modus operandi* for all future interviews. It was an accident. I have no time . . . And now I'm going to have to grovel to him. Oh, God, admit — it's a bleak prospect. Besides, when am I going to do it? . . . Darling?'

I never call Robert darling unless I want something, which is why it has the unfortunate effect, as now, of making him clench his jaw and raise one eyebrow, expressing both resignation and unbearable weariness. His face is rather like that of a Scripture teacher asked for the nth time about circumcision by a gaggle of sniggering schoolgirls.

'Yes?'

'Where does the little bit of skin come from? Sorry — I mean, I mean, couldn't we have an au pair? It would make life so much simpler. It's not that expensive and think of the things we could do. I could work properly and have the time to make the house nice. I could cook. We could go away for the weekend . . .'

Robert's mobile phone rings and while he indulges in a conversation about pagination, I drift into a daydream about Robert and me, alone, somewhere romantic — Barcelona, say — for a whole, entire, childless forty-eight hours. We'd go shopping, of course, and eat, and have drinks, in the boiling hot sunshine. And then — then what? We'd lie about in bed, of course. Hmmm. Yes. In bed. Alone. We'd . . . we'd make love. ('Make love' always brings to mind Spanish waiters saying, 'Bee-yoo-diful laydee'. Isn't that sad? I think I have arrested development.) We'd lie in each other's arms, and he'd read me poetry.

The image is somehow so improbable that I am suddenly wide awake. Part of me wants to snort with laughter— poetry! As if, as Charlie might say. But there's also a horrible raw feeling in my throat. Who am I kidding? We would not lie about. I would, and he'd pace about, not joining me, suggesting some outing or other and berating me for 'wasting time'. We would not lie in bed, except perhaps for breakfast, though even then Robert would raise the Crumb Question. Would we make love? We might, in the perfunctory way that we've become used to. The We-Are-Married kind that has to do with reassurance rather than desire. The kind that doesn't happen that often, to be frank.

I glance over at Robert, still deep in conversation. I have got to get a grip. I have got to stop thinking like this. It is a well-known fact—the best-known fact, in fact, a fact known to everyone in the entire world—that sex stops being sexy once you've been seeing someone for more than six months, a year if you're lucky. And so what? It's only sex. It's only *loins*. And at the moment it's nothing at all. We haven't actually made our very own beast with two backs for . . . well, for a little while.

Robert has pressed 'End'. 'I don't want anyone living with us,' he says, snapping me out of angst mode. 'Au pairs live with you. She'd be sprawled all over the sofa every night when I came home. She'd have to have dinner with us. She'd want to *talk*. No, Clara, I really can't bear the thought of it.'

Well, I can, I want to say. I can bear the thought. I can bear the extra sleep. I can bear the odd lie-in. I could make myself bear not having to hoover every single bloody day. But I don't say it. I say nothing. I feel tired. Bloody Sam Dunphy, spoiling my day, with his poofy eyeliner and stinky T-shirt.

I don't know what possesses me, but just as Robert is parking the car, I ask him if we could go away. Just the two of us. For a weekend somewhere—in a few weeks' time, once I've made child-care arrangements. I am displeased by the whiny, almost nagging tone of my voice. But to my surprise, Robert says yes immediately. 'Yes,' he says. 'That would be nice. I'd like it. I'd like to go back to Paris . . .'

My spirits lift. They soar. We even think alike. We are made for each other. We are the proverbial peas in a pod: Dumpea and Grumpea, perhaps.

I go to kiss Robert, but he kisses me first. And yes, since you ask, it is reassuring.

seven

I THINK I may be having a little crisis of some kind. Because it's fair to say that I am not a particularly envious person. I may have many vices, but I don't covet, as a rule. I don't yearn for things I can't have — that, surely, would defeat the point of overdrafts. I don't want to be anyone I'm not; only myself, thinner, and — oh, never mind. And yet here we are in Tamsin's little flat and I feel . . . jealous, as if my tongue might suddenly fork and hiss and my eyes turn fluorescent green. Not for long, you understand. Just for a few seconds. Minutes, perhaps.

The late evening sun is pouring yellow light in through her sash windows, the ledges of which she has crammed with herb-filled window-boxes. There's thyme and lavender, basil and rosemary, all wafting scentedness into the tiny, cosy flat (which is the size of my sitting room, I remind myself nastily, hoping to nip the j-word in the bud). Tamsin's fat, squishy junk-shop sofa, heaped with cushions and throws, takes up half the living room, but it looks like the comfiest place on earth. By it is a small, beaten-up coffee table, laden with things: glittery nail polish, a hair clip festooned with fabric roses, a pile of magazines, a glass of white wine. Elvis Costello warbles on the stereo about poor old Alison, whom this world is killing. Tamsin must have been lying on her sofa, sniffing her lavender, painting her toes and sipping her Viognier before we arrived. For some reason, the thought of this makes me want to scream with envy. There are no Playmobil men cluttering up the table, no crumbs of dried-up Play-Doh nestling inside the sofa. No noise, apart from Elvis. And nothing for Tamsin to do: no hordes to feed, no washing to wash, no swimming bags to get ready for the morning. Tamsin could drink her entire bottle of Viognier, and then another. She won't have to get up in the night because someone is thirsty or, like eccentric little Jack, 'bored' at 4 A.M. She lives in Girl World and I don't. I don't.

It's not really like I have anything to moan about. As I've said, Tamsin lives in a box. We live in a roomy four-bedroomed Victorian terraced house—one of those houses that looks modest enough on the outside (the peeling paint doesn't help, but I do so resent paying the price of a triple velvet sofa for external maintenance that nobody sees, except for the Care in the Community people who live opposite) but that extends, Tardis-like, once you're in. Okay, so it's not in the most aesthetically pleasing street anyone ever cast eyes upon, not least because there's a giant secondary round the corner and its teenage denizens like nothing more than slouching around our street, smoking and shouting and dropping crisp wrappers—but there's a cherry tree outside the house, and no one, to my surprise, has tried to nick the cluster of flowerpots that line the stairs up to the front door (Yale locks *and* Chubb: welcome to east London). I love the house, actually: my spirits rise when I turn the corner, on the way back from the bagel bakery, and see it standing there, square and comforting. God knows why I'm moaning—Tamsin's entire flat would fit into half my kitchen.

Besides, I really hate these little bursts of self-pity, which make me want to snuffle quietly as well as give myself a good slap (I could do both together—that would be attractive).

Mercifully, or not, Tamsin breaks the spell. Pouring out vast tumblers of wine, she settles herself into a tatty old armchair and tells us about last night, something of a tradition with her.

And, as is traditionally the case, last night was a disaster. I don't know quite what it is that she does — exude desperation in the way that I exude Fracas, pick her nose and offer her findings to her date with a friendly let's-share kind of smile, set fire to her farts . . . I don't know. I don't *understand*. She is, by any standards, a good-looking girl: tall, curvy, with a shock of red ringlets. (No, I know what you're thinking, but I said 'red', not 'ginger'. Trust me, she's amazing.) She has creamy skin, the kind that is absolutely smooth and unblemished, and sparkling triangular hazel eyes. What can I tell you, without sounding like Barbara Cartland? I mean, she has breasts, she's smart and she tells jokes. What more could anyone want? And yet she is very, very single. As I say, I don't get it.

'I don't get it,' Tamsin is saying to Robert, whom she seems to consider an honorary girl, to his slight discomfort. 'And, you know, I want it sometimes. I'm not a nun . . .' That's another thing about Tamsin: she is pleasantly direct.

'So last night Bill has this dinner party, and there's this guy, you know, who practically has "I Am Tamsin's Designated Date" tattooed on his forehead. I'm sitting next to him and he's chatting me up. He really is chatting me up, I'm not inventing it' — solitude makes one paranoid, I've noticed — 'and so eventually he gives me a lift home.'

'All the signals?' asks Robert.

'All the signals,' She nods. 'Definitely — big eye action, hand on waist helping me into my coat, howling at all my jokes, meaningful silences in the car. Anyway, so he comes in for coffee and we start kissing and so on, you know, and end up in bed.'

'GOOOOAAAAL!' I yell triumphantly, arms aloft, jumping up. Robert gives me a look that suggests a degree of exasperation, and I sit down again. I spend too much time with small children.

'Oh, Clara.' Tamsin says, looking grim. 'I can't tell you what it was like. I mean, I've gone to bed with some disasters in my time . . .'

'Like Mike,' I interject helpfully.

'Yeah, like Mike,' Tamsin says. 'Anyway . . .'

'And Mark,' I add, warming to my theme. 'Remember him? He had scabs.'

'Yes, he did,' Tamsin says, not looking what you'd call best pleased. 'So . . .'

'Not forgetting Tony, of course,' I pipe up again, despite myself. 'Whom you strongly suspected of having masochistic tendencies. Do you remember? "I've been a naughty boy, Miss Tamsin . . ."' The memory of this makes me snort with laughter for slightly too long, although even Tam manages a wry smile. 'I don't know how you find them,' I add smugly, as if I myself had only ever slept with National Stud Awards finalists.

'Clara, may I finish? So. We're in bed. And after a few seconds I notice he's kissing me weirdly.'

'What do you mean, weirdly?' asks imaginative Robert, a slave to detail.

I have a horrible feeling I'm about to burst out laughing again.

'Well, you know if you completely relax your tongue?' says Tamsin, demonstrating, so that her tongue is vastly wide, obscenely fat, lolling outside her lips like a distended, obese slug. 'Like this. Try it.'

Robert and I try it. If anyone came in now they'd feel very sorry for us and give us baskets to weave, not to mention bibs.

'That's it,' says Tam. 'Not a sexy look.' We all laugh wetly, tongues hanging out like retarded dogs. 'Well, that's how he kissed. I mean, he didn't even attempt to prove that the tongue is a muscle. It was flopping about all over my mouth, like a big wet dead thing. It was gross.'

'Yes, I do see it would be,' I say, fascinated. 'Did you mention it at all?'

'I tried, subtly,' she says. 'I made my own tongue exceptionally pointy.' We all have a go at doing this. It gives a strained look to the eyes, I notice. 'And after a while he cottoned on and did the same. Well, sort of the same—I mean, he made his pointy all the time. Like a dagger. He sort of stabbed my mouth. His tongue was *rigid*. I didn't like it much.'

'Surely,' I say, 'you made your excuses and left?'

'Well, it's *my* flat,' Tam points out reasonably. 'I just thought, what the hell, it'll get better when we get down to it. I mean, it could hardly get worse.' She gives a theatrical shudder as she moves off her armchair and peers into the oven, checking on our roast vegetable lasagna's progress, then comes back and pours herself another glass. 'I felt really, really randy,' she explains, unnecessarily.

'That happens,' Robert says, looking out of the window.

I am startled. Does it? To him? When? But I bite my tongue, which has had enough exercise for the evening. 'And?' I say instead.

'And . . .' There is a dramatic silence. 'And he was Mr One-Inch,' Tamsin says, looking cross but fighting, I can tell, a laughter fit. 'He was Mr "Is it in yet?". Basically, he had a weeny peeny.'

Tamsin and I explode with laughter; Robert too, although he manages to look slightly disapproving at the same time.

'A weeny peeny!' I stammer, weeping with mirth.

'The weeniest!' croaks Tam, helplessly.

'A weeny peeny and a flooby tongue,' I scream, beside myself.

'And he liked talking dirty,' Tamsin says.

'Nothing wrong with that, in theory,' I say, sobering up.

It is Robert's turn to give me an odd look.

'Absolutely not,' says Tam, wiping her eyes. 'But he kept referring to the WP'—more sniggers—'as Little Dave—he was called David. And to my—Clara, calm down—you know, as "your bush".'

'Bush?' I yelp desperately.

'Bush. "Tell me you want it. You want Little Dave in your bush." Which was silly in two respects'—Tam is very logical, as befits a primary school teacher—'since I clearly wanted it, otherwise why put up with the inept kissing? And, obviously, silly in the respect that "bush" is not what I'd call an erotic term.'

'How old was he?' I manage to ask, in between hyperventilating. 'Because it's a very 1970s, Readers' Wives kind of term, "bush". As is "pussy", although of course "pussy" sounds softer. Bush implies unkempt hirsuteness, wouldn't you say, Tam?'

'I would,' Tam says solemnly. 'He's about my age. Anyway, it was all downhill from there.'

'You don't mean you went through with it?' asks Robert, aghast.

'Well, what else could I do? I mean, the weeny peeny—shush, Clara—was in the bush, as it were—at least I *think* it was—and it seemed a bit late in the day to change my mind. The worst thing is, afterwards he went into the bathroom, had a very loud dump and came out saying, "I wouldn't go in there for a bit if I were you."'

'Oh, God,' says Robert. 'Oh, my God, how repulsive.' He looks truly appalled. As well he might do, actually. Poor, poor Tamsin. And lucky, lucky me.

'Have you thought any more about becoming a lesbian?' I ask Tam over pudding, when I've regained my composure (which actually doesn't properly happen for a few days and explains why I suddenly started sniggering like a loon by the frozen cocktail sausages in Sainsbury's at the weekend).

Tam and I once got drunk and I had the genius idea of suggesting homosexuality to her. 'People are always saying sexuality is fluid,' I'd explained, 'and that deep down we're all bisexual. Why not become a lezzy? It's very fashionable these days and you'd be bound to score. God, Tam, you could date a she-plumber—you know how your leaky tap's always getting on your nerves. Imagine! Or a she-roofer! Oh, please date a she-roofer. I still have that annoying leak in the top bedroom.' But Tam, though she didn't dismiss the notion out of hand, wasn't as keen as I'd hoped.

Now she says, 'Do you know, I'm thinking about it. What is it with the men out there? You two are so lucky.'

Robert and I try to look lucky, which in his case involves sitting up very straight and making a strangulated kind of grimace, while I sort of simper like a simpleton. 'Honestly, you don't realize. It's a bloody nightmare, the whole dating thing.'

I'm sure it is, I think to myself on the way home. I know it is—hell, I've read the books. But it has its advantages, being alone. It has its pluses. Like sunny flats with furniture lovingly sought out from antiques markets, instead of the chaos of my kitchen.

Just thinking about it makes me cross actually. Anyway. Where was I? Oh, yes. Being alone. Advantages, like lying around doing nothing with the sun streaming in. Like freedom. You know the song: 'You don't know what you've got till it's gone'. I quietly start humming it to myself.

'I hate Joni Mitchell,' says Robert.

eight

I WISH I organized my weekends better. They should really centre around me and Robert doing things with the boys. This never seems to happen, somehow, partly due to Robert's decimating 'exhaustion'. Robert, in his wisdom, chooses to spend his weekends supine on the ecru sofa in the living room ('his' room), listening to opera, with the door shut. Because he is so tired. Because his life is so tiring. His levels of exhaustion would suggest he was a particularly overworked junior doctor, rather than a magazine editor who took long lunches and came home at seven.

We used to suffer from the condition known as Competitive Tiredness Syndrome, in which each conversation consists of one partner explaining to the other that they are considerably more exhausted. I lost the game over the years: some time ago, despite myself, I started believing in Robert's exhaustion, and almost feeling guilty about it. Robert now hardly sees the children at weekends. I take them out on Saturdays and, often, Sundays too, so that the house is quiet and Robert can 'relax'.

Occasionally, the notion pops into my head that tiredness of this kind — tiredness that has no physical basis — is often a symptom of depression. On the other hand, Robert is exceptionally lazy. Either way, I am not particularly fond of the weekends. They make me feel lonely. There's nothing like another person being physically in the house but out of bounds to make one feel peculiarly forsaken.

I've bought a new outfit, one that seems particularly weekendy. Before I drag Jack and Charlie off to Stella's to play, I ask Robert what he thinks.

'Robert?'

Robert looks up from his copy of *Vogue*. 'Hmm?'

'Do you like my clothes? Do you love my trousers?'

'There are some Dries van Noten drawstring-waist ones in here,' he says. 'Embroidered chiffon, very pretty. I *quite* like yours—M&S?—but they rather remind me of Chinese plumbers. You have very good legs, but these rather suggest you have tree trunks.' He stares at them and then at me, a pleasant, open expression on his face.

'I look like a Chinese plumber? Because I was aiming for a wholesome, rustic Provençal look.' Technically, I love being able to talk fashion shorthand to my husband. I am grateful for never having to listen to him prattle on about beer or football ('My God, Clara—his *hair*' is all he's ever said on the latter). But I am forced to admit that these days he never has anything very nice to say about any clothes of mine. And, deep down, I can't say I blame him. Functional, yes. Durable, ditto. But pretty? I don't think so. Perhaps I should go shopping, or at the very least have a rummage around my wardrobe.

'Don't get in a flap,' says Robert languidly. 'It's not *my* fault. I think it's the colour—that Mao blue, so utilitarian. And of course the shape—well, the lack of shape. The rather *masculine* shape . . . Maybe with different shoes, a different top? I mean, that huge T-shirt, and those horrible hippie sandals'—Robert says 'sandals' much as he'd say 'diarrhoea'— 'You might think about shopping in normal shops. Paul Smith does a size 16 in the women's range, for instance. An 18 too, I believe.'

'I don't take an 18. Robert, do you think I'm *butch?* What's with the lesbian stuff?'

'Not normally, no. But like all tall women, you have to be careful.'

'Do you think I'm *obese?*' I often use exaggeration as a little signal to Robert to go easy on me. Am I obese? Am I hideous? Is my hair just like rats' tails? Sometimes it works. And sometimes it doesn't.

'You are slightly overweight,' Robert replies evenly, 'but not actually a porker. You aren't actually *my little porker.* You aren't my Big Pig either.' For a split second, he looks like malice incarnate. Then he starts giggling.

This is a reference to a conversation we had a fortnight ago, before Naomi and Richard came to dinner. We were trying to think of the most horrible pet names to use out loud, with the specific intention of appalling our guests. We were only quite pleased with Tiny Stubby Man as a term of endearment for Robert, although we liked the way it implied a) midgethood and b) uncomplaining acceptance of a humiliating state. But we surpassed ourselves when it came to my special name. We came up with Big Pig. The idea of calling your well-upholstered wife Big Pig in public struck us as quite irresistibly horrible.

'Pass the salad, BP,' Robert could say.

'Aaah, what does that stand for?' Naomi would ask, all eagerly. 'Bunny Pants? Booboo Pickle?'

'Big Pig,' I'd reply, matter-of-factly, dishing out the chicken (we toyed with the idea of my shouting it—'BIG PIG'—for added impact). 'It's Robert's special name for me. I am Big Pig.'

Merely imagining Naomi's repulsed and bewildered face—'But it's so cruel!'—reduced us to tears of laughter. It still does, which is why we start laughing now. As I wipe my eyes, I realize with a start that I am feeling hysterical, in both senses. Like an insect with especially acute antennae, I can feel that something is up, somewhere. Is it him? Me? I can't tell.

Robert goes back to reading *Vogue*.

I have to call bloody Sam Dunphy before we go and make amends. The idea is to persuade him to agree to a rematch. Jack has decided to position himself on my back, arms around my neck, and refuses to be shifted. I make the phone call half crouched, with his soft little head, the very centre of which still smells of baby, resting on my shoulder.

The number—something beginning 07967—obviously belongs to a mobile, but I still say, in my politest voice, 'Please may I speak to Sam Dunphy?' when he answers.

'Speaking,' he says.

'Charlie!' shouts Jack. 'Charlie! Mummy's calling Bloody Dunphy!' It's amazing what children pick up.

'Dunphy the Smurfy!' hollers Charlie from the other end of the room. It's astounding, in fact.

'Hello? Sorry about this,' I say, reaching behind me furiously to detach Jack, who is humming a little song—'Dunphy, Dunphy/Is a Smurfy/He is blue/He smells of . . . POO'—and giggling hysterically. 'It's Clara Hutt here, from *Panache*. I, er, I'm phoning to apologize about the other day.'

'Really,' says Dunphy. 'That's big of you.'

'I am big,' I say, still pulling at my limpet child. 'I mean, not physically—although I suppose that's open to argument —I mean . . . Oh look, anyway—I'm sorry. Get *off*, Jack. Sorry. Hello?'

'I'm here,' says hateful Dunphy.

'You see, the hamsters needed new bedding and I used you —they peed on your face, actually, poor you—and then I had no time to read about you properly . . .'

'Hamsters?' says Dunphy, sounding nonplussed. Then: 'Yeah, well, whatever. No big deal. Thanks for calling, anyway.'

'No, no — hello?'

'Yes?' he says.

'I need to interview you again. I won't get drunk, I promise. I got drunk by *mistake*, you see, and it all went wrong. I will do days and days' worth of research. I won't ask you about your sexuality. Hello? Are you still there? I *love* modern dance,' I add, lying. 'I live for it.'

'Clearly,' he says. 'I could tell. Anyway, no thanks. Once was enough. I'm going to Ireland tomorrow to rehearse. What's that noise?'

'Oh, just my kids. Sorry. Anyway, look — please. I could fly over. I'm really sorry . . .'

'Your kids?'

'Yes.'

'How old are they?'

'Six and three. *Please* let me interview you again. OUCH!' Jack is doing some experimental biting of the top of my ear. 'GO AWAY, Jack. *Please*. OW! Where's bloody Robert? Go and find him. Jesus *Christ*, that hurt. Sam? Are you still there? Can I please come and talk to you?'

There is a pause. 'I'm here,' he says. Then he adds, 'I don't think so,' in a softer voice. 'As I say, I'm going tomorrow. Back to Smurfland. You should explain to your kid that it's little green folk in Ireland, by the way, not blue ones.'

'Yes, yes, I will,' I say absent-mindedly. 'You won't change your mind? Look, just take my number down. I work from home. And then if you have a spare hour in the next few days . . .'

'Okay,' says Dunphy. 'What's the number?' I read it out. 'Thanks for calling,' he says again, sounding marginally friendlier. 'Goodbye.'

Buggering, buggering fuck. Araminta is going to go ballistic. I know Dunphy won't call. I quickly ring her and, thankfully, get an answerphone (a languid passage from Chopin's nocturnes, followed by Araminta sounding like she needs a Strepsil. It's the kind of message that's supposed to call to mind glacial Hitchcock blondes and pared-down elegance — 'I can't come to the phone because I'm sipping a martini in a £300 négligée, waiting for my demon lover.' If you know Araminta, whose elocution lessons haven't quite ironed out her flat Bolton vowels, this is a very funny thought). I suggest she might get a Dublin writer we sometimes use to call him; Dunphy might be more open to the idea of an interview with a sympathetic native.

Meanwhile, we're off to Stella's. You know how sometimes you are incredibly attracted to the notion of a lifestyle that you know, in your heart of hearts, is a million miles away from what you really like? I get it all the time when I read the interiors magazines that Robert brings home. For instance, I know for fact that there's nothing I despise more than the nauseatingly winsome Ye Olde Cottage look bang in the middle of town — no one's ever needed an Aga in inner London (or a 2CV, for God's sake). And yet I occasionally catch myself pining for wicker baskets, hand-painted mugs and blue-and-white gingham in the kitchen. I catch myself giving passionate looks to grotesque pottery cats in the windows of shops called things like Bramble Hedge Farm.

Stella is, I suppose, my pottery cat. Stella is saintly. Stella, basically, is Motherhood. And although I don't really want to be like her deep down, there is something potently, almost dizzyingly appealing about the way she lives her life. Stella really does 'live for her children'; they are truly the centre of her universe. You get the feeling that she was only treading water before she had them — natural childbirth, natch — and that she never, ever resents the broken nights, the lack of sleep, the ridiculously early starts. Stella *bakes cakes* while Joy and Sadie, her daughters, are at school: wholemeal pound cake and banana bread, reflecting her own wholesome hippieness. After school, Stella ferries them to ballet or drama or

French or swimming in her battered, ancient 2CV. She sits with them every night when they do their homework. She never reads the shortest bedtime story available because she's longing to be by herself for two seconds, feet up with a glass of wine and a Ruth Rendell. What's more, Stella is a single mother, which, if you ask me, elevates her virtues to those I more normally equate with holiness. She is, I suppose, entirely selfless. It is perpetually amazing to me that we are friends.

When I first met Stella, which happened when I took Jack to the parent-run playgroup which she's in charge of, I had her down as some kind of cow-like simpleton. She is beautiful, though in an unkempt bohemian way that owes more to jumble-sale finds than to shopping at Voyage. She wears no make-up. I had an innate suspicion of the bare-faced; until I met her, I'd never been friends with someone who didn't own a lipstick. Like me, all my girlfriends are, and have always been, on intimate terms with London's beauty counters, and I've always thought there was something pretty suspicious about women who weren't. Why, for a start, deny yourself the joy of looking better — unless, of course, you have yourself down as a total babe in the first place, which I suspect many of these artfully 'natural' types do. Still, who in their right mind wouldn't swoon at little sable brushes, lovely eye colours in dinky little pots, scented creams, tingly astringents? Who would say 'No thanks' when given the option of making their eyes twice their actual size? And why is it that it's always the plain ones that go about unadorned? Sometimes I see women in the street and I want to say, 'Christ! Here, have my lippy, darling. God knows, you need it more than I do.'

I have Kate to thank for my love of make-up. On my sixteenth birthday, she took me to Paris for the weekend. We went shopping at the Galeries Lafayette, where, to my surprise, she steered me straight towards the Clarins counter. 'You have lovely skin,' she said, 'but unless you work at it, it's downhill all the way from now on. I am going to buy you some products which you must use every day. I'll buy some more when they run out. I know it's boring, darling, but you're too old for soap and water now. And you'll thank me in the end.'

After a long consultation with the Clarins lady—Kate, being Kate, helpfully told her that she herself used only infinitely superior Sisley products but that these would be too rich for me, and that Clarins was 'good for teenagers'—Kate walked me to the Chanel counter. 'If you *have* to wear make-up,' she sighed, 'you might as well wear decent stuff. I don't want you to look like that slutty Tamsin. Of course, you're far too young, but I'll buy you some eyeliner, and some mascara, for parties.'

She threw in some translucent powder and, to my astonishment, a scarlet lipstick ('Red is classic. Anything else is common, apart from Vaseline—although do remember that Elizabeth Arden Eight-hour Cream makes the best lip salve *ever*'), and it was the beginning of a lifelong love affair with the de-luxe end of the cosmetics market. Apart from the fact that make-up makes you look better, I love the glamour of it, of the packaging, of the names ('Rouge Coromandel', 'Vamp', 'Schiap'). Who wouldn't? Well, Stella for a start.

So I had her down as some kind of throwback, or at the very least a ghastly lentil-chewing tree-hugger who wove her own cloth out of recycled tights. I went through a stage of bracing myself for the lecture on conforming to stereotypical patriarchal notions of female beauty, actually, but it never came. Stella isn't making any kind of point by wearing a bare face. Now that I know her, I doubt the idea of wearing rouge has ever occurred to her.

Anyway, there she was, surrounded by children that weren't her own, erecting some kind of wooden climbing frame. She said hello, and gave Jack a very sweet look, and then chatted to me about the playgroup while breastfeeding three-year-old

Joy. I don't hold with breastfeeding children once they have teeth, but I was fascinated by Stella, and I still am. She is my diametrical opposite—the kind of person for whom I normally reserve my deepest contempt. And a tiny, weeny part of me wishes I was like her.

Her home, of course, is more Cotswolds than Crouch End. There are old quilts and bits of patchwork blanket draped over the back of her cat-scratched sofas, wild flowers in lumpen pottery jugs, vaguely Bloomsburyish paintings on the walls, which are painted sludgy colours from Farrow and Ball. Stella's garden is a riot of hollyhocks and nasturtiums, and a sizeable chunk of it is devoted to vegetables. Her kitchen is Aga heaven. Her bathroom has a cast-iron bath and large, rose-patterned water jugs, suggesting she gets her water from a charming little well rather than from Thames Water plc.

The whole thing ought to bring me out in a rash—it's so fraudulent, this look, in the urban depths of north London—but, despite myself, I find it delightful. Less explicably, so do Jack and Charlie, who, mysteriously, are as quiet as mice when we're here, and don't ever whinge about there being only wooden toys and colouring books to play with—for Stella would no more entertain the idea of a PlayStation than she would tear raw battery chickens limb from limb with her bare hands for dinner. Besides, she doesn't 'believe' in television. Joy and Sadie's idea of a treat is a puzzle before bed, rather than a video of *Toy Story*.

We sit in the kitchen, while Stella reheats the soup and home-made bread she's made earlier. We have very odd conversations, Stella and I; I watch my step with her. I suppose she makes me feel protective. Certainly, she makes me edit myself. Whereas, for instance, Amber and I are always discussing whether we could ever have an affair—and concluding that no, we couldn't, since apart from anything else it would mean showing our rubbery stomachs to someone new and strange—Stella and I have sweeter discussions: about schools, gardening, biscuits, E numbers. She is so maternal that I find myself treating her rather like I used to treat the impossibly charming mother of a school friend, aged thirteen. I cannot for the life of me understand why Stella's husband—who'd left the scene by the time I first met her, when Sadie must have been about one year old—ever walked out on her.

I have been in such an odd mood recently that I am not thinking straight and so, forsaking my naturally respectful line of dowager duchess-like conversation, I decide to ask her. 'Why did Mark leave, Stella? I don't understand. If I was married to you, I'd never leave.'

'Oh, bless you,' says Stella. 'He left because I had an affair. Now, this is a green minestrone from the first River Café book. I do wish they wouldn't give recipes for industrial quantities, don't you? Well, I suppose it was because I had one affair too many. Can Jack manage with a big spoon? Can you, darling, or would you like a little one?'

'A little one, please, thank you,' says Jack, in the mysterious throes of impeccable-manners-itis. Stella hands him one and shoos the children away into the playroom.

I can barely speak, I am so shocked. 'An *affair*? What do you mean, an affair? You can't have had an affair!'

'I had lots,' Stella says. 'Sadie isn't Mark's, you see.'

'Jesus! I never knew—I mean, I never guessed. I couldn't guess. You—an affair! Jesus!'

Stella laughs. 'It happens all the time. Hasn't it happened to you yet?'

There is a strange feeling in my head, a hotness, and a weakness in my stomach.

'NO!' I shout. 'Of *course* not. I couldn't—I *wouldn't*. I could never do that to Robert' My heart is beating and the shock I feel is out of all proportion to Stella's revelation. 'What happened?' I ask, taking a sip of water. 'I . . . Well, I'm sorry to sound so, er, bourgeois. But I thought you were so sussed, so together.'

'What happened was I got bored,' says Stella. 'I woke up one morning and I had the feeling that my life wasn't all it should be. Water, juice or elderflower cordial? It's home-made.'

Part of me wants to have an epi, of course — it's not every day your most wholesome friend 'fesses up to being a serial slapper. The other part is, naturally, *agog,* And the third part is feeling very uneasy *indeed* about Stella taking the words right out of my mouth, as dear old Meatloaf might say. I mean, how often does someone quote your angst back at you verbatim? And — *Christ* — what kind of saddo am I, having Meatloaf's *oeuvre* popping into my head at times of crisis?

Stella is laughing. She is, in fact, laughing at me. 'You're very old-fashioned, Clara,' she says. 'I'd never have thought it. You, of all people, being so shocked. Eat your soup. It's going cold.'

'Darling,' I shout to Charlie in the other room, 'take Jack and the girls into the garden. You can finish your lunch there. You can have a picnic.'

The four of them shuffle off very slowly, holding their soup bowls with infinite care, trying hard not to spill. I suddenly can't bear the look of their four fragile, retreating narrow little backs and have to blow my nose.

'Clara, get a grip,' smiles Stella. 'Is your period due? Echinacea drops are very effective. I'll give you some. I've had affairs. I mean, so what? It's not like I'm unique.'

'But you're married,' I say lamely. 'You were married. I mean, did you get married in church?' I feel about twelve years old.

'Yes, I got married in church. Please, Clara, don't tell me you're some kind of religious loon?' She is really laughing now, shaking her head with disbelief, as if I were about to rip off my T-shirt and expose the foot-high Sacred Heart of Jesus tattoo underneath.

'Well, no, of course not. I was thinking more about your *vows*. I mean, I sometimes say my prayers . . .'

'You *what?*'

'Oh, for God's sake, Stella — I don't mean I spend hours on my knees saying my decades. I mean if I really, really want something to happen, or really desperately want something not to, I, er, say a prayer. Well, I sort of have a friendly chat. You know. Please, please, please don't let anything bad ever happen to the children. Please, please don't make me have cancer and die and leave them. That kind of thing.'

'"Please, please don't make me have cancer"?' It is Stella's turn to look agog, though, I notice with some irritation, also not unamused.

'Well, yes, obviously.' I shrug impatiently. 'I don't want to die of cancer and leave the boys with no mother.'

'Well, no. But why should you?'

'Oh, I don't know,' I say, getting quite exasperated. 'Why should anyone? It happens, you know, for no apparent reason. And I'd really much rather it didn't happen to me. So I sometimes say a prayer about it. And,' I add triumphantly, 'it's clearly working. Because here I am, *intact* and lump-free. Which proves my point.'

'If you say so, darling. Of course, you could always stop smoking,' says Stella, who is now laughing out loud.

I am getting pretty annoyed, partly because she undeniably has a point. I shovel some soup in silence.

'What happened?' I ask, unable to resist.

Stella takes a raspberry tart out of the larder. 'I told you,' she says, looking oddly detached, as if she were talking about an acquaintance rather than herself. 'I got bored. I met a man. We'd have very *energetic* sex in the afternoons — you know, when my sister was helping with Joy. It was very exciting for a while, being desired like that. We'd go on — what's the word — *illicit* dates. I felt like a teenager.'

'All the platitudes,' I say unpleasantly.

'Yes, I suppose so,' says Stella evenly. 'Do you want cream with that? But I wouldn't knock it. I like men. And of course I liked Mark. Loved him, actually. I have a much higher sex drive than he ever did. He wasn't supposed to find out.'

'But he did.'

'Not at first, no. But the third time it happened, I got pregnant. And I didn't want an abortion. I love children. So I told him. He asked if it was the first affair and I said no, the third. He tried staying for a bit, but he couldn't hack it. Said Sadie was a constant reminder. As you say, all the platitudes. So he left, and here I am.'

'What happened to Sadie's father?'

'Oh, he never knew. He was some student who was in London for the summer, doing odd jobs. He came to do the garden, which was how we met.'

'Horny-handed Mellors to Milady's chamber,' I say, feeling depressed. 'And you never told him?'

'No. What was the point? He was twenty-one and doing a degree. Why ruin his life?'

'I suppose. But what about Sadie?'

'Sadie is two years old and blissfully happy. I'm a good mother, Clara, better than most. My children are everything. There's no need to look so disapproving, and besides *you* asked. And I told you. It doesn't matter. I am happy and so are the girls. Why should that be a problem? Open your eyes, Clara. I'm not the first ever bored housewife. And,' she adds, giving me a sharp look, 'I won't be the last.'

'Being bored,' I say pompously, 'doesn't mean you have to go running about dropping your knickers.'

'No,' says Stella, laughing again. 'There's always macramé.'

Driving home, I am forced to consider the increasingly likely possibility that I am some kind of retro throwback. Am I really the only person around that took the 'keep thee only unto him' bit of my marriage ceremony seriously? And does this make me somehow *comical?* I feel like everything is happening in a code I can't interpret. It's all topsy-turvy, apart from anything else. It's the wrong way round—I'm not supposed to be the one to whom people shout, 'Get with it, Grandma.' I mean, I'm a woman of the world. I know people have affairs. I know marriages break up. I have two stepfathers, three if Kate really does end up marrying Max. And I myself was hardly what you'd call a blushing flower before I married Robert. Whenever I read those sex surveys in women's magazines, I'm always astonished by the frankly pitiful number of lovers most women seem to have had. I think the national average is something like four. Four! Four was my first term at university. Which I suppose makes me calling Stella a slapper deeply hypocritical. But I was an *unattached* slapper, which is, I remind myself, completely different. There's a difference—isn't there?—between going to bed with people because the sun is shining and it seems like a good idea to lie in the long grass, and betraying your husband of a rainy afternoon? Oh, it's so *grubby.* Who'd be sexually incontinent?

I park the children in front of *A Bug's Life* and march up to the living room. Robert is surrounded by the Saturday papers, nose deep into *Hello!*

'I want you to know,' I say, 'that I'd always leave you first. If I wanted to have an affair, I'd always leave you first.'

'The plain one from *Corrie*'s got married. I don't know who made the dress, but it's not a good look. Hello. Did you have a nice lunch? Where are my boys?' Robert peers at me as if I were hiding the fruit of his loins in my capacious, utilitarian pockets.

'Downstairs. Robert, listen. I would not be sneaky and grubby. I would tell you. I would say, "Robert, I love another," and I would leave first. Well, maybe I'd phrase if differently. But I absolutely would not *sneak around.*'

'Would you not?'

'No, Robert. I categorically would not sneak.'

'Well, that's a comfort.' Robert is smiling at me, as if I'd said something deeply hilarious.

'Why are you smiling like that? Christ, Robert. I come and tell you — very kindly, actually — that I wouldn't betray you on some grotty single bed, with nylon sheets probably, and hundreds of people's sweat sunk into the mattress, and a smell of sprout in the air . . .'

'Clara, how squalid. Are you planning to run off with "a Homeless"?' asks Robert, quoting Charlie. 'I had you more as a suite-at-Claridge's girl.'

'Wherever I run to,' I say, seemingly incapable of normal speech, 'it will be with a clear conscience. Would be, I mean. Hypothetically. If I ran. Which I shan't, because I, er. I, er. I love you.'

'Do you?' says Robert, still, apparently, in the throes of some side-splitting private joke. 'How sweet. I love you too.'

'Violently?'

'Sorry?'

'Well, how do you love me? Violently, or like a pet?'

Robert bursts out laughing. 'You're really the end, Clara.' He composes his face. 'I love you violently. I ache when you're gone. I drag myself around, moaning like a wounded creature.' He slides off the sofa and writhes on the floor, wailing. 'Like this. It happened just now, when you were at Stella's. I was, not to put too fine a point on it, *beside myself.* Now, I've got a couple of things to do. Will you be all right giving the boys their tea?'

I stare at him, nonplussed. He has never helped me with the boys' tea in his life.

'Good,' says Robert, for no apparent reason. 'Good.' He stands up and rubs my shoulders perfunctorily. 'There are some messages on the machine, by the way.'

56

Which is really a very long and theatrical way of avoiding saying 'like a pet'.

There's a message from Araminta, saying Dunphy's agreed to be interviewed by Niamh Malone in Dublin, thank God, which means I'm off the hook, guilt-wise. One in French, which I erase—a wrong number. Two from Kate: 'For God's sake, Clara, where can you possibly be? Call me back at once.' One from Tamsin, wanting a chat, and one from my sister Flo. I suppose I'd better call Kate back.

Before that, though, I have an overwhelming urge to be supine for a while. I need to think. I mean, one can't start despising one's friends just because they have a private life which one disapproves of. Apart from anything else, what Stella does with herself is none of my business. Who am I to suddenly appoint myself moral arbiter? And she's right: she's a better mother than I could ever be. Why, then, has our conversation affected me so much? Because I wanted her to be perfect, I suppose. I wanted to believe that people like her existed, and compensated for people like me.

But she still *exists*, I tell myself crossly. She is still the same —still a pottery cat, although not necessarily one that's been spayed. I don't know. I don't know what I think. Stella makes everything look so easy—even infidelity. Perhaps it is. Perhaps everyone's at it except me. The phone rings.

'*There* you are, Clara. It's incredibly *lazy* of you not to answer your phone.'

'Kate! I was *out*. I do occasionally leave the house, you know.'

'Do you?' Kate digests this astounding fact and then mutters, 'God knows where you go.'

'I was at Stella's, having lunch.'

Kate harrumphs. 'Is Stella that hippie one who doesn't wash? And, darling, you really shouldn't be having lunch. I've told you before—eating once a day works beautifully. I had a green apple for lunch. A beautiful fruit, the apple. So green. So fresh. It was a simple apple, but to me—a feast.'

My sense of weariness is growing by the second. I lie back on the pillows.

'What did you want, Kate?'

'On the other hand, I was talking to Lady Dalston the other day and she's absolutely melted away on the Hay Diet. You should try it.'

'Yes. Was that all? More diet stuff?'

'You're being very ungracious, Clara. I do hope you're more charming to your husband than you are to me. No, I was calling to ask you to lunch on Tuesday, to meet Max.'

'Sure. Whatever.'

'The Ivy, 1 P.M. Do try to look nice, Clara. Wear a dress.'

'Bye, Kate.'

'Have you got women's troubles?' asks Kate.

'No, I fucking have not. I'll see you on Tuesday. Bye-bye.'

'God, your foul temper,' says Kate. 'Bye.'

nine

I MUST CONFESS that I am 'aweary, aweary', like the chick from the Tennyson poem—not the one who says, 'The curse has come upon me', though she certainly cheered up O level English classes and provided one with the perfect, elegantly literary excuse to skive off swimming. Anyway: not her, the other one. The weary one. I don't know why I should be taking other people's lack of constancy as a personal affront, but I am. I mean, I'm making a bloody effort, rather than running around having scuzzy affairs, and if I can do it, so can anybody else, for God's sake. Not that one wants to sound sour or anything . . .

Speaking of feeble pant-droppers, it's about time I had lunch with Naomi, who, thanks to the literally dickheaded Richard, will now forever be known as Poor Nomes by her friends (as opposed to Rich Elves, presumably). I wonder if she knows yet about Richard's fling with Acne Girl. I do hope not. The idea of Naomi throwing herself into the role of Betrayed Wife and Martyr is simply unbearable. I can see it now—the faun-like glances, the stiff (though slightly trembly) upper lip, the wholehearted abandon with which she would throw herself into the kind of no-nonsense, capable, full-on 'coping' that would have won her medals in the war;

the faint suggestion of wimple about her head. I suppose it may work as an approach — all that stoicism and silent reproach — but I must say that if I were in her shoes (Ferragamo, flat heel, stiff grosgrain bow), I'd go for the slaphappy, full-on hysteria option every time.

None of these thoughts are good for my Doris Day streak, which has come skipping and ginghaming its way to the fore in recent days. I hate my streak, but I can't help having it, nor it me, and I've given up on trying to shake it off. My Doris streak — hello, trees! hello, sky! hello, er, Rock! — is, I think, an inevitable by-product of my family situation. It's what happens to you when your immediate family is a convoluted mass of divorce and fragmentation. At the end, deep down, you want to be the one to break the pattern (it doesn't occur to you, in the throes of the loopiness brought on by the streak, that, mad, bad or sad as they are, not a single one of my relatives actively set out to be a serial divorcé/ée).

The Doris streak is responsible for my fixation with wanting to be mother to my children, and no one else's; be married to my husband, till death us do part. The streak makes me want to be neat and nuclear; sometimes it even makes me think that I wouldn't mind being *suburban*. And, obviously, the Doris streak is often at odds with the rest of me, or at least with the parts that smoke and drink and occasionally spend a happy half-hour drying the dishes absent-mindedly while wondering what it would be like to snog strange people who really, really fancied you and were *groaning* with desire at the idea of kissing you. If they existed. And one knew them. Hypothetically.

When Doris is coming on particularly strong, I sometimes tie my hair back with a ribbon and walk around the house wearing a pinafore (a very, very bad look for size 16 woman, obviously), wondering how hard it would be to rustle up a batch of muffins for tea and humming 'Move Over, Darling' to myself. It's about to happen now. It's time, clearly, to nip the streak in the bud sharpish.

The streak is nipped for me. The phone rings. The call is from my stepfather Julian—well, my ex-ex-stepfather, if we're going to be technical about it.

'Hello, Clara,' he says. 'How are you? Very good, very good,' he continues, not waiting for a reply, which is actually quite reasonable of him, since all I ever say—Doris streak or no—is 'Fine.'

'Boys all right?' he asks. 'Robert?'

'Fine.'

'Goodo. Now, we need you down here.'

'Do you?'

'Absolutely,' Julian says.

And I imagine. I imagine what it would be like if this were a simple statement of fact: *we need you down here.* As in, I miss you sometimes. As in, *I like your children. We need you down here.*

'Gathering of the clan, as it were,' Julian is saying.

'Sorry? I missed that.'

'Gathering of the clan. At the weekend. Small party.'

'That's nice,' I say feebly. Gatherings of clans are gatherings I can do without. 'What are you—we—celebrating?'

'Francis is being baptized,' says Julian. 'Thought we'd have a do. First male grandchild and all that.'

I know he isn't my biological father, but Julian did bring me up. I have two children, I want to remind him, and even though they're not *really* his grandchildren, my boys love him as if they were. And every time Julian tells me that Francis is his first grandchild, my heart does a sort of lurch. Even though it's true.

I don't want to go. I don't want to be reminded that I'm an also-ran. I don't want my children not to understand why Francis is so much more special, so much more valued, than they will ever be in Julian's eyes. And I don't want to dislike Francis, who's only a baby.

'If you come down on Friday evening, Clara, I'll come and get you all from the station. Let me know what train . . .'

61

'Julian. Julian, I'm not sure we can make it. I need to talk to Robert . . .'

'Of course you can make it,' Julian says. 'Call me and let me know what train you'll be getting. Goodbye.'

I put the receiver back into its cradle and stare into space. It's nice at Julian's. He lives in a splendid Georgian pile in deepest Somerset. He has 'gardens', plural. Julian has *staff*, who take away your dirty clothes and wash and iron them, and make your bed and put fresh flowers in your room every day, like very helpful elves or mice. He has a big library and roaring fires in every room, as well as red lacquered bowls containing toffees on every table. He has a cook, which is arguably something of a waste, since his favourite food is boiled ham — 'good English food,' as he would put it, 'not that faffed-about stuff'.

But I still don't want to go.

My emotional well-being aside, there are other snags, like nature. Nature and I aren't what you'd call immediately compatible. There's so bloody much of it and it's so pitifully low on shops. I would love vast fields of undulating wheat much more if there was a tiny shop in the middle of each one. Nothing too de luxe: we're talking small, unobtrusive accessories boutique rather than, say, giant Harvey Nicks. A lipstick shack, that kind of thing, or a foundation hut that also stocked earrings.

And maybe fewer cows? Because while I am able to appreciate the lovable quadrupeds in an aesthetic sense — and they do look very pretty, standing there in their rather 1980s black-and-white prints, looking like backing singers for the Specials — I worry when I am actually standing too near them. Cows do that thing of completely ignoring you as you trudge through their field and then suddenly herding up, so that within seconds you have a dozen of them making a bee-line for you, not looking aggressive *as such* but not actually exuding Christian kindness either. Cows — and they have this in common with the very dim — can turn their faces from blank sweetness to intense malevolence in a matter of nano-seconds in a way that (mercifully) eludes other mammals.

Plus I eat beef. And so, when in the company of cows—most days at Julian's—I start wondering whether the cows can smell the rare steaks I've eaten over the years. When the group action starts—when they start heading towards me like so many heavy-footed, lumbering psychos—I convince myself that they can, that they are supersniffers bent on re-venge, on making an example of the stinky carnivore in their midst. And then, obviously, I fill with panic and start *running* like the clappers, stepping in the cows' vile pats as I run, leap-ing over fences and (the shame) emitting small squeaks of fear, until I get to the house and have to hose my shoes. It's a sort of ritual at Julian's and not one I especially look for-ward to.

Kate was married to Julian for fifteen years, and he is the father of Evie and Flo. He is also, through his previous mar-riage, the father of Hester and Digby—still with me?—and is currently the stepfather of Ollie and Jasmine.

I was six when Kate and Julian got together and twenty-one when they divorced. My own father, Felix, doesn't really feature much—he took off for California in 1968, grew a beard, bought a bike and manifests himself, via postcard, only once or twice a year—and it would be fair to say that Julian brought me up. Hester and Digby were brought up by their own mother, so we didn't see that much of them.

It's a funny thing, divorce. One minute—well, one *decade* really—you're someone's stepchild, a virtual adoptee, Of The Family if not actually Of The Blood, and the next—well, the next you're nothing. And it's difficult to know how to react in the long term, once you've stopped crying (because you do cry—you do the kind of unphotogenic waah-waah crying that involves snot and sobs and a swollen face).

Memories are the problem, I suppose. Memories of all of us together—me, Evie, Flo, Kate, Julian—laughing our way along a pony trek in the Lake District, say. Memories of me alone, drunk on cider aged fifteen, being collected from a party by a thunder-faced but kind-hearted Julian. Memories of missing him, sentimental as that sounds—not that Julian was any kind of paragon, but still. At least he was kind.

These memories are, fatally, ones I get the distinct impression he doesn't particularly want reminding of, partly because his parting from Kate redefined the notion of acrimony. Such memories can make a girl feel pretty damned awkward when in her cups around the Julian Armitage dinner table. Which table is problematic in itself, since it is a *new* and unfamiliar table, and not the table of my childhood. Julian bought the house after his divorce from Kate, so that although it feels like a vaguely known quantity—there are rugs and pots and bits of china that I grew up with strewn around it—it is in reality just a strange house. A house that has nothing to do with me. More than a hotel, but less than a home.

But I try and push these queries aside. If in doubt, stride through, I always say, taking very big steps and pretending you know exactly where you're going.

It'll be fine. One little baptism party isn't going to kill me. It'll be fine. I love Julian. And he, in turn . . . well, never mind. Robert will hold my hand and it'll be fine.

ten

JACK IS STARING at his porridge with unconcealed hostility.

'Lumps,' he says. 'Lumpy lumpy lumps.'

'They give you the grumps,' says Charlie.

'Yes,' says Jack, 'they do. Can I have Frosties?'

'No,' I growl, slapping pastrami on to seeded bread for Charlie's lunch box. 'It took me ages to make and I'd like you to eat it. Or at least try it. Porridge is delicious. It's muscle food. Batman cries if his mummy doesn't make it for him every morning.'

'Batman doesn't have a mummy,' says Jack. 'And Batman never cries, silly.' He starts giggling at the absurdity of the idea of a lachrymose Bruce Wayne.

'Everyone has a mummy, dumbo,' says Charlie. 'Everyone comes from their mummy's tummy.'

'Do they?' asks Jack, fascinated. 'Even Batman? Who puts you there?'

'The daddy,' says Charlie helpfully. 'The daddy gives the mummy a seed. You were a seed. A little *seed.*'

'I was not!' says Jack. '*You* were a stupid seed. I was a cool cowboy baby with cool guns. Mum-*mee*, Charlie says I was a seed.'

Both the boys gaze expectantly at me. 'You were a *sort* of

seed,' I say, vaguely, wondering if 7.45 in the morning is really the time to go into all this. 'Everyone was a sort of seed.'

'Like this,' says Charlie authoritatively, brandishing the jar of ancient sunflower seeds I once bought, emulating Stella — seedies instead of sweeties, so much better for the tooties. Needless to say, these were a spectacular nonstarter.

I say, 'Hmm.'

Both the boys stare interestedly at the seeds, then at my stomach (I must do sit-ups, I must do sit-ups), while I bustle about more theatrically than normal, finding things for their lunch boxes, hoping the general clattering around will suffice to kill this particular line of investigation. Mercifully, Charlie slides off his chair in search of his recorder, and Jack becomes distracted by a Solid Torso Action Man on the back of the porridge box, so that both of them forget to address the seed question for the moment.

(I learned about reproduction, aged seven, from a book aimed, I think, at older children — or possibly at medical students — bought for me by Kate. Kate, rightly, has a horror of sentimentality, and the book was of the biological textbook variety, with many diagrams of engorged, erect penises, looking, I remember thinking, like very pink, possibly scalded, meerkats. In my book, the act of love was represented by a diagram of the silhouette of a woman [pink] with a silhouetted man [blue] lying on top of her. His *membrum virile* was shown clearly penetrating her. Being mere outlines, neither of our happy protagonists had faces, and being mere drawings, they failed to convey any sense of how one might comport oneself in a similar situation. Which is how it came to be that, much to the discomfort of Johnny Edwardes, who took my virginity, I always believed that you both lay perfectly still during sex once penetration had occurred. I think I'll stick to the 'seed' explanation for the time being.)

Ten minutes later, Charlie and Jack are both bundled up

into their coats, ready for Naomi, who's kindly offered to take them to school this morning. I haven't seen her properly for a week or so, only waved from the car and had the briskest chat on the phone yesterday. She's looked better, in that this morning she looks like I normally look in the morning, i.e. like her anti-self: sticky-up hair, no evidence of make-up and, in her case, a redness around the eyes that suggests her husband's infidelity is no longer a secret. She says, 'How are you, Clara?' in a sad voice, and I want to hug her. Instead—she may, for all I know, look this way because she has food poisoning, and I'm hardly about to inquire in front of the children—I ask her to come round for lunch with me tomorrow. I'd go for today, but today is Kate and Max day. 'That would be lovely,' says Naomi, gathering up the boys. 'I'd really like that.'

I was wrong about Naomi. There is nothing stoical about her tottering down the stairs on her skinny legs, holding four lunch boxes and two children per hand.

I think Robert was joking when I asked him about Somerset this morning. Perhaps I shouldn't have asked the minute he opened his eyes, but I didn't get round to it last night and it's preying unpleasantly on my mind. Anyway, Robert was lying propped up on his pillows, looking coolly around the room, as is his early-morning wont, surveying the old junk-shop paintings that I have leaning against the walls, taking in the antique shawls that are draped around the sofa, the jewellery hanging off the mirror—taking in the mess, basically. So far, I've resisted his many attempts at 'stripping back' the bedroom by dumping the furniture and painting everything white. Robert says this would turn the bedroom into an 'oasis'. I say nothing. But the subject is going to come up again and I'm going to have to say something, because Robert can be very determined. I wouldn't be surprised if he had the bedroom done one day while I was away.

'I spoke to Julian yesterday,' I said. 'Wants us to go down for the weekend.'

'I can't,' said Robert.

'Robert, listen. It's Francis's baptism. There's going to be some kind of party. You know how odd it makes me feel, going there.'

'Not my fault,' said Robert. 'And I don't quite see why it makes you feel odd—you don't ever have to lift a finger when you're there.'

'Robert,' I said quietly. 'Please. I'd really like it if you came with us.'

'I can't, Clara,' Robert said, getting out of bed. 'I'm knackered and I've got things to do.'

'Like what?'

'Like stuff. Sorry, Clara, but you're on your own.'

Aren't I just? I must give it another go tonight.

I'm about to go and soak in the bath when the phone rings. It's Niamh Malone, the woman who's interviewed Sam Dunphy for *Panache*. She's after the newspaper cuttings the magazine sent me. She didn't need them earlier, she says, since she knew all about him, being a dance fan, but would I mind bunging them in the post now as she needs to check a couple of things? Sure, I say, hunting around for paper on which to jot down her address.

'He's gorgeous, isn't he?' sighs Niamh. 'Such a charmer.'

'Really?' I say. 'You could have fooled me.'

'Oh no, he's a complete dote. And God almighty, the sexiness,' says Niamh, sounding, unusually for her, positively kittenish. 'He gave me an invite to the première of the new show—you know, the London première. I'm going to come down especially. There's a huge party afterwards. There are a couple for you too. Will I post them to you?'

'A couple of what?' I ask stupidly.

'A couple of invites,' says Niamh. 'I just said, you know, to the show and then the party. If *Panache* pay me in time, I might even get this beautiful John Rocha dress I've seen to wear to it. It's black, very plain, with . . .'

'I don't think so,' I say, interrupting. 'Not about the dress, I mean. The dress sounds lovely. But you've made a mistake, Niamh. Dunphy and me, we didn't exactly hit it off.'

'Did you not?' says Niamh, sounding astonished that any-one could fail to be seduced—figuratively speaking—by the swoonsome ballerino. 'Ah well—he gave me these anyway, and said to pass them on to you.'

'Are you sure?' I ask, somewhat bewildered.

'Oh yes,' Niamh says. 'I'll send them on. I wouldn't worry about it—I think they've invited about 600 people! See you at the show, I guess,' she chirps excitedly.

'Er, yes. I suppose so. Maybe. See you. Good luck with the dress,' I say, before hanging up.

That's quite odd, I think to myself in the bath. But perhaps Dunphy is under the impression that I am some kind of reviewer or critic (he's not far wrong there, in that I could excel at personal criticism of him, the stuck-up wanker). Or perhaps he's just a Billy No-Mates who doesn't want his little show to feature too many empty seats. Maybe he is an obses-sive converter, burning with a missionary zeal to make people like me enthuse about modern dance. Still, I suppose if you're asking 600 people, the odd undesirable might slip through the net.

Anyway, Kate. The very thought of my mother's impend-ing nuptials makes me immerse myself under the scented water and stay there for as long as my lungs can hold out. I very much want Kate to be happy. I want nothing more, in fact. But Kate, like any number of serially married women before her, loves the idea of Love so much that she makes ter-rible mistakes. (I've always thought the serially married were terribly misunderstood. They're desperate romantics, as a whole, rather than desperate adventurers.) And I can't say I thrill to the core at the idea of Max, the American seer. She's a tough nut, Kate, in many respects, but the easiest of push-overs in another. She is an appalling judge of character and responds absurdly well to flattery.

Still, one of the advantages of being thirty-three instead of six is that you can at least look out for your mother's inter-ests, I reflect as I get busy with the shampoo. My fraud anten-nae are better developed than Kate's, and I will suss this man out and share my findings with her, for her sake as well as mine. And now it's time for a session of in-depth grooming. Kate would never forgive me if I arrived for lunch looking anything other than pristine. This is why Naomi has taken the boys to school: I scrub up reasonably well, but it takes a minimum of three hours in the bathroom. No wonder I man-age the full cosmetic Monty only about twice a year.

I love the Ivy. I come here for a treat, unlike Kate, who comes here at midnight and gets them to make her egg and chips, as if London's most perennially fashionable restaurant were a sweet little local caff. I love the way it smells, of success and Eggs Benedict and *fun*.

One of the many amazing things about Kate is the way in which she dominates a room. Your eye is just drawn to her, even in here, with the Ivy's usual smattering of A-list celebs and household names. She is sitting very straight along a ban-quette, facing the room, while her companion, my new step-daddy-to-be, has his (considerable) back to it.

She's beautiful, Kate, she's the real thing, with exquisite bones moving beneath her smooth, poreless skin, her huge slanted grey eyes, her sleek gloss of black hair, her generous smile. She always reminds me of one of those Nouvelle Vague French film stars. She's classy-looking, classic, to die for. If she were any taller—she's five-five—she'd be terrifying: too beautiful, too poised, too everything. But as she is, you want to protect her, to shield her. Which I am about to do. Because she may drive me completely bloody barking mad, but she *is* my mother.

Today, Kate is wearing Jil Sander: a soft, creamy white shirt that looks like whipped froth under an unstructured, floppy navy trouser suit that manages to look sexy, almost too-big, almost dressy-uppy, on her girlish frame (no Chinese lesbian she). There is colour on her fingernails, which are perfect red almonds, and on her mouth. She wears no jewellery, except for the enormous engagement emerald.

'You look fantastic, Kate,' I say, bending down to kiss her and breathing in a comforting waft of Mitsouko.

'Thank you, Clara. You're looking lovely yourself,' Kate beams back. 'Darling, you do see, don't you—it's always worth a little effort.'

'Three hours, actually,' I reply. 'Not so little.'

'Yes, well,' Kate says. 'It would take much less time if you had regular facials and just *looked after yourself* every day.'

I bite my tongue—this is neither the time nor the place for a discussion about the time, effort and phenomenal, frankly unfeasible expense involved in the kind of grooming regime which Kate considers a daily necessity. I turn to Max instead, hand extended. 'Hello,' I say. 'I'm Clara.'

He looks pleasant enough, I must say. Late fifties, I'd imagine, with a shorn head of white hair that would give him a thuggish aspect were it not for his humorous, sensitive face. He's wearing a washed-out-looking pink shirt, beautifully tailored if aged, under a faintly battered oatmeal-coloured cardigan that might be cashmere. I can see the tops of his legs as he stands up: conker-coloured cords. Which is a relief, as I was braced for the flowing white beard and matching robes, seers, in my mind, not being entirely physically dissimilar to the druid in *Asterix*—or, at the very least, braced for the 'wacky' shirt and 'fun' specs so favoured by 'crazy guys' of a certain age. His handshake is firm, and he looks amused, which is always a plus.

'Max Tilby,' he says. 'Delighted to meet you.'

'Almost like the hat,' says Kate, her head to one side. 'Quite comical. I think it's *such* a good idea to shave your head when you're going bald,' she adds joyfully, snapping off a piece of breadstick. 'Don't you, Clara, darling? Nothing worse than a man with a great thumping widow's peak. Or a bald *pate*. Which a former mother-in-law of mine — your granny, possibly, darling, I forget — always pronounced "pâté",' she adds absent-mindedly. 'A bald pâté. What a thought. All pink and moussey, like foie gras.'

'Quite,' I say, trying not to laugh and peering at Max for signs of discontent, alongside reflecting, not for the first time, on the fact that Kate, though not uneccentric, is more than capable of being a delight.

Max is roaring with laughter. 'You've put me off my starter, darling,' he says, reaching for her hand in a way I would normally find quite pukey but in this context suddenly strikes me as deeply endearing.

'So sorry,' says Kate. 'Though I do think foie gras an odd choice. Do you not see into the souls of geese, Max? Those poor creatures, so troubled. Perhaps you *choose* not to see. Very remiss of you. Have the tomato and basil galette, why don't you? Clear your conscience. Now — a bowl of consommé for Clara, I think.' Kate stares into my face. 'About 100 calories a bowl. Just think, darling, you could have *thirds.*'

'I'm having risotto, actually, Kate.'

'I do wish you'd stop eating like an Italian peasant, darling. Look at what happened to your father.'

'My *father?*' I ask. 'What about him?'

'Well, he turned into one. An Italian peasant, I mean. Within months. Sort of lumpen and coarse, when he used to be so handsome.' She sighs sadly and shakes her head. 'Because he ate risotto and *mozzarella in carrozza* all the time. And you have the same kind of bone structure, darling.'

'Kate! I am having one helping of risotto. It will not turn me into an obese mamma. Christ! Do you think we might stop discussing my diet? Especially in front of your friend here, whom I've never met before?'

'Obese mamma, obese papa,' sighs Kate infuriatingly. 'What diet?' she adds rhetorically. 'There is no diet. And it really is *such* a shame.'

'Sorry about this,' I say to Max, before turning to Kate. 'Why? *Why* is it such a shame? I don't think it's a shame. I'm happy. It's only a shame for *you*. But it's not a shame for me. So leave it, Kate, will you? Just leave it.'

'It is a shame, because you are hiding,' says Kate very steadily. 'You are hiding under the food. You are using food as some kind of substitute, and it makes me sad. It suggests you aren't entirely happy, darling. That's all.'

'Spare me the crappy psycho-babble, Kate,' I say crossly, wrestling with the horrible notion that Kate, maddeningly, is not entirely off-target.

'You asked,' says Kate. 'Now, let's order. Champagne, I think, since we are celebrating.'

'You're a very good-looking girl all the same, Clara,' says Max, with great sweetness.

'She's beautiful,' says Kate evenly. 'But that isn't the point.'

Turns out Max is only a seer in his spare time. He is not, as it were, omniscient. As far as I can establish, which isn't very far, since he is thankfully unwilling to discuss this subject in any detail, he is the kind of person that gets a funny feeling before boarding a plane, cancels his seat and then discovers while watching the news that said plane has crashed. Arguably vaguely psychic, we might say, rather than your actual Nostradamus. But apparently Kate *does* have a 'beautiful aura'. It's sort of mauve, he says (Kate: 'Darling, *mauve,* imagine! Couldn't you say pink?'). Which is nice.

And so is Max, to my surprise. He's clearly mad about

Kate, and she, in turn, is pretty smitten with him. He puts up with the lectures on geese, he laughs delightedly at her slightly off-the-wall jokes, he seems kind . . . I think Kate might be on to something this time.

When Max isn't seeing auras, he is some kind of high-flying businessman—something to do with the Internet, if I understood rightly. I know now why Kate wittered on about him being a seer. She has an allergy to the very notion of men in suits doing things in offices, a notion she finds both boring beyond belief and desperately suburban—not to mention faintly humiliating in relation to her. Kate deserves lyre-players and troubadours, she thinks, not droney old pen-pushers. Which is why Julian, for instance, was always described as 'a farmer' rather than an industrialist, based on the fact that Kate knew he liked the idea of living in the country one day. Maurice, husband number three, was, to Kate's friends and relatives, 'a sculptor', based entirely on the fact that he liked modelling things out of softened candlewax at the dinner table when he got bored. In real life, of course—as opposed to Kate World—Maurice was (whisper it) an accountant, albeit an enormously clever and distinguished one. My own father, the improbably named (for a sometime manic depressive) Felix, never actually had much of a job, which explains why I am the only one of my siblings, both blood and step, to actually need to work for a living and to fret about mortgages. Felix, Kate says, was 'a biker', which is only a very slight exaggeration.

Anyway, Max has invited us all to his 'cottage' for the summer. Kate: 'Tell Clara about your sweet little cottage.' Just as Max is about to open his mouth, she decides—as she so often does—to speak for him.

'Max has a charming cottage in the *sweetest* little fishing village,' she tells me, smiling at the recollection of it. 'A village full of simple fisherfolk. I was there three weeks ago. You'd love it, Clara. The pretty boats, the adorable people—

poor as church mice, but always willing to share their lobsters with you.'

'Lobsters?' I say. 'What do you mean, lobsters?'

'It's in America, darling, they have lobsters *everywhere,*' Kate explains dismissively, conjuring up a mental picture of poor Manhattanites fighting off the Pincer Menace on every street corner. 'Max and I went for a walk and realized we'd no supper at home, so we knocked on the door of a little clapboard house in the village and the *sweet* old peasant lady that answered gave us two lobsters! So simple, those people, but my God—they know how to live.' She shakes her head in admiration. '*That's* style, Clara, don't you think? The poorest of the poor, the dispossessed, almost, *feasting* on lobster.'

Max is grinning broadly at this stage, and so he should be, with his village full of generous, crustacean-loving rustics. 'You must come over, Clara.' he says. 'Bring your boys.'

'I'd love to,' I say. 'It sounds heavenly. Where is it, exactly, this coastal hamlet of yours?'

'It's in a place called Martha's Vineyard, on the East Coast,' says Kate. 'Too sweet. Darling, it'd be such a break for you. We could ask the neighbours to baby-sit, couldn't we, Max? They'd be glad of the cash, poor things. And then the rest of us could go and have dinner in one of those little fishermen's cafés. Rough and ready, but such fun.'

I want to say, 'What, Martha's Vineyard, as in millionaires' playground? Little café, as in $200 a head for *homard à l'Américaine?* Neighbours, as in Kennedys?' Instead, I suppress a giggle. I am suddenly filled with intense love for Kate. I am, as Elvis might put it, temporarily turned into a hunka hunka burning love. It is an indisputable fact that she enhances my life. Max is smiling at me conspiratorially and throwing Kate fond glances. Yes, I think to myself, yes. He gets her. He'll do.

eleven

I HADN'T REALIZED the post from Eire was so swift. This morning's batch, freshly landed, does indeed contain two posh-looking invitations to the Sadler's Wells première of *Contortions,* Sam Dunphy's ludicrously named show. I mean, really—you might as well call it *I'm All Bendy, Me.* The invites are printed in painfully hip type on top of a black-and-white shot of Dunphy leaping—there's probably a more technical term for it, but I don't know what it is. His skin is sheeny with sweat and he's wearing a skin-tight white T-shirty affair, through which—Christ almighty—you can see his erect nipples. Beautiful legs, though. And arms, actually—sort of *sinewy.* I have to concede that, speaking as a purely detached observer, i.e. on aesthetic grounds alone, Dunphy is a bit of a fox. Sexy, even. Speaking, however, as the kind of observer who's spent some time with him, he also, to me, looks exactly like what he is: a vain, tight-T-shirted, poofy-eyed creep.

Two smaller bits of card tumble out of the envelope. These are invitations to the after-show party, at some groovy bar in Hoxton, please bring this invitation with you, blah blah. Clocking the date—the show premières at the end of next week—I shove the whole bundle under the fruit bowl (where it joins last year's tax bill, a party invitation for Jack, a reminder from BT, a card from Selfridges advising me of some special offer on my preferred brand of cleanser, a postcard from Amber which says, 'Hello? Where are you? xxx' and our family pass to London Zoo.

I can't believe Kate said that about my 'relationship', if we're going to be all textbook about it, with food, I think to myself as I hastily give the public parts of the house a vacuum. The bloody cheek. The total *nerve*. The, er, slight psychological insight. Or not. I mean, it is simply *too* absurd to contemplate the possibility that all overweight people are unhappy. Isn't that what she said? 'Not entirely happy.' And is that what I am? I sit down on the middle step of the hall stairs, like a gigantic Christopher Robin ('Hush, hush, whisper who dares/The tubbiest of all mummies/is coming up the stairs') and switch the Hoover off.

Okay. So maybe I am not 'entirely happy'. Maybe this isn't necessarily what I had planned for myself when I was a day-dreaming teenager. Maybe this is . . . quotidian. But—and it's a big but—it's not a million miles from what I *did* have planned, because I only ever had very ploddy aspirations: to be happy, and secure, and not to have to move around all the time (Kate and I did a lot of that, around most of Europe, until she met Julian). I wanted to live in a house that would feel like home, forever, with my children. And I am. I am. I'm sitting in it.

That's that settled, then. But I am nonetheless finding it very hard to get up. My house, my kids . . . There's something else I'm not focusing on: my husband. My husband, whom I love. Because I do love him, as I think he loves me. I just don't *love* him. He doesn't make me die. He doesn't make me swoon every time I see him. I don't have to lie down each time I think of him. And that wasn't on my list. I wanted the swooning. Just a little swooning. The odd snatch of longing I wanted to feel lonely in my bed when he wasn't around.

'Nobody has that,' I tell myself crossly, remembering poor Naomi and her shit of a letch of a husband. I am talking out loud, raising my voice to myself. 'The reason I wanted the swooning is because I was fifteen, for God's sake. I had *some* swooning, at the beginning, at least. I should consider myself exceptionally lucky. How *dare* I even be thinking like this? What am I going to do—walk out because Robert doesn't ravish me every night? Fuck's sake, Clara. Get a fucking grip, will you?'

The oddest thing of all is I feel like phoning Kate. But I don't dare. Once, three months or so ago, Kate and I had rather too much wine with our dinner, and I told her—because she was looking at me like she knew—that I was feeling a tiny bit . . . antsy, I think, is the way I put it. 'Be adult, Clara,' she said. 'It's what being grown-up is about. Get on with it. You're luckier than most. You're luckier than me.' I felt embarrassed, and nodded. Kate, though, being Kate, hadn't finished. 'The thing I have *absolutely always found,*' she said breezily, 'is that provided you have *very good* sex, most of those problems just fall by the wayside.' I said nothing to this—I may have gazed at her in disbelief, perhaps. 'You do have good sex, don't you, darling?' Kate said. 'Do realize it makes me feel quite *ill* even to have to ask—I'm your mother, for God's sake, not your best friend. But it is important.'

I said, not entirely truthfully, 'Yes. Yes. It's fine.' Kate looked like she was about to say something else, but lit a cigarette instead, and we changed the subject. I can't call her now. I know one is supposed to be modern, but I simply will not entertain the idea of talking to my mother about my sex life. She was right: it's what girlfriends are for.

But I can hardly ask Naomi, who's due for lunch. Hi, Nomes, how's your sex life? Oops, not so great, I guess, what with your hubby knobbing his PA. I dial Amber's number instead, but just get her voice-mail. Stella? No, not Stella. I suspect I know what Stella's advice would be and I don't think I'd like it. Tamsin's at work. Without thinking very hard about it, I find myself dialling Robert's direct line instead.

'Hi, Clara,' he says. He always sounds so alert at work, so energetic. 'You'll have to be quick — I'm just about to have a meeting.'

'I don't have anything to say,' I say, faintly pathetically. 'We got asked to Sam Dunphy's show, and to his party. Naomi is coming to lunch.'

'Stop!' says Robert. 'Stop right now. It's too exciting. Now I won't be able to concentrate all day. Naomi coming to lunch! A ballet party! Anything else, *baby?*'

'Yes,' I say, smiling despite myself. 'I've been hoovering. And it seems to be quite sunny outside.'

'You're dazzling me,' Robert says. 'It's go, go, go, isn't it? It's a social whirl. Anything planned for this afternoon?' He drops his voice to a hyper-excited whisper. *'Sainsbury's?'*

'Perhaps.'

'The fun.' There are noises in the background, and Robert says, 'I have to go now, Clara. I'll call you later.'

'Bye,' I say. 'From funny little me, in my funny little world.'

'Bye,' says Robert. 'You forgot your funny little face.'

And I cheer up.

twelve

NAOMI APPEARS AT 12.30 on the dot, and I am glad to note that infidelity does not affect her punctuality ('Punctuality is the politeness of kings,' she once informed me, with such a regal expression on her face that I nearly asked if she had thrillingly improbable ancestry). She looks better than she did yesterday morning: the taupe-coloured eyeshadow has made a comeback, as have the tinted moisturizer and subtly outlined and glossed 'natural'-coloured lips. She throws my kitchen a mini-version of the look popularized by my mother —the 'Oh, look, an unironed tea-towel. I do believe we're in a hovel' look that mixes sociological curiosity with faint disgust—and automatically reaches for the J-cloth. Naomi's catchphrase, if she had one, would be 'You missed a bit.'

But she's a creature of contrasts, Naomi, because she says, 'I love your kitchen,' and sighs. I love my kitchen too. It may be shambolic, with its drying-rack hoicked up on the ceiling, festooned with unphotogenic garments, like my greying knickers, rather than, say, drying bunches of lavender or wispy, antiquey bits of lace, and its omnipresent bits of Lego, and I'm not entirely sure orange is the best colour for such a room—part of me keeps expecting bowler-hatted men to come marching through at any time, singing 'The Sash My

Father Wore' and looking grouchy — but at least it's big enough to have a (rather tatty) sofa in it. Okay, so the hamsters don't exactly scream 'Hygiene', and the wall space is in danger of entirely being taken over by the children's mad and not necessarily terribly aesthetically pleasing drawings — Chewbacca, in particular, looks like a poo on legs — but the kitchen is undeniably cosy.

I like to think it has other merits too, like the industrial cooking range and the lovely though minute and entirely impractical red 1950s fridge. I see the boys have been practising their spelling, because the magnetic letters stuck to it say 'BADGER' and 'HERKYOOLEES'. While impressed with Charlie's phonetic fearlessness, I don't think this looks particularly stylish. It's not a look that would get *World of Interiors* drooling, I don't think. And why 'badger'?

Unlike me, Naomi is very interested in white goods. She reads *Good Housekeeping* and cuts out the comparative features on washing machines and dryers and ovens, in order to be fully equipped when she next needs one. 'However do you cope without a chest freezer?' she once asked, absurdly, as if I was the kind of person who, given a couple of hours to spare, would automatically think, 'Hey, I know — I'll make a week's worth of casual but sophisticated dinners and freeze them.' I never entirely believed such people existed until I met Nomes, who also makes her own Christmas wreaths and decorates any cake with hand-crafted, though faintly boggle-eyed, marzipan animals.

And *World of Interiors* loves it. It photographed her kitchen last year. As you would expect, Naomi's kitchen, all pale bleached wood, Shaker units and colour-coordinated Le Creuset cookware, is the kitchen many of us long for. I am often puzzled by it, because it never looks like anyone actually uses it. It is permanently pristine, even though I know for a fact that Naomi bakes her own bread, produces three-course dinners every night and creates the kind of lunch-box extravaganzas for her children that have mine wailing about the injustice of ham and cheese rolls. ('Linus has mushroom pâté and very special cheese from the country that looks like a boot,' Charlie says, at least twice a week. 'Today Linus had a thing called lemon tart. Linus has a napkin made of cloth. Linus has carrot juice. Linus loves olives, but not Greek ones. He says Ribena hurts your teeth.' And so on.)

'I don't know about my kitchen,' Naomi says. 'It's sterile-looking, don't you think?'

'No,' I say. 'It's lovely. It's so clean. You could eat off the floor, if you were pretending to be a doggy. I'd love a kitchen like that.'

'You know, don't you?' Naomi says, in a neutral tone of voice, rooting through her bag for her Canderel while I put a coffee in front of her. 'You must know.'

And I am in a quandary. I know many things, as I am always telling the boys. I am omniscient and packed to the gills with information, which I impart to Father Christmas every December; I even have eyes in the back of my head. But I know too much, in this particular circumstance, and I'm not quite clear what part of my deep and profound knowledge Nomes is referring to. The difficulty of keeping a kitchen immaculate? The cost of said kitchen? The recipe for salmon baked in a salt and herb crust? Or the fact that her husband's a philandering bastard?

I am wet, and Option A seems safest. 'You must spend all day cleaning it,' I say. 'I mean, God knows I try — you wouldn't believe the amount of Mr Muscle we get through in a week — and it still looks like this.' I gesture at the pile of newspapers on the table and at the delicate towerlet of crumbs under Jack's chair, a testimony to his love of Jammy Dodgers. 'So yes, I *do* know. I don't know how you do it, though. I wish we had cleaning ladies, don't you? Robert says they're a waste of money, but I don't.'

'I mean,' says Nomes, briskly clicking her saccharine dispenser twice, 'about Richard.'

Arse. Now what? Do I lie? Do I feign ignorance and mime shock and outrage when she tells me? Do I nod grimly, and deal with her asking me what kind of crappy friend I am for not telling her the moment I found out? Arse. Arse. Big, giant, outsize arse—Richard's arse, in fact. Thinking on my feet, I decide to cling to the possibility that the Richard news is non-sexual. Perhaps he's been promoted, or been given a bigger company car, or a huge bonus (to match the size of his behind). Perhaps he's been sacked, I think maliciously, which would serve him right.

'Know what?' I say feebly, burying my face right inside the fridge. 'I'm just looking for the pumpkin ravioli. Where can they be?'

They are, in fact, literally in front of my nose. But I am quite liking it in the fridge and feel a marked reluctance to come out. Especially when Naomi says, 'Know that he's having an affair.' I feel a great love for the inside of the fridge at this moment. A passion, almost. A longing for more of its Arctic embrace. 'Hmm?' I say spastically, panic rising. And then: 'Where are the *fucking* ravioli of *fuck?*'

'Language, Clara,' says Naomi automatically.

I reluctantly close the fridge door. My heart is beating horribly fast and a part of Selfless Clara The Good Friend wonders whether I might be a candidate for a heart attack. I mean, I'm hardly the Exercise Queen.

God, what a thing to think at a time like this! I am going to punish myself by not lying.

'Yes, I know,' I say, as gently as I can, except it comes out as more of a shout. 'With Parmesan, black pepper and cream, or with olive oil?'

'Plain, please. Calories,' Naomi explains. 'How long have you known?'

'About a week,' I stammer nervously. 'They're disgusting by themselves. At least have oil. There's some basil somewhere. I could shred that? *Chiffonade de basilic,* Nomes—that ought to float your boat. It sounds rather chic. No?'

'No,' Naomi says, brushing aside my helpful culinary suggestions.

'Look, Nomes, I would have told you, but—well, you know, no one likes to deliver that kind of news. Think of the poor messenger, you know, being shot. Bang bang. Ow.' I clutch my breast melodramatically and stagger a bit.

'Clara . . .' says Naomi. 'For God's sake.'

'I'm sorry,' I say, sobering up. 'I'm so sorry. I've known a few days. Robert told me. I'm sorry.'

'What did he say?'

I must say, Naomi is looking very composed. In her shoes, I'd be red in the face and practically hyperventilating by now.

'He said Richard was, er, having a really pathetic and utterly insignificant fling with Acne . . . with his PA.'

'That's about the size of it,' Nomes says, apparently satisfied. 'A fling.'

'How did you find out, Nomes?'

'The usual way—credit card bills,' she says. 'We have a joint account and as you know I always go through the bills —which I'd strongly advise you to do, Clara, by the way. I noticed an entry from an Ann Summers shop.'

'What?'

'You know, those sex shops. I thought maybe Richard had bought me some kind of joke present—'

I interrupt, agog. 'Does he often buy you joke presents from sex shops?'

'It has been known. Anyway, I waited a week or so—'

'Like what?' I ask, cutting in again. 'What kind of thing?'

'Do let me finish, Clara. Oh, like padded handcuffs'—she smiles at the recollection—'or see-through nighties. A maid's uniform, once. Very cheap fabric, actually. Appalling seams.'

'Right,' I say feebly.

'Anyway, the present didn't appear, and I went back to the statement, and there were lots of restaurant bills, for amounts that were clearly for two people—seventy-odd quid here and there, and even Richard doesn't eat that much. His work entertaining goes on his other card. So I asked him what he'd been doing in Ann Summers.'

'And?'

'He said he bought a joke leaving present for a woman at the office—a woman who was retiring. I could tell he was lying. I asked what the present was and he said a dildo.' Naomi allows herself a terse little smile.

'A *dildo?*'

'Yes. Hardly the thing for Vera from Accounts, as it were, I said.'

'Well, er, quite. Hardly the ideal gift for an elderly stranger.'

'No. Anyway, I said I'd noticed some odd restaurant bills that weren't on his expense account—I'd checked the dates and they were all when he was supposed to be working late. Richard's a very bad liar. So he told me. Said he'd been seeing this . . . woman . . . for a few weeks.'

I've had my back to Naomi all this time, poking around the cooker and fiddling with what she'd no doubt refer to as 'condiments'.

'So,' she says. 'We need to make a plan.'

'Make a plan?' I repeat stupidly. 'What kind of plan?'

'Well,' says Naomi, allowing herself a proper smile. 'We need to decide what I'm going to do, obviously.'

'In what respect, Nomes?'

'You know,' she says. 'A plan of action. We need to get organized.' She rustles through her handbag again. 'I made a list earlier. Where can it be?'

'What do you mean, you made a *list?* What kind of list?'

'A list of options. I haven't done anything so far. When Richard told me, I said, "I see."' She looks at me for approbation, but I stare back like a startled fish. 'I haven't made a *fuss,* Clara. He does so hate fuss. But I need to decide what to do next.'

'Chop his balls off?' I mutter to myself.

To my utter amazement, it seems to me that Naomi is actually quite enjoying this. To her, her husband's infidelity constitutes a new task—and God knows she loves tasks. The curse of the stay-at-home mother, I've always thought, first strikes when the children start going to school, when the carefully orchestrated days—nutritionally balanced lunch at 1 P.M., toddlers' swimming group at 3, creative play at 4, piano practice at 5—stretch emptily ahead, and women like Naomi start wondering what they are actually *for*. Workless, hobbyless and childless for much of her day, Naomi needs something to keep her mind occupied. And Richard—the thoughtfulness!—has provided it.

'You could go shopping,' I say. 'On his card, I mean. That's always quite cheering. Are you sure about these ravioli?'

'Yes, thanks,' Naomi says as I place a steaming plate in front of her. 'Is that salad dressed?'

'Only lightly. Of course, you could always get incredibly fat as revenge. You could become obese and grow a moustache. You could lie around all day eating. That would serve him right.' The idea appeals to me enormously—for a minute, I feel half-sorry that it isn't Robert who's putting it about.

'I don't think so, Clara,' says Naomi. 'Do try and be serious.'

'Well then, what? Take a lover?' As if.

'Hang on, I'll get my list. Right. Here we are. These are my options. Are you listening? Okay. One, make his life hell.'

'Sounds good to me.'

'No. It was tempting for about three seconds, but really—think, Clara. If I make his life hell, he's hardly likely to come back to me with his tail between his legs.'

'Do you want him to?'

Naomi puts down her fork. 'I do love him, Clara,' she says, in the tone of voice someone might adopt were they considering putting down their ancient dog. 'I'm used to him. We're comfortable together. And then, of course, the children . . .'

'Well, yes, the children,' I say, clinging on to the notion —not least because the idea of staying with someone because you're 'used to them' somehow lacks appeal to me. I mean, I'm used to my ancient Birkenstocks, but it doesn't mean I've stopped buying shoes, or window-shopping, for that matter.

'And the thing is, Clara,' Naomi says, warming to her theme, 'the thing is that I've *invested* a lot in Richard.'

Eh? 'What do you mean, *invested?*' I ask.

'I really wanted to get married, Clara. I'm not like you. I'd wanted to get married since I was a little girl. I knew what kind of dress I was going to wear by the time I was twelve. I'd picked all my hymns and worked out the order of service. I'd thought about the flowers. I wanted to live in the kind of house we live in, with the kind of man who would make me feel . . . comfortable. I never wanted to work, as you know— I'm not ambitious that way—and I wanted children. I invested everything I had in getting Richard. He was a good catch.' She looks up. 'He still is.'

'I don't understand "invested",' I say, wondering whether this might not be the time to explain the basics of feminism to Naomi. I give it a quick try. 'Once, Naomi, more recently than you'd think, women didn't have the vote . . .'

'Who cares?' says Naomi. 'I never vote. Don't start telling me about that boring Pankhurst woman. What I am trying to say is, I studied men like Richard for a long time. I saw what they wanted. They work hard, you know, and after they've finished their couple of years of playing hard, they want a woman who's going to make their life easy.'

'I don't believe I'm hearing this,' I say. 'I don't believe this.'

'So I made myself into that kind of woman,' Nomes continues. 'I was kind of like that to start off with, which helped. I've always dieted. I go to the hairdresser once a week. I have beauty treatments. I've learned to cook. I can talk to his colleagues. I produced nice children. Our house is pretty impeccable. I buy flowers twice a week and polish the floorboards myself. I make him nice dinners and ask him about his day. I never moan about having my period or about being depressed. You know.'

'Naomi,' I say, my appetite having—almost uniquely—deserted me. 'Listen. I know we're different in the way we think. Everyone wants to feel secure, I can understand that. But really—you don't have to reinvent yourself. You don't have to be a *hausfrau,* even a glamorous one. You're what—thirty-five, tops? Is that really what you want? Because maybe this has happened to make you re-evaluate. I mean, I hate to sound like Kate, but it is possible. Don't you want mad love? Passion? Risk? To be able to talk about you every now and then? Because as requests go, it's hardly an outrageous one. Don't you want not to have to *work* at it all the time?'

'No,' says Naomi. 'Absolutely not. I want what I have. I want Richard. I've always wanted that and nothing's changed.'

'Okay,' I say, feeling weak but also faintly admiring. 'What's on your list?'

'Okay. Here we go. One, make his life hell. That's no good. Two, meet the woman and explain it all to her.'

'Explain what?'

'That he'll never leave me. That he likes *boeuf en croûte* and Janet Reger underwear, not . . . oh, I don't know, Pot Noodles and Bhs knickers. That he might be *fucking* her'—Naomi blushes slightly, though less than me—'but that he *makes love* to me. That he loves his children . . .'

'Okay,' I say. 'I get the picture. I wouldn't do that quite yet. It's a bit mini-series, as an approach, and it implies she's more of a threat than she is.'

'Yes, I think you're right,' says Nomes. 'Which leads us to option number three. Be more like her.'

'What, like Acne Girl?'

'That's rather a good name for her. Yes. Be more common. What do you think?'

'I think you've just told me that he likes you for what you are.'

'Hmm. She wears very cheap scent. I've noticed. Number four: do nothing.'

'Nothing at all?'

'Nope. Not a thing. Carry on entirely as normal.'

'I see. And what does this achieve?'

'It shows him I'm not humiliated. It shows I'm not going to get hysterical.'

'But aren't you humiliated?'

'Not as much as I thought I'd be.'

'Right. So keep on with the fillet steak at home, as it were, until he tires of the Little Chef burger?'

'Yes.'

'What if he thinks, hey—I can keep on having both?'

'He won't.'

'You sound very sure.'

'I know Richard, Clara. I've studied him. I know him inside out and back to front. Actually, I think this might well be some kind of midlife crisis. Men get them, you know.'

I am staring at the half-eaten ravioli on my plate. The cream and Parmesan have congealed somewhat; the rocket leaves on the side, though still glossy, have started to wilt. It's not unappetizing as such. There's nothing wrong with it. But it could look better. It could make me want it more. It could make my appetite rear up and roar. It's like my life, I think to myself in that dazed, half-lit way you sometimes find yourself drifting into in the middle of a conversation. It's my life on a plate.

'You're lucky to know Richard so well,' I say, getting up. 'I mean it. I don't know what I'd do in your shoes. Good luck with it, Nomes. I'll do anything I can to help.' And I get up and clear the dishes. I hold our plates under the tap and the water washes the debris clean away. The food grinder roars into life briefly, crunching up the remains of our lunch.

'Thanks, Clara, darling. I do think Do Nothing is best,

don't you? Gosh, do you know, I'm almost looking forward to it,' she says, with a giggle. 'Don't just stand there, Clara! Shall I make us some coffee?'

'I hate coffee,' I say.

'So you do. Well, tea then. Earl Grey?'

I am holding the plates in my hands, ready to load them into the dishwasher. One little slip and they'd come crashing down, scattering their bone-hard whiteness all over the floor. But I don't slip.

'Tea would be lovely,' I say instead. 'One sugar, no cancer-inducing sweetener.'

'There was another option, you know,' Naomi says, giving my arm a squeeze as we stand by the kettle. 'There was an option five, but I was too embarrassed to say. I've cheered up so much though, now I know what I'm doing. Shall I tell you what it was?'

'What was it?'

'Be more like you,' Naomi says with an affectionate look.

'Be more like me?'

'Yes. Go with the flow, you know, and see the funny side.'

'The funny side? Of an affair?'

'You know what I mean—I mean, get angry, and then get even, and then joke about it. Just—be more like you.'

'I don't think you want to do that,' I say. 'I don't think . . . Well, ha ha, I don't think, full stop. Shall we have the tea upstairs?'

thirteen

AND NOW IT'S FRIDAY and we're off to Julian's. Without Robert. But never mind, never mind. I mind a lot, actually, between you and me—I mind more than I can say. I don't often ask him for much in terms of emotional support. It's humiliating even to *have* to ask. Surely when you've been with someone eight years, they know what upsets and discombobulates you, as well as what makes you laugh. No? Well, evidently, no.

I've already mentioned some of the problems—cows, nature—that I experience in the countryside. The main problem at the moment, though, is sartorial. Charlie and Jack are already wellied-up, with hideous Man U woolly hats perched on their little round heads, raring to go.

It's okay for them, I reflect mournfully as I stare at the contents of my wardrobe for the fourth time this morning. My wardrobe is undeniably, problematically urban. It has mummy clothes—big jumpers, stretch trousers, boring shirts, tweedy skirts (so ironic). I don't like the mummy clothes, practical though they are. They're fraudulent in some way that, at eighteen minutes past nine on this Friday morning, I suddenly find deeply offensive. I'm not like that, I want to tell the clothes. I used to be a babe—no, really. On the spur of the moment, I peer into my capacious pyjama top. Hello, bosoms. Remember when I exposed part of you at parties, cleavage peering out of low-cut satin dress? The bosoms are silent, as well they may be. It's been so long since bosom-outings that they've probably developed Alzheimer's.

Nonetheless, they're still there, and they're not bad, if you like that kind of thing. When I get back from Julian's, I think I might go shopping for — what, my lost youth? Well, yes.

A framed photograph of Kate sits by the bedroom window. I am on her lap, aged about two. I can't help but notice that Kate, though undeniably a mummy, is wearing a tiny little Pucci dress and showing a generous amount of toned, golden leg. I glance back at my clothes, feeling exactly — but *exactly* — like Demis Roussos.

The wardrobe also contains a scattering of pre-mummy clothes: sexy little things in fabrics you want to stroke, A-line skirts that land just on the knee, tight cashmere cardigans, a fitted coat. I make a mental note to get these dry-cleaned when I get back. If I can squeeze myself into them, that is.

Angst aside, I need to address the fact that the wardrobe absolutely doesn't contain a single garment that works in the country. One of the greatest mysteries of life, if you ask me, is the question of how people — women — dress in the country without looking almost incredibly unfeminine. If I dress for the country, I look like drag: like a middle-aged truck driver in a bad frock. How to avoid this look? This is what I need to know. This is the information I must have. Because, I think as I reach into the closet and come out with a Nicole Farhi knitted two-piece consisting of anthracite-coloured wide 'pants' (snigger) and a matching loose, tunic-like top, this kind of thing only works with heels. And even I know kitten heels are allergic to mud.

So this outfit, which is perfectly presentable, is going to have to be worn with the only pair of robust flat shoes I own: tan suede lace-ups. I try them on: where's my lorry? I kick the lace-ups off and try the outfit with slim, two-inch heels: leggy, and quite foxy. Lace-ups again: I am a hefty man and call myself Paulina at weekends. The heels: almost minxy. The flats: Pat from *EastEnders,* but butcher, as it were—Butcher, even, I snigger, delighted with my own joke.

What else? Perhaps a dress. I fish out a Ghost slip dress from the Old Me collection and bung on a huge sloppy Joe on top. Hmm—not bad. Not exactly flattering, but not bad. Faintly teenagey, perhaps. But the lace-ups, once on, render it instantly ridiculous. Trainers? I can't say I go a bundle on giant, paw-like feet, but needs must. The trainers make me look absurd. There's nothing worse than a size 16 woman pretending she's on her way to the gym all the time; it's like having a tattoo on one's forehead saying 'I am seriously delusional.'

Jeans? Don't make me laugh (or cry). A skirt, then. Stepping gracefully over the discarded pile of clothes on the floor, I head for the skirts. A tweedy number, perhaps: very rural. I put it on. What looks vaguely funky in the city turns me into an instant relative of Miss Marple, with a touch of simple-minded elderly milkmaid thrown in for good measure. The only alternative to the flats are my trusty Birkenstocks, which make me look like the kind of saddo that 'creates' artwork using a cunning combination of menstrual blood and woad.

'Fuck it,' I say, scooping up the whole pile and bunging it into the suitcase, along with a couple of evening frocks—we change for dinner at Julian's—some underpants, a selection of monstrously unsexy bras and a handful of tights. 'It's Somerset, not the Milan catwalk.'

'You said the F-word,' says Charlie delightedly. 'I know the F-word. I also know the B-word and the S-word.'

I know I should really tell him off for this knowledge, but I am curious. 'Come and whisper in my ear,' I say. 'Tell me.'

'Okay,' says Charlie, swaggering. 'I will whisper very quietly, because Jack is too small for the words.'

'So are you, darling,' I say, as Jack wanders off to find Bun, his favourite teddy. I kneel down, my ear level with Charlie's mouth. 'Tell me, darling, and then let's not ever hear the words again.'

'Furg,' says Charlie, before letting out a squeal of hysterical delight. 'Bollorgs.' He peers at me quizzically, not sure whether to carry on. 'Bumbum. Shit. Shit. Shitty.'

'Charlie!' I exclaim, shocked. 'That's terrible. How do you know those words?'

Charlie shrugs proudly. 'School. I never say them, though. Mummy, what are bad words for?'

'For when you're very, very angry and a grown-up, darling.'

'Sometimes I say bumbum,' Charlie explains helpfully. 'Like when that annoying Milo won't stop bothering me.'

'Well, bumbum isn't too bad,' I say, giving Charlie a hug and surreptitiously sniffing in his delicious little boy scent — sweeties and grubby hands mixed with warm body. 'Now, go to your room and find some books to bring with us.'

'We've got a secret, haven't we, Mummy?' Charlie says, beaming, as he karate-kicks his way out of the room. 'A bad-word secret.'

'We have, darling,' I confirm, wandering into the bathroom. See, that's another thing about the country: it doesn't go with make-up. You look absurd on a wet walk wearing scarlet lipstick. And, as we have seen, I don't suit the fresh-faced, natural look — not unless it's artfully contrived, anyway. I throw the contents of my product shelf into my sponge bag, and chuck in a pair of lipsticks, some eyeshadow and a tube of foundation anyway. I now know for a fact I'm going to spend the weekend looking ridiculous, but what can I do? It's scrub-faced lezzy or painted harlot in inappropriate clothes, and though neither of the looks is one I particularly aim for in normal life, the latter strikes me as preferable to the former.

We don't have a particularly enjoyable journey. Trains can be tricksy when you're accompanied by two small children, both given to racing off in any direction on the spur of the moment and, more problematically, prone to palling up with every weirdo they can spot. My children insist on roaming up and down the carriage and ignoring beaming, cuddly old ladies and their fellow small boys entirely. Instead, they like striking up long, loving conversations with skinheads, football supporters and the very drunk — their ideal new friend would be a shaven-headed, pissed Millwall fan, although they are also quite partial to tramps.

I am carrying our huge, heavy travelling bag, a basket containing teddies and books, a paper bag containing sandwiches and an armful of newspapers (fat chance). I emerge from the train a couple of hours later looking, I expect, as harassed as I feel. There are crisp crumbs down my front and a fruit juice stain on my sleeve.

Julian is at the station waiting for us. The boys spot him first.

'Julian!' they shout, beside themselves. 'Hello, Julian! We love you! We brought you a picture of a mouse, didn't we, Jack?'

Jack nods shyly, holding out his hand for Julian to hold.

'I do football at school now, Julian. I like Man U,' squeaks Charlie.

'I like mouses, and David Beckham,' Jack says. 'Do you?' But he says it too quietly, staring at his toes, though beaming, and Julian doesn't hear, so that my first words to him are a reproach: 'Jack was saying he likes David Beckham. And mice.'

'Does he indeed,' Julian booms. 'Do you, young man?' He ruffles Jack's fluffy hair affectionately. 'And why is that?'

'Because I love him,' says Jack, thinking hard. 'He can run so so fast.'

'He can,' says Julian. 'Hello, Clara,' he adds, kissing my cheek. 'Good journey?'

'Fine,' I say. 'Grubby-making' — I point at my juice-flecked cardigan — 'but fine.'

'Goodo,' says Julian. 'You were always good at getting food down yourself.'

What am I supposed to reply to this — 'Well, you know me and my Down's syndrome, Julian'? But he's not expecting an answer, and besides there's no need for me to be so defensive. The remark wasn't made unkindly.

'Anyway,' he says, gesturing to the car. 'Let's go.'

The house is beautiful: solid, Georgian, wisteria-covered. Its drive is very long. The boys shout out greetings to the sheep and cows we pass. Julian and I make small talk, rather as if I were his maiden aunt: super weather, lovely cow parsley, oh look, a pheasant. The house is full, he tells me: me and the boys are here, Evie and Flo are arriving after lunch, as are Digby, baby Francis's father, and Digby's wife, Magdalen. Miss Johnson, Julian's closest neighbour, is coming to lunch today, which cheers me up. Hester, Digby's sister, might come up tomorrow with her children.

We eventually clamber out of the Land Rover and on to the gravel, to be greeted by the frenetic barking of Julian's many dogs. Julian's third wife, Anna, is standing by the door in jeans and cashmere sweater. She looks effortlessly rural and plainly a stranger to the lorry-driver clothing dilemma. I wonder how she does it, and immediately feel inappropriately dressed.

'Welcome,' she says, kissing us. 'Lunch in half an hour. You're staying in your usual room. Do you need a hand with your things?'

'We're okay, thanks,' I say. 'Come on, boys. Charlie, could you hold this basket, darling?'

'We want to stay with Julian,' Jack wails. 'We want to see the chickens.'

I look at Julian, who nods, amused. 'I'll take these creatures to meet my fowl,' he says. 'We'll have a drink before lunch, I think — drawing room, quarter of an hour or so.'

'Okay,' I say. 'Thanks. And boys,' I add, looking stern, 'please behave.'

'We will,' they say in unison, and go marching off towards the chicken coop, leaping and skipping around Julian like a pair of puppies.

We're staying in the Cherry Room, a scarlet extravaganza that features cherry-printed curtains and a cherry-strewn bed-spread. The room is large, and someone has laid two small camp beds at one end for the boys. We won't be needing them. Sans Robert, they can sleep with me in the massive four-poster. I feel a twinge of irritation—deep grievance, if we're going to be technically accurate—at his absence, and shoo it away. Now is really not the time.

I brush my teeth—trains, like planes, always make my mouth feel plaquey—and wash my hands. I sit on the bed. I want to change my clothes, but don't. A small vase of blue-bells is by my bedside. I look at my watch: ten minutes to go. I wish I didn't always feel such a guest. I sigh, bounce on the bed as if testing its springs, glance at my watch again: eight minutes. I might as well go down early.

I've been coming to Julian's for some years, but even though I know my way around, I still don't know where anything lives. The house is quiet as I stiffly come down the stairs, and fragrant with the smell of furniture polish and flowers. There's a muted noise coming from the kitchen, but I turn left and start walking towards the drawing room instead.

When I reach it, the first thing I notice, as ever, is the bank of family photographs that dot every available surface. I don't know why I always clock, chippily, that there are a dozen or so pictures of Julian's blood-children on display and one of me (on my wedding day). They are not going to change, these photo displays, and yet I always glance towards them hope-fully every time.

97

Standing by the fireplace, Julian, fine-boned, grey-haired, faintly fierce, is looking patrician and talking to Miss Johnson, who is wearing a three-piece suit and sitting in an armchair with her legs squatly open, like someone about to burp in an eighteenth-century print of life at the Garrick Club. Short and stocky to the point of boxiness, Miss Johnson wears suits, smokes cigarillos and likes nothing more of a morning than shooting the rabbits that scamper across her lawn. These are known as 'the buggers'.

'Clara,' she says, looking up at me with her beady currant eyes. 'Bloody good to see you, my girl.'

'Hello, Myrtle,' I say, bending down to kiss her. I rather love Miss Johnson, whose possible sexual orientation is never mentioned.

'Snorter?' says Miss Johnson. She is, I notice, drinking a whisky on the rocks. 'Give the girl a snorter, for God's sake, Jules.'

'Something soft, please, or I'll fall asleep.'

'Can't have that. I was hoping you might walk the boys with me,' says Miss Johnson.

'Er, yes,' I say, confused. 'Where are they, Julian?'

'In the kennel,' roars Miss Johnson.

'I, um, why?' I ask, feeling—as I often do down here—that I don't know the script, or even the language. I feel like a foreigner, like I should be pointing at things, or indeed people, with a simple smile, saying, *Pliz, what is?*

'Best place for them,' says Miss Johnson.

I stare at her, mouth slightly open.

'Jack and Charlie are in the kitchen with Anna. They collected some eggs,' says Julian, smiling broadly. 'Myrtle's referring to her dogs. Clara.'

'Oh, I *see*,' I practically shout, dizzy with relief. 'I thought . . .'

'Thought I'd locked the blighters up,' chortles Myrtle.

'Well, yes.'

'Wouldn't harm them,' Myrtle says. 'Wouldn't harm them a jot. Plenty to learn from our canine brothers.'

'All the same . . .'

'Where's that man of yours, Clara?' asks Julian, handing me a glass of cranberry juice. 'Arriving on the evening train?'

'He couldn't make it—he's got tons to do,' I say, noticing, as I utter the words, that they sound pretty feeble. Julian raises an eyebrow, but says nothing. He often does this vis-à-vis Robert. It annoys me.

'Lunch is ready,' says Anna, who's just come in. She's nice, Anna—she's just like Julian without the willy. Prettier, I suppose, but talk about birds of a feather: Julian and she are so finely attuned to the inaudible intricacies of *comme il faut* upper-middle-class country life that they barely need to communicate at all.

Anna's two children are away at boarding school; she misses them, she says, as she leads us into the kitchen. 'But you know how it is. I was sent away at seven myself and you *do* get used to it. You love it, actually, after a while,' she adds affirmatively, risking a coda: 'Adore it, in the end.'

I've given up staring at her in slack-jawed horror whenever she mentions this—which she does surprisingly often for one so contained—but the ghost of a shudder still passes through me as I imagine what it would be like if Charlie, this time next year, were waiting for the train at Paddington station, all packed up and ready to go, clutching his tuck-box, his bare knees and trembly lip prepared for the decade of boarding school ahead.

'It's wonderful now, you know,' continues Anna, unprompted. 'It's not like in my day—or even yours, Clara. They all have mobile phones and they wear their own clothes most of the time.'

I smile at her in a manner which I imagine to be comforting, don't tell her that mobile phones are hard to cuddle up to, and try to push away my own memories of lacrosse, grey meat and the kind of wet mornings when you missed home so much it hurt all around your chest.

*

Lunch—steak and kidney pie, mash, carrots, apple crumble —is a jolly affair, mainly because of the boys and Miss Johnson's boisterous high spirits. I eat quietly, quickly, lavishing praise on each mouthful in a way that strikes me as peculiarly ingratiating.

Julian sets off again after it to collect Digby and Magdalen from the station. I lie on the lawn near the children, who wander off and bring me back interesting things—stones, twigs, bits of sheep wool—to examine. The children's forays are so comprehensively exploratory that Jack is soon covered in mud from the stream that trickles through the garden; both the boys' wellies are covered in duck poo. We go back up to the room so that I can change Jack's clothes.

'Is it cartoon time yet?' asks Charlie, throwing his muddy self on the bed and flicking on the television.

'Not quite, I don't think,' I tell him, dragging an immensely reluctant Jack into the bathroom. 'And get off the bed, Charlie, for God's sake. You're filthy.'

How is it possible to get mud into your actual nostrils? I scrub at Jack with a flannel, ignoring his squeals of protestation, and wander back into the bedroom in search of clean clothes. The flickering TV screen catches my eye.

'And coming up after the break,' says the female presenter, 'we have modern dance's newest sensation, Sam Dunphy. Don't go away.'

'I'm coooooold,' Jack howls from the bathroom. 'I need my cloooothes.'

'Is Jack all bare?' asks Charlie. 'Where are the cartoons? Can I play with my Gameboy, Mummy?'

'Muuuuummmeeee,' hollers Jack.

'Yes. Coming,' I say, rifling through our bag for a T-shirt and trousers and running back into the bathroom. 'Quick, Jack, let's put these on,' I tell him. 'Quick! I want to watch something on the TV.'

'My name is Squirtle, Mummy,' says Jack, putting one leg

into the trouser hole and pausing. 'Like in Pokemon. Because I like Diglet and Squirtle best.'

'Hmm,' I say. 'Can you manage now, Squirtle?'

'Yes,' says Jack. 'I'm nearly four.'

'Shout if you get stuck—I'll just be through here.'

Charlie is sitting on the bed in his vest and pants, holding his Gameboy, which is making an extraordinarily loud noise.

'Charlie, could you turn it down? I'm trying to listen.'

'Bee beep, bee beep, BEE BEE BEEEP,' says Charlie in time to the noise. I don't think he's heard me.

Jack wanders back into the room. 'Diggy dig, diggy dig,' he says. 'That's what Diglet says in Pokemon.' The sound pleases him enormously and he repeats it. 'Diggy dig, diggy dig,' he says, louder this time. The phone by the bed starts ringing.

'BEEP!' says Charlie. 'Gotcha!'

'Diggy DIG!' shouts Jack, as Dunphy's face fills the screen.

Why isn't anyone picking up the bloody phone?

I press the volume button on the remote. 'He's a hunk,' I say, out loud.

'I'm a hunky monkey,' says Charlie.

'I'm a hunky lunky,' says Jack, who loves rhymes. 'I'm a hunky dunky.'

I can't hear properly, though at least the phone has stopped ringing. 'Great to be in London,' Dunphy is saying. 'Intimidating . . . big venue . . . staying with friends.' I press Volume again, to no avail. The boys are in full flow and it's like being in the zoo. 'Walking along the river,' Dunphy says, 'something something, restaurants.' Outside, Elvis the dog (named by Evie) starts barking.

'That's it,' I shout at the children. 'Complete silence, *now.*' They look at me, unimpressed. 'Complete silence,' I repeat. 'The first person to speak is a baby girl.'

'In nappies?' asks Jack.

'In nappies and a bib. Now, silence.'

Jack sits on the bed, his hand clasped over his mouth. Charlie buries his face in a pillow and turns the sound off his Gameboy.

'What's been your most memorable experience of London so far?' the presenter, who is called Candy, asks Dunphy.

'Well,' says Dunphy. 'I like the buildings a lot. And I love Kew Gardens.'

'I suppose you go there to get away,' says Candy. 'You've been getting an awful lot of media attention . . .'

'Speaking of which,' says Dunphy, 'there was a, ah, memorable interview. Perhaps I shouldn't say this . . .'

'Do,' says Candy.

'The girl, the woman—she gave me nits.'

'Nits?' says Candy.

'Yeah,' says Dunphy, smiling a very white smile. 'She insulted me and then she gave me nits.'

Candy, sniffing a good anecdote, leans forward. So do I.

'How did she do that?'

'The insulting? By asking me if I was a Morris dancer.' My mouth drops open. 'Actually, by asking me if I was a gay Morris dancer.' Candy raises an encouraging eyebrow, but Dunphy is busy laughing softly to himself.

'I lost my temper a bit,' he says, still smiling his—oh, okay—sexy smile. 'I shouldn't have, really. It's quite funny, in retrospect, don't you think? And then'—he shrugs—'the next day my head started itching. I think they came from her.'

'Well,' says Candy. 'There you have it. The professionalism of the press. I don't suppose you'd tell us who she was?'

'Mm,' says Dunphy. 'No.'

Oh, my God. Oh, Holy Mary, Mother of God. Oh, utter *fuck*.

'Hey,' says Charlie. 'Was that the Smurfy man?'

'Yes, darling, it was.' My head is suddenly itching me like mad. I switch the television off, jump off the bed and start pacing about the room.

'Has he got our nits?' says Charlie.

'I think he might have.'

Charlie hops off the bed and takes my hand. 'Don't worry, Mummy. Don't look worried. He was nice about it.'

'Yes,' I say. 'Yes, I suppose he was.'

'He was happy,' says Jack. 'Diggy dig.'

'We need a chemist,' I say, dialling Flo's mobile number. I leave a message on her voice-mail—'Nit lotion, Flo, urgently needed. Please stop off on your way down.'

Christ. How embarrassing. And how . . . thought-provoking, in certain respects.

Soon the gravel crunches again with the sound of Julian's tyres.

You know how the Sloane Ranger is supposed to be defunct? Well, it isn't. There are still plenty of people around whose idea of a good time is having a food-fight and then debagging someone named Piggy or Fruity or Jumbo. Digby, whom I love despite myself, is the only person I know who taps the side of his nose meaningfully to impart the news that someone is Jewish, even though no one asked. Digby can make himself weep remembering the Empire. He worships Churchill. He thinks wars are 'sexy' and, when he thinks something is 'sexy', feels compelled to shout 'Woof', accompanying the unlovely exclamation with a vague, malcoordinated swivel of the hips—a swivel which tells you all you need to know about his prowess on the dance floor, or—God forbid—in the sack.

What is it with posh men and dancing, incidentally? Why does any well-bred dance floor resemble a red-faced, slack-tongued spastics' convention? Actually—let's not beat about the bush—what is it with posh men and *sex*? Why can't they do it? Kissing: comprehensive, Labradorial facial licking. Foreplay: one squeeze on each breast, as if testing avocados for ripeness. Rumpo: 'Bloody hell, bloody hell, waaaah!'

They simply can't get the hang of it. And then, six seconds later, a complacent, self-congratulating 'Did you come?', the question posed almost rhetorically, as if the answer — 'Yes, baby, oh *yes,* yes, torrentially' — was obvious, the implication being that, thanks to Jumbo or Fruity or Piggy's expert ministrations, you have, for the first time, realized that women can be multi-orgasmic, and are on the verge of weeping with joy and gratitude.

Where was I? Ah yes, Digby. Well, here he is: rah rah rah. Six foot one, ruddy-faced, wearing moleskin trousers, a shirt from Thomas Pink and a 'fun' waistcoat embroidered with . . . well, naked black women wearing banana skirts, it seems, though surely this can't be right. I'd hate to make him sound like a cartoon (he'd be Foghorn Leghorn). I sidle closer to him to get a better look.

'Hi, Dig.'

'Clara! Marvellous that you came. How are you?'

'Very well. Hi, Magdalen.' I kiss Digby's demure, fragrant wife and stroke Francis's forehead. 'Your waistcoat, Digby. It's, uh, unusual. Where's it from?'

'Excellent, isn't it? Really excellent. Magdalen' — he gestures at his wife — 'got it for me last Christmas. It's some bird called Josephine Baker, famous dancer, apparently, Paris, 1920s.' He rolls his eyes and waves his palms about. He's going to say it, I think to myself. Any minute now, he's going to say it. Any minute . . . 'Marvellous sense of rhythm,' he says, on cue, while I let out a snort of laughter — I gave up on the indignation years ago. 'Those people. Johnny, er, Bongo, as I know you like me to call them, Clara. Bloody good dancers.'

'Good dancers? Takes one to know one,' I say sweetly.

'Yah, Dig's a bit of a devil on the dance floor,' says Magdalen, bursting with pride.

Digby shouts 'Yah!' and breaks into an exuberant little routine of his own device, wiggling his not inconsiderable bottom to and fro and pumping his arms up and down to an imaginary tune all the way to the drawing room. We follow him meekly.

'Queen,' he says. 'Bloody love 'em. And Bryan Adams, but he's better for the slow stuff.' Another swivel, this one pregnant with promise.

'Digby,' says Julian, 'do you mind?'

'Sorry, Pops. Just showing the girls how it's done.' He winks at me horribly. 'Eh, Clara? Does the old eyes good, eh? Eh?'

'Woof!' I say. 'Woof, Digby.'

'Steady on,' says Digby, delighted.

'"Pops",' says Julian, taking my arm. '"Pops"! I wish he'd desist.' He shakes his head, but there's a twinkle in his eye and his complaint is wrapped in palpable affection. 'Pops!' he says again, smiling to himself. 'He is a card, isn't he, Clara?'

'Joker in every pack, Julian,' I say.

fourteen

EVIE AND FLO arrive shortly after Digby, and Anna and I race outside to greet them. After the hugs and a whispered 'Evie's driving me *mad*' from Flo, I notice that the car's back seat is covered in carrier bags and gift wrappings.

'Been shopping?' I ask, pointing through the window.

'Yes!' yells Flo, unlocking the boot. 'Presents! We have gifts for you all.' She is wearing the shortest skirt I have ever seen —it's as wide as some of my *pants,* frankly—accessorized with a T-shirt that says 'Jesus Loves Me' in glittery writing and a pair of giant fur-lined boots of the kind favoured by Eskimos.

'Yes,' says Evie guilelessly. 'And Clara gets hers first because she's the guest. We get ours last because we're home. Home, home, lovely home,' she half sings, doing a little dance.

'Shush, Evie No-Tact,' says Flo, throwing me a concerned glance. I smile manfully back. 'Clara,' Flo continues, 'gets hers first because she'll love it so much.' And she produces a giant beribboned parcel from The Cross in London—my favourite shop, and hers. 'Open it when we get inside,' she says, and starts yanking at a giant wicker hamper that has Fortnum & Mason printed on its side.

'Now, here is another gift, which is the gift of food.' They really do talk like this, my sisters (half): part Nancy Mitford, part excitable, slightly solemn child.

'Mm,' says Evie, 'I love food.' She looks like a sweet little mushroom, her cat-eyed, heart-shaped face peering out from under the brim of a vast, lavender-coloured velvet hat, which matches the stripe in her 1970s Missoni knitted dress. This particular ensemble is tailed by a pair of sparkling silver Nikes. 'Food's yummy.'

'You don't think that when you sick it up,' says Flo bluntly. 'This present is for Anna. It's a hamper. From Fortnum's. For Christmas. Except it's not Christmas, so they had to make it especially and there's no plum pudding.'

'I don't sick it up any more,' says Evie, looking hurt.

'Thank you so much, girls,' says Anna delightedly. 'How lovely.'

'I got them to put some marzipan pigs in it,' says Flo. 'They weren't part of the original hamper. So when you bite into a marzipan pig, you can think of kind-hearted me. Kind-hearted *us*, actually—the pigs were Evie's idea.'

'There's a lot of calories in marzipan,' says Evie. 'But I don't care. And I like the pigs' sweet faces, don't you, Anna? Where's Robert? And where are the boys, Clara?'

'Robert's in London. And the boys are playing hide-and-seek, I think. They'll be out in a second.'

'But we want them *now*,' says Evie, who is an exceptionally devoted auntie. 'Boys! BOYS!' she shouts, like a nun who's lost her vocation. 'WHERE ARE YOU?'

'Here we are,' Jack and Charlie shout back, galloping over the gravel and lobbing themselves into their aunts' arms. 'We saw a cock.'

'Cool,' says Evie, in her blithe twenty-three-year-old way. 'Whose was it?'

'A boy hen,' says Jack. 'Called a cock.'

'Oh,' says Evie. 'That's nice. Let's go inside for the rest of the presents, Flo. I'm starving.'

*

Laden with elaborately wrapped gift boxes, we stagger into the roomy, stone-floored kitchen, where we deposit the girls' presents on to the table. I open mine, the first layer of which contains an intricately embroidered pink cardigan, complete with sequinned flowers. The second layer hides a fabulous silver lace skirt (drawstring waist, oh joy), and the third—good grief, there's more—a couple of dozen very thin, glittery, beaded bracelets.

'Do you love our presents?' says Evie.

'Passionately,' I reply truthfully. 'You are angels of sweetness.'

The boys start racing around the kitchen, shooting each other with their brand-new pop guns while wearing a stegosaurus outfit (Jack, delirious with happiness) and an extravagantly mustachioed pirate's (Charlie, ditto). Miss Johnson, whom Evie finds and wakes up from her nap, gets three bottles of flavoured vodkas with a silver flask to decant them into ('Capital!' she booms, causing me, not for the first time, to wonder whether I've stumbled into a 1930s play). Elvis, the Labrador, gets a red velvet collar with diamanté studs; Anna gets a vast bunch of lilies, to add to her hamper; Mrs Dunn, who does and is elderly, gets some cashmere slippers, 'for your poor feet'; Mrs Hoppy (really), who cooks, gets candied fruit from Carluccio's; and so on. Digby, who's off somewhere walking with Julian, gets a pair of pants that say 'CAUTION: HEAVY GOODS'.

We're falling about laughing at these when Julian returns. 'What a jolly scene,' he says, divesting himself of his Barboun. 'Hello, my darling girls. Is it Christmas?'

'Daddy!' They rush to embrace him. 'No, but we might not be here for Christmas'—Julian raises an eyebrow—'so we thought we'd bring the gifts now. And then if we are here we'll bring more, so, you see, it's a win-win situation,' Flo explains. 'Anyway—come and open yours.'

Julian seems delighted by his first edition of *The Diary of a*

Nobody, a book he is able to quote from at considerable length. The first time I ever saw Julian laugh hysterically, with tears, was when quoting from it to Kate. The second parcel contains *Three Men in a Boat,* a tome which has an equally dramatic effect on Julian, reducing him to hyperventilation on many an occasion and even, once, to falling off a loo with a very loud thud.

'But how brilliant!' he exclaims. 'My two favourite books, from my two favourite girls! Er,' he adds, giving me a glance and looking around for Magdalen, who has taken the baby off for a feed. 'Well. Er. Oh. Yes.'

'I love that bookshop, Heywood Hill,' says Evie. 'They're so professional. They know your credit card number off by heart.'

'How odd,' I say. 'It's hardly as if you live to read, Evie, darling. How often do you go in there?' The notion of Evie as bookworm is, as it were, novel and not entirely convincing. I don't think Evie's read anything since being devastated by *Charlotte's Web,* aged eleven, although she shows some familiarity with the more upmarket mail-order catalogues.

'No, silly—I mean they knew Daddy's credit card number.'

'Oops,' says Flo. 'Oopsy doopsy doops. Do you want to play football, boys?' And she scoops them up and whirls out of the kitchen.

'And why would they need my credit card number?' says Julian, for whom the penny is slowly dropping.

'Well, to pay for the presents, of course, silly,' says Evie. 'Me and Flo can hardly be expected to buy things at Tiffany's with our measly allowance. Miss J, show Julian the lovely flask.'

Miss Johnson does.

'Very smart,' says Julian. 'So, darling, correct me, are all these lovely presents—very cosy-looking slippers, Mrs Dunn. Cashmere? Hmm—effectively, ah, from me?'

'Well, effectively,' says Evie. 'I mean, obviously, they're

from us. From me and Flo. We chose them, you know. But you paid for them.'

'I . . .' starts Julian.

'Oh, Daddy,' says Evie, sidling up to him. 'Don't make a fuss. I mean, you get all the benefits. Especially of the hamper, which has marzipan pigs with the *sweetest* faces. Look.' She thrusts a pig into his face. 'Really examine the sweetness.'

'I suppose,' Julian sighs, having conceded that, yes, the snouts are especially adorable, and that, yup, it is indeed a particularly gorgeous shade of pink. 'I suppose it makes some kind of sense. But really, Evie, I'd have been just as happy with an old paperback.'

'I wouldn't have been just as happy with some rag from Oxfam,' I say supportively. 'Mrs Dunn wouldn't have been just as happy with flip-flops, would you, Mrs D?'

'No, Clara,' says Mrs Dunn, gazing lovingly at her warm, snuggly toes.

'The thing is,' Julian says, 'that you all have to stop buying lavish presents like this. You're so like your mother. It's completely over the top.'

'Top, schmop,' says Evie. 'It's lovely. Who doesn't love lovely great big presents? Hands up.'

We all keep our hands down — Evie actually sits on hers — including Julian, who seems mollified.

'Oh, all right,' he says. 'All right. Not that it's exactly the first time this has happened. But all right. I suppose. Now, I'm going to do my paperwork.' And he wanders off, Pooter under his arm.

The christening of Francis Cornelius Xavier, during which the baby beams sweetly and looks adorable in Digby's own ancient christening gown, passes off without a hitch; it even makes me cry. Some braying friends of Digby and Magdalen's are to be godparents. During the party that follows, I discover that none of the women works and that all the men work in the City. Francis is given lavish presents of the solid-silver variety and photographed, in his gown, in his proud parents' and grandfather's arms. I hug my boys close to me throughout.

We get the train home early the next morning.

fifteen

BACK FROM SOMERSET, I realize with a start that the sexy weekend away with Robert beckons, not, I must confess, especially alluringly. I'm not ready. When I imagined us romping through Paris—actually, bizarrely, I pictured me more doing a Toulouse-Lautrec kind of a louche cancan, red rose clenched between teeth, Robert watching, slick with brilliantine—I had the New Clara in mind: groomed, chic, sleek . . . and, much as it pains me to say it, slightly thinner.

Unless something very dramatic happens in the next six days, I'm going to hit Paris in full Jabba the Hutt mode, with two chins and nothing foxier to wear than a pair of tracky bottoms—except perhaps a lesbian-look Country Casuals outfit to change into for dinner, one that will stand me in depressingly poor stead when I whisper, 'Coffee, tea . . . or me?' at my dear husband. More (Roseanne) Barr than Bardot, and thus guaranteed to cause detumescence at twenty paces.

Clearly, I'm going to have to hit the shops. Equally clearly, a little dieting wouldn't go amiss. There's only one snag—a snag that's as considerable as my waist size: I don't believe in dieting. Me, I'm anti. I constitutionally disapprove of any slimming regime, on the heartfelt principle that Life Is Too

Short (which principle also applies to aerobics, pooper-scooping and anal sex).

The kind of women who ogle a biscuit and then, guiltily, take a bite, squealing a winsome, 'Ooh, it'll go straight to my hips,' are among the women I despise most in the world. The kind of women who, on being told that there's a tablespoon full of oil on their salad, or a couple of glugs of cream in their pudding, pat their flat stomachs and say, 'It's awfully rich,' with a panic-stricken face, make me want to slap them. The kind of women who eat sad fat-free dinners and sugarless cheesecake, not realizing — fools! — that they're munching on the kind of carcinogenic sugar substitutes and creepy E numbers that'll make them so sick in later life that skinniness will be theirs forever make me incandescent with irritation.

Diets! Ha! I suppose one might consider them if one weighed twenty-two stone, and broke the paving stones as one walked along, and had to cope with the sound of cracking cement and pedestrians' wails echoing forever in one's shamed, burning ears as they slid down, down, down through the cracks to their doom. But otherwise, who'd turn themselves into a freaky giant rabbit, nibbling away at greenery?

Well, actually, um . . . perhaps I would. Nothing drastic. We're talking a few pounds. Even though I'm not a pavement-pulverizer yet, I can't help feeling that Paris — and the satin-sheeted, four-postered, 'honeymoon'-type suite Robert has booked for us — deserves a little effort. A hint of cheekbone or a well- or at least better-defined jawline wouldn't go amiss.

I might even buy some pants of the non-added-stretch, non-nice-and-cosy variety. It's been ages since I owned a pair that didn't come up to my waist, spurred in part by comfort but also by the hard-held belief that a woman in lacy, bum-bisecting knickers is a woman whose definition of 'erotic' is uncompromisingly suburban. Provincial, even. 'I've got a treat for you tonight, Barry,' followed by — tadaa! — the sateen, flame-retardant *peignoir* flung open to reveal a nylon set of suspenders and a tawdry half-cup bra, probably in burgundy, with matching 'panties'. 'Cor,' says Barry. 'Giggle,' says the wife. 'Fancy an early night?' 'Not half,' says Bazza, who later wipes himself up with a sibilant 'tiss-yoo' or perhaps a stray serviette. It's not a scenario that floats my boat. It's a scenario that keeps me in Big Pants.

But hey — why not live a little? I think to myself, rootling through a pile of magazines to find the address for über-lingerie shop Agent Provocateur. These garments must exist in non-man-made fibres and non-acrylic lace, surely? I must call Evie for the Cabbage Soup Diet, too. And — why not? — book the facial Kate's always banging on about. And a leg wax. Perhaps I'll even try a bikini wax, for added sauce at bedtime.

The prospect of bedtime, underwear, waxing and sauce sends me spiralling into something that, if I didn't know better, I would certainly describe as . . . well, worry. But it can't be worry. We've been married eight years, remember? We have two children. We have sex. Sometimes, though not recently. Not since . . . Jesus. Still, I'm not worried. Worry? Me? Ha! What for?

Amber has finally been located and is dropping in this morning for coffee — 'With my foul godson, do you mind? I said I'd look after him, but God, Clara, he's simply *the* most unattractive child ever. I can hardly bear to look at him, poor thing.' She shudders theatrically down the phone.

'He's not *that* bad,' I say disingenuously, since, actually, he is. 'Poor little boy, having a godmother that hates him.'

'Oh, *don't,* don't make me feel worse than I already do. And anyway, I don't hate him. He just makes me feel a bit sick.'

'Amber, that's terrible. Anyway, bring him round. Is he wearing his bag?'

'What bag?'

'The brown-paper number, with the holes for the eyes, that you force him into the second his mother leaves.'

'Clara! Don't be horrible,' Amber says, her outrage tempered with the beginnings of a giggling fit. 'He's wearing a lovely Babar hat, aren't you, Sammy?'

'Yeah,' says Sammy in the background. He has a disconcertingly deep voice for a two-year-old. 'Babar.'

Amber sighs. 'Can we come right away? I don't know what to do with him. I'd take him to the park, but someone might think he was mine.'

'Sure,' I say sympathetically. 'Come now.'

'See you in a minute,' says Amber, sounding wildly relieved.

You're either reading this as a parent, in which case you'll understand the above exchange perfectly, or you're not, in which case I'd better explain.

It is always assumed that, if one loves one's own children, one loves other people's, or at the very least that one has boundless patience with them. 'She's very good with children,' people say admiringly. This is simply not true. Some of us are, instead, very good at acting. Okay, lying.

Charlie has some friends I can hardly bear to have in the house ('William was an angel! So sweet! Can he come again soon?'), and I've come across such a number of grossly unappealing babies ('Oh! But he's *lovely!* Makes me feel all broody!') in my time that I ought to be awarded an honorary PhD in Deception. Once, Robert and I went to see the new-born child of some very dear friends at Queen Mary's in Paddington, a shockingly ugly infant, combining skeletal, very unbonny thinness with terrifyingly adult, big-nosed facial features, a tiny, amphibian-style slit for a mouth and a tufty gingerness around the (vast) head.

We nearly lost it, despite our years of practice, but composed ourselves at the last minute and managed to make the requisite cooing noises, and even to say reverently, 'Can I hold her?' After the ward door had shut behind us, we turned to each other and retched. No, I know it's not very nice, but believe me—it happens. Quite a lot, as a matter of fact. There are a lot of really grotesque children out there, either in looks or in temperament. And many of them, sadly for all concerned, belong to one's friends.

Amber's charge, Sammy, has neither looks nor an appealing nature. He is huge and jowly, which isn't his fault, but rather that of his mother, who felt such pride at his robust infant's appetite that she started padding out his bottles with baby rice and got him on to solids about three months too early. One of the many unhappy results of this maternal enthusiasm is that Sammy—who really looks much more like a Dave or a Terry, possibly because he shows a hefty slice of buttock cleavage at all times, or possibly because his favourite word is 'Yeah'—has weirdly adult tastes in food. I don't mean he guzzles Aqua Vita and screams for pesto, but rather that he's partial to . . . Well, you'll get a demonstration later, no doubt.

Within ten minutes, Amber and Sammy are at the door. Sammy is, indeed, wearing a Babar hat, which fails to obscure his distinctly porcine features; you can see right up his nose.

'Babar hat,' he growls, pointing upwards and flashing extra, unpristine nostril.

'That's lovely,' I say. 'Come in, Sammy, and let's get your coat off.'

Sammy totters in. 'Pee-pee,' he says, pointing at his crotch. 'Done pee-pee.'

I struggle to squidge him out of his coat—his mother refuses to accept that she really should buy him clothes made for five–six-year-olds, so he is always sausaged into his outfits in a way that tugs slightly at the heartstrings.

'Why,' says Amber, 'is this child in nappies if he's aware of the act of peeing?'

'I don't know, Amber. Maybe his mum wanted to make it easier for you. Maybe he's only just started being potty-trained.'

'But she isn't making it easier,' Amber wails, 'because now I'm going to have to change his *nappy*.'

'Nappy,' says Sammy, doing an oddly adult, wriggly little dance, as if the disco floor of a Saturday night held no surprises for him, thank you very much, babe, fancy a spin? 'Sammy's nappy's full.'

'For God's sake,' whispers Amber. 'See what I mean? Why couldn't he just say, "I need the loo" *before* the event?'

'Because he's two,' I say sternly, taking Sammy by the hand. 'Stop being mean. Pass me the changing bag. I'll do it. Come on, Sammy.'

I take him up to the boys' room and do the necessary. Is there anything more revolting than changing someone else's child's nappy, especially when it is, as Sammy accurately pointed out, indeed very 'full'? Having done the business with the Pampers and the aloe vera wipes (using half the tub through fear of making contact with Sammy's poo), I smile briskly at Sammy, who smiles back beatifically, says 'Better', points at his crotch again and takes my hand in his own squidgy one, quite touchingly, to go downstairs.

'Are you hungry?' I ask. 'You could have an early lunch.'

'Want tea,' he says, in his sonorous basso profundo. Honestly, the child would be the pride of any Welsh choir. 'Want my tea.'

Had he not done this before, I would simply assume Northern parentage and provide him with a bowl of pasta. These days, I know better: Sammy wants a cuppa. I don't know why infantile tea—and coffee—drinking should repulse me so much, but it does. Sammy's PG Tips seem lacking in innocence, somehow. What kind of woman gives her two-year-old mugs of tea?

I try what I always try: 'Ribena, Sammy? Apple juice, milk, water, Vimto?'

But Sammy replies what he's always replied: 'I want my tea.'

Back in the kitchen Amber, who's made herself a pot of coffee and dug a fruit cake out of the tin, practically throws herself at me. 'You did it! You did it! Oh, Clara, you're an angel! It must be easier for you, having kids of your own, of course. You must be used to it. I just can't deal with all that poo. Will you do it again if *he* does it again?'

'Can't we at least take turns? Because it's in no way easier, Amber, actually,' I reply. 'Poo, let us not forget, is poo. You can *just about* get to grips with your own flesh and blood's, but believe me, anyone else's grosses me out as much as it does you.'

'Want my tea,' says Sammy, who is sitting on the floor and has started taking off his shoes.

'Coming up,' I sigh, flicking the kettle on again. I wander into the playroom—well, the boxroom that has toys in it—and come back with some wooden bricks, a nodding dog on a string and a pile of picture books. 'Here, er, darling,' I say, depositing them on the floor by Sammy, who is now struggling with his socks. 'You have a play while I talk to Auntie Amber. Would you like a biscuit?'

'Where's my TEA?' shouts Sammy, momentarily distracted from the business of tending to his extremities. 'Want my TEA.'

'Keep your hair on,' I mutter, abandoning the 'I am a kind lady' tone I'd adopted earlier. 'Give me a chance.'

'Ooh, I'm parched,' says Sammy, who is normally looked after by an elderly childminder and whose vocabulary can, therefore, err on the Mavis Riley side. 'Ooh.'

'Coming up,' I repeat, retreating back to the table and to Amber, who is looking at Sammy and shaking her head. 'I'm never, ever having one,' she says. 'Imagine if it came out all Samoid! And it was yours! And you had to love it! I'd have a breakdown.'

'You wouldn't notice, if it was yours,' I say.

'Course you would. Motherhood doesn't make you *blind*, for God's sake.'

Amber and I always have this argument. She claims that she would never be able to love a plain child as much as she would a photogenic one. I claim that she would, though actually I claim this for argument's sake, since I am not convinced. Certainly, when the boys were born, I scrutinized them very closely indeed. And I decided they were lovely — the bee's knees, the ant's pants of glorious babyhood. But then, I am their mother.

'Clara,' says Amber, tucking into her fourth slice of cake, 'you know perfectly well you would be *distraught* if you had a plain child.'

'But I wouldn't *know*,' I say. 'Unless you told me. Would you tell me, Amber?'

Amber munches thoughtfully. 'We always said we would, remember, before you had Charlie? But then you loved him so much . . . And, thank God, he was lovely.'

'He still is.'

'Yes, of course he is. No, I wouldn't tell you, but I'd confirm it if you told me.'

I get up and make Sammy's tea, pouring the brew into a child's Peter Rabbit, two-handed mug to make myself feel better about feeding a baby caffeine and tannin.

'Two sugars,' says Sammy.

'Sugar rots your teeth,' I say briskly. 'I am not giving you two sugars, Sammy.'

'Milk and two sugars, please,' says Sammy uncompromisingly and looking at me squarely, slightly like a dog that's about to bite.

'God's sake,' I mutter. 'It was only one last time. What do I do, Amber? Do you give him two?'

'Yes,' says Amber. 'Otherwise he has amazing tantrums.'

'Thank you,' says Sammy, as I put the mug on a low table beside him. 'Tea.'

'You're welcome,' I say, noting that he may look like a pig/dog, but at least he has nice manners.

'Cara,' says Sammy, as if he were a suave, hand-kissing Italian, or—less charmingly—I were a type of easy-roast potato. 'Cara?'

'Yes?'

'I've got cheesy feet,' Sammy says, in his open-mouthed, faintly breathy way.

I reel back, nauseated. 'I'm sure you haven't, Sammy,' I mumble.

'I have,' he says stolidly and matter-of-factly. 'I've got really cheesy feet, Mummy said.'

'Amber!' I say furiously. 'Can't you have a word with his mum? It's a completely inappropriate thing to say to a little child. I mean, I *kiss* my children's feet.'

'She was just stating a fact, I think, Clara.'

'Nonsense. Two-year-olds don't have stinky feet.'

'Don't come over all Dr Spock with me,' says Amber. 'I don't know about two-year-olds' feet and I don't wish to know.'

'Penelope Leach, actually,' I say. 'Do keep up.' I am suddenly filled with compassion for big, ugly, foot-odoriferous Sammy, whom I pick up. His big, slightly bovine, brown eyes stare up at me. I hoick him on to my hip and bring him to the table. 'Shall I read you a story?' I ask.

'Yeah,' says Sammy. 'Lovely tea, that. Nice cuppa tea, that,' which banter he feels compelled to qualify with a loud, exhaled 'aah' in the manner of a freshly sated builder who has drunk his tea, smoked his fag and burped a loud, rich burp.

Three minutes into some dreary saga about train engines, I am forced to concede that Sammy's mummy has a point after all.

'It's putting you in a bad mood, isn't it, having us here,' states Amber, with some accuracy.

'It's just it makes me feel so *guilty,* Am, not having charitable or Christian thoughts towards him. It makes me feel like the most horrible, monstrous human being.'

'Sammy farted,' says Sammy, from my lap.

'And now he's farted on my *thigh,'* I hiss, putting Sammy down. 'And my thoughts are getting worse and worse.'

'Perhaps he'd like a nap,' says Amber hopefully. 'He has one, late morning.'

'Doesn't look remotely sleepy to me,' I say. 'Not when there are more feet to examine, and more wind to expel.'

'I'll take him to the park, then,' says Amber, looking disconsolate. 'We haven't even had a proper chance to chat and I haven't seen you for weeks. Come with us to the park, why don't you?'

'Mm — you know how much I love nature. But okay, just to catch up.'

'Sammy did a pee-pee,' says Sammy, holding his crotch.

sixteen

WHILE THE OTHER MOTHERS at the park are devoted to
their charges, smiling contentedly and making unabashedly
competitive, elaborate sandcastles with turrets and moats, we
head straight for the bench in the corner for a smoke and a
gossip. Amber has taken the precaution of wedging Sammy
into a toddler's swing that he can't clamber out of by himself
and we watch him swoop happily into the sun-flecked air as
we chat, emitting loud, deep 'Waah's' of excitement (Sammy,
I mean, not us).

The reason Amber hasn't been around, or at least not
around at the same time as me, is that she has met a man. Not
just any old man, she explains, but The Man; The True Love;
The One. She met him at a dinner party, which just goes to
show that those hellish evenings devised by married people
for their own cruel amusement — 'Which retarded ugly-bug
shall we sit next to your desperate single friend with the plum-
meting self-esteem, darling, this time? The dwarf with halitosis, or the letchy fat one with dandruff? Decisions, decisions . . .' — do sometimes yield results.

She's quite hard-boiled, Amber, and she doesn't fall easily.
I glance over at her and I must say that she *looks* in love. She
has that kind of radiant glow more often associated with

pregnant women. 'He's just fantastic,' she says. 'He's just *amazing*. It's like we're the same person, cut into two — look, I'm even saying naff things, that's how in love I am, yuck, but also yippee — except he's much sexier than me. Oh, God, Clara, he is just so sexy. He's incredibly good in bed — the sex, the sex, my God . . ' She drifts off and stares into the distance, smiling a faintly irritating smile, so that I have to pinch her.

'Ow, Clara, what did you do that for? Anyway — I can't believe it, can you? He's handsome — he's incredibly handsome, actually. Almost abnormally. He's *freakishly* handsome. He's funny. He's good in bed. He's cleverer than me, which I always like. He even has money!'

I do see how this would appeal, since Amber has spent large chunks of her life supporting impecunious, hopeless types, all of whom claimed to be 'artistes'. ('Yeah, piss artistes,' Tamsin once said succinctly.) 'And I'm moving in with him at the weekend.'

'What, already? How long have you known him?'

'Two weeks. But he was away for five of those days. Actually, it's two weeks, six hours, eleven minutes' — she squints at her watch — 'and . . .'

'Yes, okay, I get the picture,' I say, laughing. 'You don't think you're jumping the gun at all?'

'I *know* I'm not,' says Amber, grabbing my arm quite hard. 'I've never felt this way about anyone before. I can't wait for you to meet him.'

'I still think . . .'

'I get out of bed naked!' says Amber triumphantly, raising her voice.

'What, no draping yourself in king-size duvet so you have a train? No blanket? No sheet? No lying there getting cystitis from dying to pee but not wanting him to see your thighs?' I am, it must be said, quite impressed.

'Nope. Naked.'

'Naked as a worm? No cheating? Actually *showing* the thighs? Exposing the buttocks?'

'Naked as a naked thing. Completely starkers. And not even retreating so the buttocks are concealed. Actually *turning around*, Clara. Now will you believe me?'

'It does put a new light on things,' I admit.

Amber has, shall we say, poor body image; her years of bulimia have seen to that. Unfortunately for her, she is a classic English pear shape, so no matter how much she diets, or how sick she makes herself, she still looks like she's wearing jodhpurs even when you can see her ribs. I'm only being matter-of-fact here, you understand, rather than mean; it's simply the truth. Amber is lovely-looking, but she has the world's biggest arse—an arse so vast that she is forced to sway from side to side as she walks.

I would never get out of bed naked now, I think to myself, if I were ever in a situation that called for it, which of course I wouldn't be. I am full of admiration for Amber, tinged with, perhaps, a tiny flicker of jealousy. What's she doing getting out of bed naked, when my arse is smaller and I still couldn't? Thank God for marriage and cosy pyjamas, I think to myself with a shudder. Still, there's no denying this is good news for Amber.

'God, Amber, that's so brilliant. Congratulations!' I give her a hug. 'Have you told your counsellor?'

'About Mark? Not yet.'

'Because it's the most amazing leap forward, the naked out of bed thing. I'm really pleased for you.'

'Yes,' she smiles—and she really is looking dementedly happy. 'I'm pleased too. The amazing thing is, he actually seems to like my bottom. Oh, GOD,' she shouts, smacking herself on the forehead, 'oh, GOD, I forgot to tell you the other news.'

'What other news? You're not pregnant?'

'No . . . but guess who is?'

One of the other mothers is walking towards us, looking worried. 'Excuse me,' she says, gesturing towards the swings, 'but is that your child?'

'NO!' we both shout in unison.

'I mean, sort of,' says Amber.

The penny drops and my stomach lurches. 'We forgot about Sammy!' I scream, horrified.

'It's just he's been swinging for about fifteen minutes,' says the mother. 'All by himself.' She is not beaming with approbation exactly. She is looking at us much as, earlier, I looked at Sammy's nappy.

'Oh, God, oh, fuck, oh, godding fuck,' says Amber, which doesn't do much to improve the mother's facial expression. 'Fucking buttfucks up the BUTT,' she adds, for emphasis, stubbing out her cigarette and running towards the swings.

I race after her. A group of small children has gathered around Sammy the Incredible Swinging Toddler—'He just Swings On and On'—who, mercifully, seems to be enjoying their attention, although he does look a little dazed.

'Sammy! Oh, Sammy! Oh, poor thing,' says Amber, swooping him out of the swing and kissing the top of his Babar hat. 'Oh, darling Sammy, I'm so sorry.'

'Sammy swing,' booms factual Sammy.

'God,' says Amber, 'poor little boy.' She looks up and notices the other mothers, and can't help adding, 'He's not mine, you know. I'm just minding him. See?' She squishes her face next to his. 'We don't look at all alike. Because he's not mine.'

'Funny way of minding a child,' sniffs a woman in dungarees. (We have come to Stoke Newington, after all, where people eat nut loaf and millet as if the past three decades simply had not happened, a state of denial that extends to the sartorial. Want to buy a tie-dyed T-shirt and matching Jesus sandals? Fancy a lentil bake? You know where to come.)

'The poor little thing,' says another. 'We thought he'd been abandoned.'

'Well, he hasn't,' says Amber. 'I just got caught up chatting to my friend. Come on, Sammy, let's go and play.'

'Whee,' says Sammy, sounding unconvinced. 'Sammy go whee! Swing.'

We slink out of the playground enclosure, swift with guilt. Amber straps Sammy into his buggy. He's asleep within minutes, exhausted from his surfeit of involuntary exercise.

'I think you'd better not visit anyone when you're with him,' I say to Amber. 'Just concentrate on him. It's as much my fault as it is yours, though — God, how awful.'

'Well, he's fine now,' says Amber. 'He remains unsnatched. That's the main thing.'

'I was just so enthralled by what you were saying,' I say, suddenly remembering. 'So, who's pregnant?'

'Oh yes,' says Amber. 'You're not going to believe this one.'

'Amber, come on. Tell me.'

'Guess,' says Amber.

'No, I don't want to. Come on.'

'Tamsin.'

'NO!'

'Yup! She found out a couple of days ago.'

'But whose is it?'

'Ah,' says Amber. 'Ah, yes. The paternity question.'

'Please don't tell me she doesn't *know*,' I say, aghast. 'She's a fully grown woman. Fully grown women know who they're pregnant by. Jesus. It drives me mad, that. It's like when women in their thirties tell men they want to hold on to, "I think I'm pregnant." I mean, talk about fuckwits. You pee on a stick and you find out. You don't dither about like Mavis bloody Riley.'

'Tamsin *did* pee on a stick. And she *does* know who she's pregnant by,' says Amber.

126

'Well? *Well?*'

'The one-night stand.'

Oh no. Oh *no*. I grab Amber's arm. 'Please tell me you're joking, Amber. The weeny peeny? The man who had a dump in her loo? No. No. Please, Amber, are you joking?'

'I swear I'm not.'

'*Fuck*. What's she going to do?'

'She doesn't know. She's in a bit of a state. I mean, you know as well as me that she's been madly broody for years now . . . But, you know—even in that kind of situation, would one want a weenster as a dad?'

I leave Amber in the minicab office—why is it that none of my friends can drive?—and walk home via the nice bakery that does hot bread. Back in the house, I drag a battered old quilt down from my bed, make a pint mug of tea, hunker down with a hunk of said loaf and dial Tamsin.

'Why didn't you tell me?'

'Hi, Clara. I was a bit freaked out. Also, I kept getting your answering machine.'

'How far gone are you?'

'Only six weeks.'

'What are you going to do? Have you told him?'

'I don't know. And no. No, I haven't.'

'Are you feeling sick, darling? Because, ginger biscuits.'

'What?'

'Ginger biscuits by the bed—they help with the sickness, and also they're quite yummy, plus if you put on biscuit weight nobody notices. They still want to pat you.'

'I haven't been that sick—actually, I only really feel nauseous in the evenings—but thanks, I'll bear it in mind.'

'Oh, Tamsin.'

'Oh, Clara.' There is a long pause. Then: 'What am I going to do?'

'Fuck. I don't know.'

'You *know* how much I want a baby . . . Clara, are you in a tunnel?'

'No, I'm right down under the eiderdown. With worry, Tam. I've burrowed. Yes, of course I know about you wanting babies.'

'But I don't necessarily want a baby *by myself*. I mean, how am I supposed to work it? Pay someone all my wages so that I can go out to work and never see it? Stop working and not be able to pay the mortgage? And surely I wouldn't be the first single mother—Clara, how do other people do it?'

'They do it by not ever asking themselves those kinds of questions. Honestly, Tam, no children would ever be born if one approached the whole subject with any kind of logic. Or rather, children would only be born to people who had pension schemes and Tessas and savings—imagine the creepiness.'

'Savings!' Tamsin says wistfully. 'Ha!'

We both fall silent again, imagining what it would be like to have no overdraft.

'Don't you think you ought to tell him—what was his name, again?'

'David. And his penis was called "Little Dave".'

'Don't remind me, Tam, or yourself. Oh, God, I don't know what to say.' I think for a bit. 'The thing is, he was good-looking, right?'

'Ish.'

'And intelligent? I mean, not actually simple?'

'No, intelligent, as far as I could tell.'

'Well, then. It's nurture, anyway, not nature.'

'But, Clara, what if he's passed on the crap-shag gene? Or the crapping gene, full stop? More to the point, what about me being a mummy on my own?' She is beginning to sound tearful.

'Oh, Tamsin.'

'Oh, Clara.'

I feel panic-stricken on her behalf, I really do. I pop my head out of the eiderdown and reach for a cigarette.

There's a small silence for a while, during which we both sigh, which I do extra loudly, to show my support.

'I'm racking my brains, Tam.'

'Me too.'

I take a sip of tea and spit it out again with excitement.

'Oh,' I say, 'Tamsin! I know what will help. You need to do Madonna.'

'I don't think . . .'

'Darling, doing Madonna never failed us. Remember?'

'How could I forget? We did it for years. It was our *life*.'

'Exactly. And did it ever, ever fail?'

'Umm . . . No, I don't suppose it did, except when you came to my dad's fiftieth birthday wearing a rosary and a dirty nightie, remember?'

'I'd forgotten, actually. God, imagine wearing that.'

'That was the Madonna thing.'

'Yes, but that was a *sartorial* aping, Tam, which is not the same thing. Doing Madonna has never failed. And we haven't done it for years. I really think it's your best option.'

'Okay,' says Tam, with a sigh. She's stopped sounding weepy, though. 'Let's do Madonna. Let's do it now. Or shall I come round?'

I sit up again, drawing the quilt around me.

'No. I think in emergencies it's okay to do it on the phone.'

I feel like I'm travelling back in time. Tamsin and I spent our entire teenage years — actually, it went on well into our twenties — doing Madonna. It's perfectly simple: you hum a bit of 'Express Yourself' to cheer yourself up, and then ask yourself, *What would Madonna do if she were in my shoes?*

The marvellous thing was you could apply this simple question to everything and it always gave the right answer. The day Tam and I started playing it was the last time any sweating weirdo ever tried to press himself up against us on the tube on the way to sixth-form college. Pre-Madonna, faced with this unhappily frequent circumstance, we'd move away, or give feeble dirty looks. Post-Madonna, we started hurling very loud abuse (it took a couple of goes before we decided there was no real need to do this in an American accent): 'Don't ever do that again. Don't fuck with me, or I'll cut your balls off.'

It worked. But that's only one example of literally dozens. If we fancied a boy but felt too shy, as ourselves, to do anything about him, we'd do Madonna and ask him right out. That worked too, more often that not. Treated badly by a friend or boyfriend? Well, Madonna wouldn't lie around sobbing on her Snoopy duvet, and neither did we. Doing Madonna worked brilliantly later too if anyone ever bullied us at college, or later still if people were mean at work. Doing Madonna quite literally shaped our lives. The last time I did it was on my wedding morning.

'She's never failed us before, Tamsin. Ready?'

'Ready. But, Clara, she has evolved a bit since then, don't you think? She might not have knee-jerk reactions any more. I mean, she might have stopped saying "Fuck" and going for it and putting her hand down people's pants.'

'Bollocks. She's fundamentally the same, except older. Like us.'

'I feel silly doing the singing.'

'Okay, do it in your head. Or I'll do it. I'm going to do it, Tamsin.'

The lyrics pop out of my subconscious, fully formed. I start singing, quietly at first. But although I am embarrassed, I have faith. I sing Madonna's words—I think of her more as Maddie, at time like these, or even as Madge—as though they were my own.

'Wooh, baby,' I tell Tamsin. 'Let's go.' And I sing the first line. Surely I don't need to tell you how it goes? 'Express Yourself'? The pink corset peering out of the pinstriped suit?

The blonde curls? Our youth, if you're anywhere near me in age. Course you remember it. Unless you were busy dissecting frogs while breathing through your mouth and cursing the hussy Maddie, who'd anyway look much nicer if she wore something sensible in easycare Crimplene. In which case, please stop reading: you're banned.

Tamsin sings along, quietly. Then she interrupts herself.

'Clara?'

'Uhh, mmm, mmm,' I say, carrying on.

'Why are you making those sorts of squeaks? You sound like Michael Jackson.'

'No, I don't,' I say. 'I'm moaning provocatively, Tamsin. Do you remember nothing? Moaning provocatively is part and parcel of the Maddie experience.'

'It's a bit off-putting,' Tamsin says. 'And besides, she doesn't moan in "Express Yourself". She moans in "Like a Virgin".'

'Hardly an appropriate track for you, darling. Bit late in the day.'

'Don't be mean,' says Tamsin, giggling.

'*Touch Litt-el Dave,*' I sing, to the tune of 'Like a Virge', as it's colloquially known to us aficionados. '*Go on, you know you want toooo . . . Touch Li-i-i-tlle Dave . . . He's a penis . . . With a na-a-a-ame. A-a-a-aaame.*' I emit a manly, Dave-style—I imagine—grunt.

'You're the most juvenile person I've ever met,' says Tamsin, snorting with laughter. 'Can we get on with it now?'

'I'm only trying to cheer you up, sweetheart. Besides, she always moans,' I say. 'But you go first then. I'm listening,' I add, like Frasier Crane.

She does, shyly at first, then with mounting enthusiasm as she reaches the bit about making him—and I paraphrase loosely—pipe up and share his emotions. I join in, and within a couple of seconds am bellowing down the phone and gyrating on my own sofa.

'Clara?' Tamsin says, interrupting a second time.

'Now what?'

'We're singing the wrong bit. That bit's about boys. My quandary isn't about boys.'

'It is, kind of,' I point out. 'No boy, no boy-penis. No boy-penis, no boy-spermatozoa. No boy-spermatozoa, no baby. Quod est demonstrandum. Express yourself!' I growl, in a fairly impressive approximation of Ms Ciccone.

We really get into our stride round about verse three, which informs us that—I paraphrase again, for reasons too tiresome to go into here—all we need is to feel like queens on thrones, all the time. 'Too right, Mads,' ad-libs Tamsin.

'Yes!' we both scream in unison as the song ends.

'I feel so much better,' says Tamsin.

But I don't, momentarily. For some reason the lyrics make me think, fleetingly, of my marriage. Well, I say fleetingly— actually, they make me think, and think, and think until it feels as if my head is going to burst.

Is that really what I used to do, not believe in second best?

'Clara?' says Tamsin. 'Clara? Have you gone off to find your Gaultier corset dress? Clara? The old MAC Russian Red lippy?'

I feel sick—I could vomit, since you ask—but it passes, as does the simple-minded, two-D-ness of youth. It passes. Sympathy vomiting . . . I must love Tamsin a lot.

'Here I am,' I say. 'So. Let's cut to the chase. What would Madonna do?'

'Clara, she'd have the baby,' says Tamsin happily. 'I *know* it. If she wanted to have a baby, she would have a baby, and sod the consequences.'

'My feeling entirely,' I agree. 'She wouldn't have an abo, anyway—she's Catholic. She'd have the baby and somehow end up having a fabulous time.'

'I'm keeping it!' says Tamsin. '*I'm gonna keep my baby, ooo eee.*'

132

'Different song, but same thing, I suppose. Have you cheered up, darling?'

'You bet,' says Tamsin. 'You can be godmother, if Madonna says no.'

'See you later, darling. I told you it would still work.'

'Oh, it does, it does,' says Tamsin, sounding like she's tap-dancing. 'It still works.'

A baby! Tamsin's going to have a lovely little baby. Which doesn't stop the fact that, personally, I think those lyrics are adolescent and simplistic, I reflect, as I put the phone back into its cradle.

God! I think to myself. God, we were such intensely *silly* girls. Thank Heavens we grew up.

That's it. She's gonna keep her bay-bee, oo ee. And I'm going to Paris with my husband of eight years, oo err. And I've got to sort myself out; I've got to take myself in hand. And speaking of oos, what's this? I have butterflies and my breathing is hard and . . . Well, if I didn't know better I'd think it was a panic attack! Ha! Imagine. Me—a panic attack. As if. *As if.* I really should cut down on my smoking though. It's disgusting to breathe like that, in tiny breaths, like you've been punched.

Anyway. Anyway. Speaking of song lyrics, *Le jour de gloire est (presque) arrivé*. I've got to get my Paris self in gear. I've got a leg wax at 4, plus the bikini thing, and Robert's taking me out to dinner in Islington. Robert, Robert, Robert whom I love and who loves me, and look at our life, how could he not, how couldn't I?

Speaking of dinner, I seem to have mislaid my appetite over the last few days. Nerves, probably. France nerves. My face, as reflected in the hall mirror, actually looks quite nice.

I phone Charlie's friend Rollo's mother to make sure she's okay about picking both the boys up and having them to play, give the kitchen a quick wipe and hoover—I don't understand what happens to my kitchen, I just don't get it; it's not like I while away the hours staging my very own dirty protests — and get in the car.

It's funny. I actually used to be a high-maintenance girl, by my own standards, if not by my mother's. When Robert and I met, I weighed the right kind of weight and had nice arms with a hollow down the underside and went for manicures when I could afford it. I was so nicely dressed all the time. I could spend entire Saturdays shopping for an outfit to wear that night — a feat which I considered deeply sad the second I got married and had children and preoccupied myself with casseroles and educationally sound toys instead, like a grown-up.

And now I'm not so sure. They were such fun, those shopping expeditions, blowing half the week's wages on a hot little dress that I thought might make him want to kiss me. He used to tell me he loved the way I dressed, in between telling me he loved me.

Is my period due or something?

seventeen

FUCK. *Fuck*. I am lopsided. I am wrong Down Below. Now what?

There are many conspiracies of silence in the world—the fact that no one, not even your mother, ever tells you how much childbirth hurts springs to mind, for starters. And now this: the bikini wax. Why did no one tell me? Why did Amy, the beautician, not say, 'And now I'm going to traumatize your pudenda with hot wax'? Why do people even have this stupid treatment performed, unless they're yetis?

Anyway, I couldn't go through with it. It hurt too much. It hurt so much that I grabbed Amy by the hair and pulled, while screaming a primitive-sounding kind of scream.

Amy said, 'Uh, oh dear, is it that bad? I'll try and do the other side quicker.'

I said, 'Amy, if you ever fucking try that again, I swear I'll kill you. Don't come near me. Pass me my pants.' (A hard sentence to utter in a dignified manner, incidentally, that last one.)

Amy: 'But I can't let you go home with one side done and not the other.'

Me: 'I forbid you to do the other side. I'll sue you if you try.'

Amy: 'But, Clara . . .'

Me: 'I *said*, pass me my pants.'

There followed an awkward silence while I struggled into said underwear, one side of me still tacky with warm wax.

'Clara?'

'Please don't talk to me, Amy. That was worse than childbirth.'

'But you're going to look very odd . . .'

'I don't care.'

But, actually, I kind of do. I look *mad* around the, er, middle. I don't think this is a quandary that could be solved with the help of nail scissors or Immac. Perhaps I should shave the whole thing off? It seems the only sensible option. But then I'll look grotesque, like a porn mag. Oh, what am I going to do?

The phone rings. It's someone called Electra, from some PR company. One of the perils of working from home is that you're subject to these phone calls all the time. I can't really pay attention to what she's saying, because I am thinking about my pubis and feeling depressed. 'Something something party,' she says, sounding reproachful. 'Are you coming? You haven't replied.'

'What party is that?'

Electra doesn't sound like she has lopsided pubic hair. Electra sounds like she's wearing Gucci heels and a dinky little top for people with no breasts, in a size 6, and probably a couple of glittery butterfly hair clips in her hair. My spirits are, frankly, low.

'In Hoxton? For *Contortions?*'

'Oh,' I remember, wanting to laugh. 'Mr Dunphy. I don't think so, Electra.' Uninvited, a picture of Dunphy suddenly appears in my head. Dunphy smiling, in a T-shirt.

'You can't make it?'

'No, I can't.' He's still there. I rub my brow with my right hand.

'Oh.'

'I'm sure it'll be great, but, you know . . .'

'Oh,' she says again. 'I guess I'll have to rework the seating plan.'

'I guess you will. And now, if you don't mind . . . What seating plan? I thought it was a drinks party. For 600.'

I walk over to the table lopsidedly and fish around for the invite. Here it is: it says 'champagne, canapés'.

'It's *drinks*,' I say. Why are these people always so dim? 'It says "champagne, canapés". So there's no need to make me feel guilty over seating plans. And now, Electra, I've really got to go.'

'I'm not talking about the drinks,' says Electra, sounding surly as well as thin. 'There's a little dinner afterwards, at the Groucho Club. The show at 7, the party at 9 and dinner at midnight.'

I am parked in front of the kitchen mirror. I've definitely got cheekbones. It's a miracle! I wonder if they'll last. How *pathetic* of me to get excited about cheekbones, though. Especially when I've got horrible deformed pubic hair.

'You've made a mistake,' I say flatly. 'I am not invited to dinner. I really, really have to get on with my day now, so if you don't mind . . .'

'Well, you're on my list,' says Electra, sounding non-plussed. 'You're on my dinner list. What am I supposed to do now?'

'Oh, for Christ's sake. It's just a mistake.'

'It isn't.'

'It must be.' Mustn't it? Why would he want me to come to dinner? And why would I want to go? I rub my face again and exhale loudly. 'Are you sure you haven't made a mistake, Electra?'

'I'm certain. I've got the list.'

'How many people at dinner?'

'Twenty.'

'And I'm on the list?'

'Yes,' says Electra. 'I keep telling you.'

'Well . . . Don't cross me off yet then,' I say very quickly, not quite understanding what I am saying, or why. 'I'll try and come.'

'Cool,' says Electra. 'See you at the party.'

My heart is pounding and I feel very hot.

'Electra?' I say, despite myself.

'Hmm?'

'Is, um, Sam Dunphy gay?'

There is a silence. I fill it. 'Never mind,' I say. 'Forget I asked. Please.'

'Gay?' splutters Electra. '*Gay?* No, Clara. No. He is not gay.' She snorts with laughter. 'Why do you . . .'

'See you,' I say, and hang up.

There's only one possibility here, I think to myself, and I am not even going to entertain it. *I am not even going to entertain it.*

I hate to bang on about it, but there is definite bone-action going on about my face. I call Kate, on the spur of the moment, to book an appointment with her facialist—who, fortuitously, has a cancellation on Friday morning. Kate is full of the joys of spring, and full of the joys of Max. Kate is happy ('Darling, isn't life *bliss?*'). For some reason, this slightly throws me.

I collect Jack and Charlie from Rollo's house, and the very sight of them fills me with that passionate love you sometimes feel for your children, for no reason, in the ordinary middle of ordinary days. We make macaroni cheese for tea and build an entire Lego village before bathtime; I almost want to cancel dinner with Robert to spend more time with them. Jack squeals with delighted fear at his bedtime story, which involves me being a growly monster; Charlie sits in his bed, twirling his hair like he did when he was a baby.

Robert's keys in the front door signal my own bathtime. I've half an hour to get myself in order before our dinner reservation. Of course, if I believed what I read in women's

magazines, I'd simply put on some heels, a darker lipstick—
and put my hair up, perhaps—and, hey presto, a sophisticated day-into-night look, just like that. I wonder, and not for
the first time, who writes that crap. (The answer, of course,
being me—I write that crap: 'Try a darker eyeshadow and a
black liner for a night-time look that's as sophisticated as it is
sexy.' Ha!)

Lying in the bath, I can hear Robert and the boys giggling
downstairs. He's being a monster too, one that tickles as well
as growls. There's nothing, really, to beat family life when it's
like this. Nothing. And I think my period really must be due,
because the thought of this kind of happiness, inexplicably,
makes me want to cry.

I don't think I've really told you what Robert looks like. His
hair is a dirtyish, messyish kind of blond; he's five foot nine—
about my height; and his features are the right side (for a
man) of pretty. There's something slightly cruel about the curl
of his mouth, but this is compensated for by his kind eyes: the
kindest eyes I ever saw, in fact—you need to be careful, with
eyes like that, or you get taken in, since Robert is not, actually, particularly kind. The eyes are a dark, flinty sort of grey,
which makes their kindness all the more startling, and are
very long-lashed. He has a prominent, aquiline nose, but is by
no means beaky. (I do think, though, that beaky is preferable
to pug, when it comes to men's noses.) He is very slim and his
clothes, his impeccably tailored clothes, hang off him properly, as if he were a mannequin.

He's handsome, Robert, I think to myself as we sit at our
candlelit restaurant table for two. He's handsome, and he
isn't my type. He has very nice hands. He looks clean. You
could lick him and only ever taste Creed Green Irish Tweed
(*tiens!*) aftershave.

My clean, fragrant husband and I sit very straight and order
two glasses of champagne.

'Looking forward to Paris?' Robert asks.

'Yes. God, Robert, I had a bikini wax and it went wrong.'

'How?'

'I couldn't bear to let her do the other side. So now I'm all misshapen.'

'God, Clara, does it hurt that much?'

'Like you wouldn't believe. But anyway—if we, you know, in Paris, do try and keep your eyes averted.'

Robert gives me a long look, one that combines—if you ask me—both mirth and faint disgust. But then he surprises me by saying, 'I don't mind, Clara. I really don't mind. Don't worry about it. It'll be okay.'

And this is a kind thing to say; it matches his eyes. But it makes me feel pitiful somehow, not quite right, as if I were the kind of person you make allowances for. The kind of person you don't sleep with much, perhaps.

'Do you think we're happily married, Robert?' I ask, passing him a menu. 'And do you remember the lemon risotto we had here last time? It was so delicious.'

'Yes,' says Robert. 'Yes, it was—but it's not on today, they've got pumpkin and sage instead. I'll have that. And a plate of antipasto to start.' He flicks his eyes towards the waiter. Robert is the kind of person who always catches waiters' eyes. He's also the kind of person who's never had spinach in his teeth, or not had a tissue to sneeze into while trying to impress a companion.

'I'll have the tomato salad and then the squid, please,' I tell him.

'And some *pommes allumettes,*' says Robert automatically, on my behalf.

'No, not today, thanks,' I tell the waiter. 'Just the salad and the squid.'

'A first!' says Robert, leaning back in his chair. 'Why don't you have some? They're your favourite thing.'

'I don't know—I keep not being starving,' I tell him. 'It's really weird. I keep not wanting my favourite things.'

'Actually,' says Robert, leaning back further and narrowing his eyes, 'I think you've lost a bit of weight.' He pauses. 'You're looking lovely.'

'Hmm. It'll all come back on again, so I wouldn't think about it too much,' I say, made gruff by the direct compliment.

'I don't care what weight you are, Clara,' says Robert, sounding resigned and not exactly tender.

'You didn't answer my question. Do you think we're happily married?'

Robert sits back in his chair and runs an impeccably manicured-seeming hand through his impeccably tousled hair.

'What do *you* think?' he asks, unnervingly, and fixes me with his kind, flinty, paradox eyes.

There are some situations where it just won't do to be seen to dither and this strikes me as one of them. Though, clearly, not him.

I say, 'Basically, yes.'

'Why?' Robert asks. 'Why do you say that?'

'We're such good friends,' I say, and Robert nods. 'You're my best friend, or as good as. We like the same jokes, and the same things, and the same food.'

'And the same children,' Robert adds drily.

'And we love our children.'

'And do we love our lives?' he asks. 'Really.'

The waiter places a second glass of champagne in front of me.

'You love yours, I think,' I say to him. 'And I love mine. I mean, I don't know what it means, loving your life. I don't have any points of comparison. There isn't another me and you I can measure us up against.'

'But you're happy?'

'Yes, of course, Robert. Aren't you?'

'Yes,' he says slowly, stretching the word out like a Southern plantation owner. 'I'm happy enough.'

I hate 'happy enough'; I hate middling, compromisey, half-arsed, horrible, ungenerous 'happy enough'.

But I say, 'That's the mature thing, isn't it, to be happy enough? Not delirious, or depressed, but happy enough. That's what shows you're a functioning, emotionally sussed adult.' I do hope my face is composed, because Robert is able to detect even the smallest lie. Confusingly, the next sentence isn't a lie, though, I don't think. I say, 'I'm happy enough too.'

'Not delirious . . .' Robert says, gazing into the distance. 'Clara, you know I love you.'

'Yes. And I love you.'

'I'd never hurt you.'

'Nor me you. Are we playing Mills & Boon?' I say, trying to lighten the oppressive atmosphere that's suddenly gathered around us.

'Yes. I am about to press you into my manly chest,' says Robert, which does the trick. 'You will feel my strong heart beat and your insides will liquefy with desire.'

'Robert, are you trying to say something?'

'No, Clara,' he says, pushing his antipasto around his plate. 'I'm not trying to say anything. Except that we're spoiled people and sometimes I think that we should count our blessings. Chin-chin.' He raises his glass.

'Cheers. I do that all the time,' I blurt, having taken a sip. 'I count them all the time.'

'Do you?' says Robert, raising an eyebrow. 'Anyway, let's talk about something else.'

I start telling him about Tamsin; he fills me in on Richard's affair (still ongoing), and passes on gossip. We leave the table at 11 P.M., faintly woozy (me), and, back home, both go into the boys' room to kiss their sleeping heads good-night. Robert stands, framed in the door, while I stroke Jack's fluffy little head, and when I look up he smiles at me so sweetly that, were we still playing Mills & Boon, I might say something about breaking and hearts.

*

I have decided to give myself the day off. It's Thursday, the day before Dunphy's party, and I am going shopping. Flo has come round to look after the boys. I have hours, and hours, and hours to myself. I am going to buy a lovely dress, and make-up, and shoes. I am, not to put too fine a point on it, beside myself with excitement. I am not going to buy a single practical thing. I am not even going to *look* at price tags. I am going to do the kind of shopping I haven't done for years.

Flo has given me a list of shops. I don't mean that I am the kind of simpleton who doesn't know where Selfridges is, but as I say, I haven't done this kind of shopping for years and the kinds of little boutiques du jour I'm after are no longer in my address book. I don't want to look like anybody else. I want the most beautiful things my money — or Messrs Barclays' money — can buy. It's been at least eight years since I spent more than £100 on a dress. I can't wait.

Following Flo's directions, I find a narrow little street in naff Covent Garden and, sure enough, half-way down, as promised, is exactly the kind of shop I was after. Its tiny little window glitters with promise. Frothy, beaded, sequinned, feathered dresses hang from pale-pink, padded satin hangers in colour-coded blocks: azure, candy-pink, scarlet, violet. From the street, I can see a pea-green dress that's exactly like a mermaid.

I can also see some tiny little assistants, with tiny little twiggy arms, and suddenly, right there on the pavement, I mutate into Two-Ton Tessie, destroyer of pretty frocks, seam-burster. Mercifully, Madonna, fresh in my mind from Tamsin, comes gallantly leaping to the fore once again. Would Madonna stand on the pavement, feeling shy of a few skeletal creatures with a couple of brain cells between them? No, she would not. And neither will I. I push the door open and totter into Aladdin's cave.

What's this? Not a mean look, not a whisper, not a 'Have you tried Evans?' in sight (not that anyone's ever said *that*, thank God, but in my more paranoid moments I can't help think it's only a matter of time). Instead, one of the twigs clicks forward on her tiny kitten heels and says, 'Can I help you?'

'I want to look fabulous,' I say, feeling like one of those old boilers you get on morning-television makeovers: puddings on legs who want to look like Monroe—'I want to *ooze sex,* Brian,' they say delusionally.

But I persevere. 'I want to look *fantastic.* I need a dress, and shoes, and maybe some kind of cardigan or wrap. Can you help?'

'Stay there,' says the angel in a size 4 top, steering me towards the changing room. She returns a couple of minutes later, arms laden with exquisite frocks. 'There are a few here to choose from,' she says, 'but my colleagues and I think the green one. We thought so the minute you walked in. Would you like to try it on first?'

The green dress is the diaphanous, glittery mermaid's dress I saw through the glass. It is the most beautiful dress I've ever seen. The assistant discreetly withdraws while I struggle out of my old clothes. The dress—a 14, I notice with some sur-prise—fits like a glove. My stomach sticks out a bit, but so what, really? It just looks like a normal stomach, as opposed to the concave bodies featured in *Vogue.*

'That's incredibly flattering,' the assistant says approvingly. 'It's bias-cut, which is what's making your body look so long.'

'It's amazing,' I say truthfully. 'But what about my arms? I'm not wandering about flashing my arms.'

'I brought you some wraps, and this cardigan,' she says, 'which I think is just beautiful.' She unfurls a tiny wisp of heavily beaded cream satin; the shimmering beads form tiny pink roses. I don't know what's going on, but it fits too.

'It fits!' I shout, feeling mad with joy.

'It fits beautifully. And then, I thought, some heels, some-thing delicate,' says the girl. 'We don't want to look too colour-coordinated. I had some very pretty sandals, with straps made out of ribbon, but I think we may have sold out. What's your shoe size?'

'It's 7,' I say. And to myself: 'If they have the sandals, my life is going to change,' much in the way that, aged fifteen, I'd say, 'If it's an even number of steps to the corner shop, X will ask me out.'

The sandals would make the outfit perfect. I have to have the sandals. 'I could maybe squeeze into a 6,' I call after the assistant.

'You're in luck,' she says, returning with a box. 'We have one pair left, in pink — to match the roses — size 6.'

'I won't try them on,' I say, feeling panicky in case they don't fit. 'I'll just take them.'

'Are you sure?' says the girl. 'Wouldn't you like to see the whole outfit?'

'No,' I say. 'I'll try them on at home. Now, do I need anything else?'

I leave an hour later. As well as the dress — God, the dress: I could snog it — and the cardigan and the ribbon shoes, I have cream-coloured clip-on fabric roses for my hair, some tiny pearl and crystal earrings for my ears, and a bottle of the house scent, which smells of crushed mangoes.

'You're going to look beautiful,' says another assistant as I sign the Visa receipt. His gaze rests on my wedding finger. 'He's going to love it.'

'I hope so,' I say, feeling panicked again. 'That's the idea.'

eighteen

'IT'S DUNPHY'S THING tomorrow evening,' I tell Robert later that night. The boys are bathed and combed, ready for bed. They've been allowed a quarter of an hour's worth of Playstation as a treat. 'I've been shopping. Do you want to see?'

'Are the two related?' asks Robert, smirking slightly. 'Are you making a *special effort* for the special party?'

'Please don't talk to me as if I were retarded,' I snap, feeling a surge of anger rising. 'It's bad enough that you do it at all. But don't do it now. I'm really not in the mood.'

'Oooh!' says Robert, sounding like Frankie Howerd. 'Have you come home from the shops *all cross?*'

'No. I have come home from the shops in a good mood. Don't spoil it.' But he has, already, in a small way. It's always in a small way.

Robert perches his perfectly toned bottom on the arm of the sofa, lights a cigarette and pours himself a drink from the tray of gin, tonic, lemon, ice and heavy tumbler he's brought up from the kitchen. 'Okay,' he says. 'Let's see.'

I sit on the floor cross-legged, surrounded by bags. I'm so excited about my purchases that I can't be bothered to sulk.

'I bought some make-up,' I say. 'Here, look. This is black

cake eyeliner. Do you remember, I used to wear it all the time?'

'Very *Dolce Vita*,' says Robert. 'Yes, I remember.'

'And these are some glittery eyeshadows. Can you see — they catch the light. Look at the silver one, it's lovely.'

'Very pretty.'

'False eyelashes . . .'

'I see we're going for the whole full-on Fellini-starlet effect, then?'

'Well, yes. There's hardly much point in being faint-hearted about it. I mean, if you're going to dress up, you're going to dress up.'

'Quite. What's this stuff?'

'Powder that shimmers. For the limbs.'

'Foxy,' Robert says succinctly, making foxes' ears with his fingers, à la *Wayne's World,* and immediately making me honk with laughter. 'What shall I wear?'

'You?'

'Me. Moi. What shall I wear? Is it black tie?'

'Oh. Yes. No. I don't know. The thingy's downstairs some-where.' How could I have forgotten about Robert?

He wanders off in search of the invitation and returns brandishing it. 'It says "Dress: Up",' he announces. 'Which is just as well in your case. I think I'll just wear the new suit. You know, the one with the purple lining. I can wear it to the office and come straight from there.'

'Very nice.' I nod. 'So you're going to come, are you?'

'Yes,' says Robert, giving me a long look. 'Why? Would you rather I didn't?'

'No, no — I'd love you to come. It's ages since we've been to a party.'

'Clara,' says Robert, 'what are you talking about? We went to a party a couple of weeks ago. We go to lots of parties.'

'No. I mean a proper, glamorous, dressy-uppy party, as opposed to a party that's full of moaning couples who don't have sex any more and talk about property.'

'It *was* a glamorous party,' says Robert, nonplussed. 'With dancing. With caterers. Don't you remember? Fred's thirty-fifth?'

'Whatever,' I say vaguely.

'I don't *have* to come,' says Robert, sounding huffy now. 'If you'd rather go on your own.'

'Oh, Robert, pipe down. I want you to come. We'll look very photogenic and it'll be charming. Now look, here comes the dress.' I start loosening the tissue folds it's wrapped in and feel another pang of passionate love as a corner of the pea-green fabric appears. 'Ta-daa!' I yell, somewhat over-excitedly, as I pull the dress out.

'Christ!' says Robert. 'Christ, Clara. That's *amazing*. It is by . . .' He jumps off the sofa to come and look at the label. 'Yes, I thought so—it was in *Vogue.*' He strokes the fabric. 'Brilliantly cut, Clara, do you see?' he adds, pointing out the seams. 'Bias, of course. Does it fit?'

'Yes, it fucking well does,' I say, feeling, to be perfectly frank with you, outraged.

'Try it on, then, and keep your hair on. I was only asking. Did you get shoes?'

'Yes,' I say, showing him. 'And I did try it on, obviously. You'll have to wait until tomorrow to see. I'm not doing it again now.'

'Perfect shoes,' Robert says, nodding approvingly. 'Perfect outfit, actually. Very good, Clara. It's ages since you bought anything this nice. Months. Years.'

'Close on a decade, I expect,' I say 'Close on my wedding day.'

'Hardly my fault, darling. I'm always telling you to go and buy clothes.'

'You're always telling me who stocks size 26, which is hardly the same thing, Robert. Anyway, I'm glad you like it.'

You'll notice Robert is not asking me how much the outfit cost. This is one of the things I like him for. It's another blessing to add to my list, actually, because I know for a fact I would die if I were ever involved with anyone mean, and Robert's the least mean person I know. Financially, at any rate.

You'd think I'd never been to a party before. I can't sleep. I make up all sorts of little scenarios as I lie next to Robert in the dark: my splendid pea-green entrance, the colour of my frock matching the face of every other woman in the room. I replay the scene again and again in my head, until by the end I am, in fact, Madame de Pompadour wowing jaded Versailles to a choir of seraphim. Then I feel guilty and include Robert in my fantasy game. He becomes an irresistible, studly, gigolo-but-classier type, with eyes — but of course — only for me, despite the pleading entreaties of the assembled throng, who turn away from Dunphy as one.

Oh. Where did that come from? I wish I could go to sleep. I turn my head and peer at Robert in the darkness. He even sleeps neatly. He gets into bed and doesn't shift position until the morning. He looks like a picture of someone sleeping. His T-shirt is very white. His pyjama bottoms are — I lift the duvet and have a little peek — pristine: washed silk. Robert never dribbles or drools in his sleep. He doesn't snore. He could be dead.

I must have gone to sleep at some stage — the last thing I remember is counting all the shades of Chanel nail polish I own, like the highbrow creature I am — because now it's the morning. Rise and shine!

Robert's already in the shower, and emerges briefly to kiss me on the cheek before racing off muttering something about the inevitable meetings. 'I'll meet you there,' he says. 'I might not make Sadler's Wells, but I'll see you at the party afterwards. I've got the invite in my pocket.'

The slamming of the front door coincides with the appearance of Charlie and Jack, the latter clutching his stomach melodramatically and wailing about being 'starving'.

'Please feed me, Mummy,' he begs. 'I have woken up so so weak. Mummies need to feed their little children,' he adds reproachfully.

'Jack!' I say 'You've only just woken up. I'm not refusing to feed you, you silly child.'

'I am a *starving* child,' Jack sighs, lying down weakly on the hall carpet. 'I am a child that always, always starves.'

'You are a fathead,' says Charlie. 'Mummy, can I have Coco Pops for breakfast? Also, I need my swimming things. Also, can I have ham sandwiches instead of cheese? I really hate cheese these days.'

'Since when?'

'Since yesterday. But I really love ham.'

'Ham is from pigs' bots,' yells Jack, jumping up, his famished state temporarily forgotten.

'*You* are a bot,' says Charlie. 'A pink, piggy, bottomy bot.'

'Muuuuuum . . .' Jack starts, welling up.

'Okay. Clothes on, faces and teeth, and downstairs,' I bark. 'Charlie, don't tease Jack. Jack, don't be so wet. Come on,' I add, clapping my hands—why? I know from experience it's hardly likely to galvanize them—like a sergeant-major. 'Let's go.' I have the feeling that, all things considered, today might be a long day.

I haven't spent this much time getting ready since I was a teenager, when the promise of a party was always far more thrilling than the angst-inducing, what-if-the-spinning-bottle-lands-on-me reality: the long afternoons spent comparing pink, usually frosted Rimmel lipsticks in Woolworths (in defiance of Kate's orders); the hours spent deciding which plasticky, glittery Miss Selfridge earrings that week's pocket money should be spent on (ditto: 'Pearl studs, darling, so classic'); the 35p facepacks from Boots that practically took a layer of skin off; the endless fiddlings with gel and Babyliss tongs—

all performed with a minimum of two girlfriends, each of us coming on like Diana Vreeland in stripy legwarmers ('No, you use the frosted highlighter here. It really opens up the eye'). Tamsin, who was always of our number, had a passion for wigs. She spent her weekends between the ages of thirteen and sixteen going to parties looking like Dolly Parton, with cascading, shiny white-blonde curls and a bra stuffed with Kleenex.

I could do worse things than ask Tamsin along tonight, I reflect, as I head off for my massively expensive facial. She might like to come round and get ready with me, for old times' sake. I leave a message on her machine before getting into the car, and then drive the forty minutes it takes to get to Knightsbridge.

I am wary of facials. I've had some extravagant disasters in the past. In fact, did I not trust Kate implicitly in the matter of treatments, I wouldn't be here now. I've had facials before, in anticipation of a party or date, that have left me . . . well, I don't think 'deformed' is too strong a word. Certainly in need of a brown-paper bag: red, swollen, with raised, furious welts all over my newly treated face, left to roam the streets of London wailing, 'I am a human being,' like John Merrick. I have suffered. I have been the Elephant Girl.

Most facials, I reflect as I park the car, are a bloody disgrace. And then of course there's the small talk: 'Now, since you have enormous pores, I'll just apply our special Big Round Shiny Acne Face toner.' Or perhaps: 'There's a lot of grease around the nose area, and of course the chin . . . Well, we haven't been cleansing very thoroughly, have we? I'll just smear on some Kill Yourself Now, You Human Oilslick cream over the worst bits.'

Kate swears by Karina, though, and I have faith. And indeed, an hour later, I emerge miraculously smooth of face, with a firmness about my cheeks which was not so before. I don't know what she did—no doubt it was perfectly revolting—but I no longer appear to have any pores. I reflect, once again, on how money is wasted on the rich. I always think this when I'm walking down Sloane Street (which, admittedly, is not very often): all those old bints with tight faces, dripping jewellery and labels and personal trainership—and they still look terrible. If I were married to an incontinent, elderly millionaire, I'd look amazing—and I wouldn't look people up and down like that, like that woman's looking at me right now, the cow. Still, she's probably envying my porelessness, if not my cosy track-suit bottoms 'n' giant sweater combo.

There's a message from Tamsin on my machine as I arrive home; also one from Charlie's headmistress asking me to call her. I dial the number in a frenzy of panic, the worst, most macabre scenarios popping, uninvited, right into my head—skulls cracked open like eggs in the playground; teeth flying; little limbs broken and askew; purple lips. Miss Robarts, the school's secretary, who sounds about twelve, puts me on hold for a while. The stentorian, barking tones of Miss Fitzgerald eventually come on, reducing me, as they always do, to a state of gibberish.

While other parents—the kind who don't turn up to school in pyjama bottoms and jam stains—impress me wildly by appearing to be able to communicate normally, adult to adult, with Miss F, I immediately revert to my unangelic twelve-year-old self. Apart from the fact that even standing in her vicinity makes my scalp tingle in the old, familiar way, I always want to blurt out that I'm sorry and that it won't happen again. And then I want to run away shouting 'Bum', though so far I've managed to control myself, on this front at least.

But Miss Fitzgerald has a more sinister confessional effect on me too. She makes me volunteer the kind of headmistress-hostile information I should really keep to myself of a morning: 'God, Miss Fitzgerald, my hangover,' that kind of thing.

I don't think she likes me—and why should she, when I blush and stammer like some drug trafficker with a bottomful of condomed-up cocaine every time I clap eyes on her?

'Ah,' she says. 'Mrs Hutt.'

'Good afternoon, Miss Fitzgerald. I've just had a facial.' See what I mean? Why did I tell her that?

'Yes,' she states, as if, being omniscient, she knew all about it. 'Now, Mrs Hutt . . .'

'Yes, Miss Fitzgerald. Is everything all right? Is Charlie okay? I'm sorry about his language, by the way . . .'

'It's Charlie I'm calling about,' she says, in no apparent hurry to put me out of my misery.

'At least he doesn't swear,' I say, feeling deeply guilty. 'He just talks, ah, robustly.'

'I'm not calling about his *language,* Mrs Hutt,' she says, sounding—unimpressively for a primary school teacher, really —on the irritated side. 'I'm calling about his *head.*'

Because Miss Fitzgerald makes me feel mad, or bad, or both, I am incapable of thinking logically.

'Is he conscious?' I ask, feeling briskly efficient, though obviously chilled. 'I'll be right over.'

'He is perfectly all right, Mrs Hutt. But he does have nits.'

'Nits?'

'Yes. Head lice. As you are no doubt aware, schools no longer have nit nurses, so you'll have to deal with the problem at home. Charlie's teacher informs me that he has had the lice for some weeks now.'

'But we de-loused ourselves last week!'

'Unsuccessfully, it seems. She apparently sent you a couple of notes, feeling this was more appropriate than "collaring" you, as it were, in public.'

'I never got them. The notes.'

'So she gathers. I must remind you, Mrs Hutt, that parents are requested to empty their child's work-drawer once a week, and that this may contain communications from staff.

Charlie's seems to have a good fortnight's worth of completed worksheets in it. Plus, of course, the notes from his teacher.'

'Oh dear, sorry. I always think the ongoing homework is more interesting that the stuff he's already finished,' I say pointlessly. Miss Fitzgerald is silent. 'Anyway,' I add, suddenly feeling hideously scratchy around the scalp, 'thank God he's all right. I'll go and get the poison shampoo now and delouse him again tonight.'

'We'd be most grateful, Mrs Hutt,' she says royally. 'You'll need to do the whole family, of course. Good afternoon.'

My head is very itchy, but it's probably psychosomatic. God, I think, sitting down on the kitchen sofa (grubby). I am an appalling parent. I am an *atrocious* mother. My poor little boy has nits and it takes me ages to do anything about it and even when I do it doesn't work. I light a stress-relieving cigarette (bad mummies are like the baddies in US blockbusters: we all smoke). I am such a *lamentable* parent, I think, that I don't even notice what's going on on my own child's head. I am a freak. I am a monster. I am obsessed with nail polish and facials and parties, while my sons' heads could—urgh, what? I wonder what happens if nits are left untreated for months? Does the problem become *internalized*? Does the grey matter become prey for the vile head lice?

Tamsin interrupts my internal monologue, just as I am wondering whether I should miss tonight's party and do delousing penance.

'Tamsin, I'm a lousy mother. Literally, ha! I made a joke. Though God knows why at a time like this. Tamsin, the boys have nits,' I practically sob.

'Oh, Clara, for goodness' sake. All kids get nits. All the time. I know from school—it's nobody's fault.'

'But he's had them for weeks. And he did say, "My head's itchy," a couple of times, but I just bunged the stuff on and ignored him.'

'Never mind, Clara. You know now. Tea tree oil works very well, by the way. Now, about this party . . .'

'Do come. You could come here and get ready with me. I thought it might cheer you up—assuming you need cheering, of course. Do you, Tam?'

'Well, I could do with a party. But I'm hardly lying in bed weeping about my fate, if that's what you mean.'

'Still happy with your decision—about the baby, I mean?'

'Yes. Ish. It's a bit of a freaky thing to take on. I mean, it just feels completely unreal. I look the same, I feel the same . . . but there's a baby growing inside me.'

'Yuck, don't make it sound like *Alien*.'

'Foetuses are parasites, Clara.'

'Spare me the human biology class, Tamsin. They're not parasites, they're lovely little fluffy noo-noo babies. And anyway, if we're going to be pedantic, shouldn't it be foeti? Have you told work?'

'Not yet. I need to decide what I'm going to do, financially and stuff. I'm hoping for a job share. But anyway,' she sighs. 'I'd love to come to the party with you. I've been reading about your Mr Dunphy all over the place, actually. He's a bit phwoar, don't you think?'

'If you like that kind of thing,' I say haughtily. 'He's a deeply unpleasant human being,' I add, sounding like a dowager duchess. 'And, for some reason which I absolutely can't fathom, I've been asked to this dinner afterwards, at the Groucho.'

'How extraordinary,' says Tamsin, sounding puzzled. 'The dislike can't be that mutual, then?'

'Dunno.' I don't know, I don't know, I don't want to know. 'Anyway, come round about 6-ish? The invite says "Dress: Up", so, you know, bring a decent frock. Bring a wig.'

'I'll see you later,' says Tamsin, laughing. 'I won't need the Kleenex, at any rate, my bosoms are outsize. I'm practically an H-cup.'

nineteen

'YOU'VE LOST WEIGHT,' says Tamsin accusingly, standing on the doorstep a couple of hours later. 'Why didn't you tell me?'

'Only a couple of pounds, I think,' I reply. 'Hardly earth-shattering. Did you want a telegram?'

'Makes a difference, though,' she says, frowning. 'Especially around the face.'

'It'll all come back on in a couple of days.' I shrug. 'Anyway, I still look pregnant around the stomach. I look more pregnant than you.'

'You do, actually,' says Tamsin, cheering up and coming in. 'So, what are we wearing?'

'I went shopping,' I say, leading her into the living room. 'Oh, the door again. That'll be Flo—she's baby-sitting, bless her. Notting Hill café society must be in mourning.'

It is indeed Flo, wearing what appears to be a purple nightie, trimmed with rather pretty orange lace, a pair of pony-skin clogs and a giant, tufty coat that looks like it's made of monkey fur. 'Am I the most devoted sister in the history of the world?' she asks rhetorically, as she kisses me hello. 'Yes, I am. I am a paragon, Clara, and by the way Evie doesn't know what that means.'

'How is Evie? I haven't spoken to her since we last met.'

Flo sighs and places her car keys in a small Hello Kitty plastic purse. There are tiny transfers of pansies on her fingernails. 'She's a bit depressed, actually, Clara, and it's my fault.'

'Why?'

'I explained apartheid to her yesterday — she asked what it was — and the very idea of it sent her into a decline.' I nod sympathetically. The same thing happened when I explained the Holocaust to her a couple of years ago. 'Do you remember when we were little,' Flo says, giggles mounting, 'and you had that record called "Free Nelson Mandela" and she said you ought to complain because you hadn't got one?' She starts laughing out loud, as do I, at the memory of a twelve-year-old Evie, indignant on my behalf, shaking out the record sleeve with a disgusted face, saying, 'Someone must have nicked it. What is a Mandela, anyway?'

'Oh, bless her. I must give her a ring,' I cry. Being a disastrous mother is bad enough, without being a crap sibling into the bargain. 'Anyway, Flo, thanks for coming. The boys are playing upstairs. I've given them a bath and de-loused them . . .'

'Gross,' says Flo.

'Yes, it was. Jack had about six, but Charlie had *hundreds*. I was nearly sick, and they keep moving on the comb in the most repulsive way. They've got to sleep with the stuff on their heads, so make sure there are towels on the pillowcases, and don't let them rub themselves all over the sofas.'

'God, don't tell Kate,' says Flo. 'She'll tell you about slums and wonder if they have TB. Anyway, I'll go up, then, and play with them,' she adds, shedding her monkey fur. 'Do you want me to help with your make-up? I've been reading this really great book.'

'Ah, maybe,' I say, touched by her offer but not entirely trusting. 'I'll come and present my face later.'

'Okey-pokey,' says Flo, marching up the stairs.

Back in the living room, Tamsin gives me another long look. 'I must say, you're looking very well,' she says.

'Don't sound so delighted. Drink? And then I'm going to have a bath. You can too, if you like.'

'Do we have to share?' says Tamsin. 'Only, we might not fit.'

'I mean in the children's bathroom,' I say. 'With the ducks and the bubbles that change colour.'

'Okay,' says Tamsin. 'I need to shave my legs. Got any gin?'

'As long as you want it for legitimate purposes only,' I joke, realizing, slightly too late, that the joke isn't very funny. But Tamsin doesn't seem to mind, and we clink our glasses together before wandering off to our respective tubs.

Apart from a spot of bother with the eyelash glue—there's a flaky spot on the edge of my left eye that suggests occhial dandruff—I am forced to admit that I've done pretty well. I look like I used to, I realize, with a yelp of joy.

I don't want to disappoint you here. I love transformations in books as much as the next woman—that 'I was a great big fat caterpillar but now I am a bee-yoo-tiful itsy little butterfly' stuff always thrills me to the core—but we need to be realistic. I'm still a size 16 (or a big 14, if my dress is to be believed), my legs haven't grown longer and my curls are not cascading down my back, though, as someone once said, it is indeed a privilege to live in the same era as John Frieda's Frizz-Ease hair-taming serum. But I look pretty nice, in a slightly round kind of way. In a dim light, I could be mistaken for Sophia Loren's slightly porkier and possibly lightly pregnant sister. It's a good look, all in all—green dress, green eyes, black hair, black, improbably long lashes, and the foundation they sold me in the specialist make-up shop is working wonders to emphasize my temporary porelessness.

I wiggle into my bedroom—the dress is on the tight side—

to try on the lovely strappy ribbon shoes. They're an extremely snug fit. They're not the comfiest thing ever and it hurts to walk, but they look great, and one must suffer — or so Kate always told me — to be beautiful (*'Il faut souffrir pour être belle'* were her exact words). I hadn't borne in mind that the heels would make me roughly six feet tall, but there you go. Better than being four feet, I always think, although boring and slightly giraffey to have to bend one's high-up head to kiss one's little husband.

More to the point, the shoes arch my feet in such a way that we're talking va-va-voom on the bosoms and bottom front. I stand in front of the mirror, admiring myself, much as you'd admire somebody else. I mean, I know it's me, but, basically, wow. And I do hate it when people pretend they look crap if they know perfectly well that they don't. So I admire myself some more. Sod modesty, frankly, at times like these.

'Fuck!' shouts Tamsin, who has wandered in in search of a hair-dryer. 'You look fabulous.'

'Why, thank you,' I simper. 'Do you really think so? It's not, you know, a bit much, as a look? I have to be careful, with make-up — as you know — because make-up-wise, my primary role model is the drag queen.'

'It's fabulous,' Tamsin repeats, frowning. 'Not draggy, no more showgirl, as if you should have feathers on your head. I haven't seen you look like that for years.'

She walks around me, rather as one might pace around a horse before buying it — I'm ready to bare my gums and kick back my hooves for inspection. 'What are those shoes?' she asks suspiciously.

'They're new. Do you like them?'

'They're sexy,' she says, in the same tone of voice.

'That's because I am a gorgeous minx of utter go-on-my-son foxiness,' I say, feeling really marvellously buoyant and light-headed and taking another sip of gin.

'*And* your dress is sexy,' Tamsin continues.

'It is allowed, you know, Tam, once in a blue moon.'

'Hmm,' says Tamsin. 'It takes getting used to.'

'Why?'

'I don't know. Because I'm not used to it. Because I'm used to you slobbing about in tracky pants.'

'Please don't say "pants",' I say. 'We're not in America. You make it sound like I roam the streets of London in padded underwear. And I don't slob. I relax.' Tamsin raises an eyebrow. 'It's true! Besides, I do dress up sometimes, Tam.'

'Not like this. And you've never done your make-up like that before.'

'Yes, I have. I always used to do my make-up like this. Tamsin, why are you being such a complete poop?' I ask. 'Is this a subtle way of telling me I don't look nice? Do I look like mutton?'

'No,' says Tamsin. 'You look very nice. Very nice indeed. Lamby. It's just a shock, that's all. You're a mummy. You're married. You're—sorry, darling—a bit boring.'

'Tamsin!'

'It's true, though. Sartorially, I mean. You're not supposed to dress like that and look good. You're not supposed to dress like you're on the pull.'

'Oh, shut up. And *grow* up. It's the Noughts, darling. Married women don't have to wear pinnies or carry feather dusters. And I'm not on the bloody pull.'

'Of course not,' says Tamsin. 'But still.'

'Still what? Are you trying to tell me you're jealous? Like when I had Aquatic Sindy and you didn't? Like when I snogged George "Tongue" Hartley?'

Tamsin snaps out of her fit of grumpiness. 'Slightly,' she smiles, coming over to give me a hug. 'A bit. But I'll get over it. Come and help me get dressed when you're ready. *And* I'll have you know I snogged George "Tongue" Hartley as well.'

'No! Where?'

'Ritzy Cinema, Brixton, 1983,' she says triumphantly. 'By the way,' she adds as she heads for the door. 'You would.'

'Would what?'

'Pull. You'd pull, and I'd have to take the bus home and listen sadly to Barry Manilow songs and practise French-kissing my pillow, imagining it was the Tonguester.'

'Don't be silly, Tamsin,' I say, feeling very delighted indeed at this generous compliment. 'I've just got to find some earrings, and I'm coming.' After all, I've been jealous of her often enough, and not had the honesty to tell her. I suppose this evens things out.

I hum 'Copacabana' to myself as I fumble around for my new crystal earrings, affix them to my lobes (which shimmer with, er, shimmery powder, as would my collarbones, if I actually had any) and go off to present myself to Flo. Her verdict, I am pleased to say, is rather more enthusiastic than Tamsin's.

'You look really lovely,' Flo says kindly. 'A bit like a sweetie in a shiny wrapper, though with hair, obviously. Yum. Well, not yum to the hair, but otherwise, yum. People might try and eat you.'

'You look beautiful, Mummy,' says Charlie in a small voice.

'You look like Maid Marian,' says Jack, scrabbling for superlatives. 'All cool and fighty.' He strikes a Robin Hood pose, imaginary arrow waiting to be fired, and beams at me. It is, frankly, the ultimate accolade. I totter out of their bedroom feeling a million dollars.

We skipped *Contortions,* the actual performance, partly because Tamsin was having an epi about her 'frumpy' dress (actually it's anything but, being a red and pink velvet affair that looks amazing against her orange hair—the generous amount of pregnancy-boosted bosom on display doesn't do any harm either); partly because I wanted to read the boys their bedtime story, to alleviate some of my guilt at leaving them to go to a sexy-sounding, non-boring and thus unmotherly party looking like I was on the pull; and partly . . . partly because when it was actually time to go, I started getting cold feet.

Flo had to physically restrain me from peeling off the eyelashes and from *running* upstairs to change into something less tralala-ish. (Tamsin: 'Change, by all means, if it makes you feel more comfortable.' Flo: 'Shut up, Tamsin.' Me, miserably: 'Maybe we should just watch *EastEnders* and order a pizza. Maybe we're too old.')

Flo had to practically push us out of the door and into the waiting taxi. Now we've arrived outside the fiendishly trendy bar in Hoxton where the party is being held, though, I feel butterflies of trepidation.

'Do I . . ' I ask Tamsin.

'You look great,' she replies gruffly.

'So do you,' I tell her truthfully, at which she snorts unattractively. 'Do that more, Tamsin, it's very sexy,' I tell her, my nerves getting the better of me, as if I were some gimpy teenager about to hit the school disco.

Tamsin gives me another furious look.

'Come on, then,' I cry—I'd actually be hopping up and down if I weren't trying to look vaguely cool—'let's go.'

We're about half an hour late and the bar—East End boho, I'd describe it as: dim lighting, second-hand leather armchairs, a curved, beaten-up wooden bar, pebbles in the fireplaces, Casablanca lilies in giant clear vases—is already heaving. We stand at the top of its stairs and look down.

The dancers, Dunphy's troupe, are instantly recognizable. The place is dotted with people with long, sinewy twig-like limbs wearing very small clothes, thus prompting a repeat of that sinking, I am the Elephant Girl and may as well pack my trunk now feeling. There are girls whose entire bodies are highlighted with glitter, sparkling in the relative darkness; and men—ooh, hello—wearing white cotton vests and artfully cut, buttock-enhancing cargo 'pants'. One tanned, razor-cheekboned man, standing slightly back from the general mêlée, is wearing a dazzlingly crisp, white outfit, based loosely on a shalwar kameez. Swathed in an extravagant fuchsia-coloured shawl, he looks a picture of bored, faintly jaded beauty, like he should have been sketched by Harold Acton.

There are also a lot of people in black, of the kind with unisex facial hair-goatees for the men, the merest soupçon of a 'tache for the women. These are presumably critics, or a general gaggle of eager balletomanes. And a handful of your artier celebs are scattered about too—a pair of the more outré fashion designers; ironically bespectacled gallery owners; a couple of already-pissed, staggering artists, one of whom has the thinnest legs I've ever seen; a brace of the pop stars who like hanging out at private members' clubs because it makes them feel cerebral; a comic who fancies himself as a bit of a latter-day Marcel Duchamp.

'God,' says Tamsin, as we make our way down the stairs. 'He's certainly packed them in tonight. It's quite scary. You don't get this in Belsize Park. Or when we go for drinks after the PTA.'

'Life on the edge, eh, Tam? They're just rent-a-crowd,' I say, though I am, in truth, slightly impressed that Laughing Boy should command this calibre of celebrity fan.

We go down the stairs, extremely slowly and precariously in my case—I can barely walk in heels that fit, let alone heels made for people with irritatingly narrow feet (mine are almost perfect squares—if I were less delusional, I'd throw the shoes away and wear the boxes). I navigate each step with the utmost care, raising each foot like a pony. It's not the most graceful entrance ever made—my shoes make a terrible clunking racket on the metal staircase—but needs must.

Robert is standing at the bottom, holding two glasses

of champagne. 'You look fabulous, Clara,' he says, smiling broadly, though with a slight frown of puzzlement. 'You look the best you've looked in years. Better.' He hands me the flute with a dazzling smile and offers the second one to Tamsin. 'Hi, Tam,' he says, kissing her on the cheek. 'You look amazing too. Beautiful dress. How're you feeling?'

'Not sick, if that's what you mean,' Tamsin says. 'I'm feeling fine. God, look at all these people. Have you been here long?'

'About ten minutes,' Robert says. 'It's full of people I vaguely know through work.'

'Hello, Clara,' says a voice down by my right breast—thank God I'm not too drunk, or I'd think I had magic chatty bosoms. I look down and say hello to Niamh Malone, the Dublin writer who interviewed Dunphy somewhat more successfully than me.

'Hi, Niamh. How was Sadler's Wells? We didn't make it in time.'

'Oh, it was *amazing,*' she says. 'He was so brilliant. He got a standing ovation, you know. Oh, look,' she adds, pinching my arm with unnecessary force. 'He's just over there. Will we go and say hello?'

I look in the direction towards which Niamh is pointing. Dunphy is standing, surrounded by a large crowd, at the other end of the room. He's changed—I imagine, unless modern dance happens in what I recognize from Robert's expert tuition as a Helmut Lang suit—into a very narrow trousered, fitted-jacketed black number, which he is wearing with a white shirt, open at the neck, and no tie. His hair is slicked back, but falling forward in an absurdly rakish, slightly sleazy way. His teeth look very white, and he is laughing. Coiled around him like a serpent is a long-limbed, blonde-haired creature, who brays loudly at everything Dunphy says.

I don't really have the stomach for it. 'Later, Niamh—but you go over now if you'd like,' I tell her.

'I think I will,' she says, practically panting with anticipation. 'I'll catch up with you in a mo.' And she winds her way through the crowds, though not, I notice with delight, before giving Robert a long, approving look from beneath her considerable (real) eyelashes.

Tamsin has wandered off to chat to someone she knows, and Robert takes my arm as we stroll through the assembled mass. He is looking very handsome, and I like the feeling — pretty much forgotten in recent months, not to say years — of us looking photogenic together. We look like a sexy couple. It turns out there are a number of people we know at the party, and I am soon on my fourth, and then fifth, champagne flute, feeling very jolly indeed.

Wildly irritatingly, I've been putting off going to the loo ever since we arrived. This always happens to me at parties. I don't want to miss anything and I can't face the hassle of walking down some endless corridor to find one unlovely lavatory with, inevitably, no loo paper. So I hold on and on until I suddenly think I'm going to pee right there.

It's happening now. I detach myself from Robert, whose hand I was holding, and head off towards the large, fluorescent TOILETS sign, designed, it seems, for maximum humiliation, so that when you're having a drink in the bar and conversation stalls, you can give knowing looks to every poor soul who comes back from the loo. Years ago, Amber once got very drunk and shouted, 'Number twos, was it?' at a hated rival, who'd been taking her time, before collapsing into a hysterical heap.

The loos are, unusually, clean and well lit, and there is loo paper. I pee, and come out to find the lissom blonde who was hanging on Dunphy's arm, as well as on his every word, staring at herself in the mirror. She is very pretty — 'If you like that sort of thing,' as my mother would say, the sort of thing in question being a Pamela-Anderson-but-classier kind of look. The girl is wearing a butter-coloured tiny leather skirt which shows off her long, golden legs, and a halter-neck top that looks like it's cashmere: the kind of sexy-but-casual look which is impossible to carry off unless you're a size 8 and live in a gym.

She leans over the sink, reapplying copious amounts of putty-coloured lipstick to her rather pinched mouth, lining it first with a pencil — one I recognize as Spice from MAC, as it happens. She overlines her mouth, adding a precious millimetre to plump up its circumference, and stands back to watch herself again. She smiles. She turns her head, shakes her hair. And then — I think it's fair to assume she hasn't seen me — she lifts one beautifully toned arm and then the other and sniffs her own armpits.

At which point, despite myself, I chuckle like a loon. The girl focuses her laser gaze on me and glares, fouffing up her mane of hair, then turns on her pretty little heel — tippety-tap, all the way down the corridor's flagged tiles.

Back in the bar, Robert is howling with laughter at something one of the artists has said, and I go for a little spin round the room on my own, fortifying myself with another glass of champagne. Clothes are strange things, I reflect philosophically to myself. A lot of people who wouldn't normally look twice at me are coming to say hello, introducing themselves and offering drinks. Here comes one now, in a too-sharp suit and a ton of hair wax: Mr Smoothie, Mr Git, Mr I'm Too Old to Wear My Hair Like That, Mr I Drive a Very Big Car Which is in Inverse Proportion to the Size of My Penis. You know the type.

'Hi, gorgeous,' he drawls. There's something loose and slack about his mouth. 'I'm Gus.'

'Hello,' I say reluctantly, without smiling.

'Top-up?' he asks, sniffing loudly and wiping his nose with his hand (cocaine, I think, rather than a chesty cold).

'S'pose.'

My new friend whistles loudly to catch the attention of a passing waiter. I hate people who are rude to waiters.

'So, gorgeous . . .'

'Would you mind not calling me that, please,' I say, made bold by my drinks. 'I don't know you and it's very familiar. In quite a vulgar way. Unless you're going to sell me half a pound of Maris Pipers. In which case it's okay. Is that what you do—vegetables?'

'Wooh,' says Gus, which rhymes with pus. He leans forward. 'I was only being friendly. You've got beauddiful eyes.'

'Yours are on the small side,' I say, exhilarated by my own rudeness. 'Can you actually see out?' I screw up my face and mime desperate attempts at peering out of my newly narrowed eyes, and this, unattractively, makes me laugh and laugh. I always have this problem with my own jokes, especially— though not exclusively—when drunk. It is grotesquely unappealing and it makes me ashamed, but I can't help it.

Gus walks away. I am still snorting, *honking* with laugher, when a voice behind me says, 'Clara.'

'Oh, Robert,' I cry, fishing in my handbag for a tissue to wipe my eyes before my elaborate eyeliner starts streaking, 'there was a man here and he was such a creep, such a slime-ball, and he said I had nice eyes and I asked if he could see out of his, because they were so small.' The memory of my *bon mot* brings on a new laughter fit. I turn around. It isn't Robert, of course, but then you probably guessed.

'Hello,' says Dunphy. 'It is quite a good joke, but do you always have to be so bloody rude?'

'I was being sort of experimentally rude,' I say. 'You know, rude in the way you can be when you're dressed up.' I look Dunphy up and down and register his puzzled face. 'You probably wouldn't understand. Anyway, he really was the most ghastly man. Look, over there. Sort of lizardy. Kind of man that buys you fruit-flavoured edible knickers. Kiwi, probably. A pointless fruit, though rich in vitamin C.' Oh dear. I seem to have had much too much to drink. 'Called Gus,' I add, seemingly incapable of stopping talking. 'Short for gusset, I expect.'

Dunphy surprises me by roaring with laughter. 'Oh, God, him,' he says. 'You can be as rude to him as you like. My, er, friend's brother—not actually invited. Are you having a good time?'

'Yes, thank you,' I say soberly. 'Are you? How are your, er, nits?'

'Gone,' he says. 'Tea tree shampoo. Refill?'

'Why not?' I yelp. The waiter refills the glasses. 'To, er, your dance thing,' I say, clinking my glass against his. Which, if you must know, feels curiously intimate.

'My show?'

'Yes. I hear it was marvellous.'

Dunphy shrugs. 'They all seemed to like it,' he says, with a rather dazzling smile.

We stand in silence for a few seconds.

'I like your dress,' Dunphy says.

'Goodo,' I trill. I'm feeling a bit woozy, actually. A bit squiffy, if the truth be told. 'Goodo,' I repeat, like one of my stepbrother's stripy-shirt and red-braces City friends. 'Woof,' I say, and start giggling again.

'You look very, er . . . very, um . . . nice.' Dunphy grins.

'A compliment!' I cry. 'From you. Who'd have thought?'

'Not you,' he smiles. 'About dinner . . .'

'I thought that was a mistake,' I say, suddenly feeling entirely sober.

'What, you can't come? That's a shame.'

'You actually *asked* me? What on earth for?'

'I thought it might be nice,' says Dunphy.

'Nice?' I echo stupidly. 'Nice? How?'

'I don't know,' he says, looking me straight in the eye. Blue, blue, blue. His eyes are very blue. 'But you can't come?'

I want to go. Suddenly, and I don't quite know why (no, really, I don't, I categorically don't), I want nothing more than to go to Dunphy's dinner.

'I might be able to,' I say. 'It's just that I thought it was a mistake.'

'Try,' he says, very quietly, and it strikes me that, really, Dunphy would be quite good on the radio. He sounds like honey, but very *male* honey, if you know what I mean: honey made by he-bees. If I were a housewife listening to him, I'd probably come over all funny.

Actually, I *am* a housewife listening to him.

'Try,' he says again.

'I will,' I say, making a concerted effort not to blink rapidly.

'Good,' he says, just as the blonde from earlier arrives.

'Sam! There you are,' she says, kissing his cheek. 'Come and talk to me, baby' She takes Dunphy by the hand and leads him off into the crowd.

I stand and stare at my glass. Of course, Irish accents are sexy per se. It has nothing to do with the person speaking; it's just the *accent*. Irish people can't help sounding sexy, except for Ian Paisley. It's a simple fact of life. I try it myself: 'Begorrah,' I husk. 'Jaysus.' Yes, very sexy. It's just the *accent,* you see.

The *accent.*

I really must find Robert, and some water, though not necessarily in that order.

Robert walks me round and round Hoxton Square, instructing me in breathing. 'Deep breaths, Clara, through your mouth,' he says helpfully. 'Here, I've got some Evian. How come you're so drunk?'

'I am not drunk, Robert,' I say sternly. 'I just feel a bit dizzy.'

'Because you're drunk,' says Robert, but he says it kindly, and strokes my hair.

'I'm supposed to go to this dinner now, Robert. What shall I do?'

'What dinner?'

'Oh, God. I had the feeling I hadn't told you. A dinner at the Groucho for Dunphy. For Sam Dunphy.'

'Here, have some more water. Do you want to go?'

'Who was it who said, "Never drink water; fish fuck in it"? The dinner—I don't know. I did want to go, but now I'm not sure. It depends who I'm sitting next to. If it's that man Gusset, then no.'

'It might be fun,' says Robert. 'What a revolting thought, about the water.'

'Isn't it just? Would you rather I stayed with you?'

'It's up to you, Clara. We could go and have dinner somewhere, or I could go home and rescue Flo.'

'Would you like us to have dinner together? Would you *love* it?'

'Of course,' says Robert. We sit down on a bench and I snuggle my head against his shoulder. 'But we have lots of dinners together and you might have a good time. I think you should go.'

'You don't mind?'

'No, I don't. I'm knackered, anyway.'

'Okay, I'll go. How am I looking?'

'Your nose is a bit shiny, but otherwise you look great.'

'It's because my make-up is industrial strength and applied with professional tools,' I say, and we both laugh.

Robert leads me on a final tour of the square, holding my hand. 'I'll drive you there,' he says, and does. When we get there, he kisses me good-night. Properly, if you know what I mean.

twenty

I HAVEN'T BEEN TO the Groucho for years. Nothing's changed: all heads still crane every time someone new comes into the room; there are still too many balding middle-aged men with shirts open to their navels, escorting much younger, pert-breasted women; there are still celebs; there is still co-caine. I wind my way—fairly unsteadily, but it's not the kind of place where anyone would notice—through the down-stairs bar and up the stairs to the private dining room. Some-one wolf-whistles, which is nice—why do some women have a problem with whistles? They make my life—until I realize that the ghastly Gus is behind me.

I'm a bit annoyed by this, especially as, when we walk into the dining room—the dozen or so other guests are already seated—we give the impression of doing so as a couple.

'You made up, then,' says Dunphy, apparently finding this intensely comical. He points to an empty seat and I notice he has nice hands. 'And you made it. You're over there,' he says. 'Next to Christian.'

Christian, it turns out, to my joy and delight, is the impec-cably groomed man in the raspberry-coloured shawl—which, on closer inspection, turns out to be a heavily beaded and embroidered sari. He has very prettily plucked eyebrows.

'Hello,' he says. 'You're the interviewer.' He lets out a little bark of laughter. 'I thought I was going to be sick with laughter when Sam told me,' he adds. 'Funniest thing I ever heard.' He talks incredibly fast.

'It was awful,' I say, blushing. 'And I gave him nits.'

'Ha!' screams Christian, still laughing. 'Darling, don't worry about it. It made my week. And his—he's dined out on it a few times.'

'That's nice,' I say. I feel a touch put out, but can't help thinking that yes, giving Dunphy nits is actually on the comical side, and that it's quite nice of him—Dunphy—to see the joke.

'Just remembering makes me hysterical,' says Christian, lighting a filterless oval, Turkish cigarette from an embossed, turquoise cardboard box. 'Especially thinking he was a nancy.' He lets out a snort of laughter. 'Now, where's hubby?' he asks, more composed.

'At home.'

'And you have children, I gather? I'm terribly nosy.'

'Yes, two. Whom do you gather from?'

'Your fan,' Christian says, rather sarcastically. 'Sex?'

'Sometimes,' I quip.

'My sister has children,' Christian muses, exhaling. 'I'm always telling her to mind her pelvic floor.'

'Really?'

'Mm. Women are so lucky having pelvic floors. Means anyone at all can become a terrific fuck. Unless you've had six children, when I gather it's rather like chucking a welly down the Finchley Road.'

'Christian!' I say, half appalled and half wanting to scream with laughter. For some reason, he rather reminds me of Kate. This is exactly what she'd be like if she were the type of gay man who liked Baudelaire. 'That's a terrible thing to say. And it isn't true.'

'How would you know, Missy?'

'Well, I have two children, and I like to think it's not like chucking anything down anything.'

'Caesareans?' asks Christian, looking knowing.

'Well, yes, as it happens, but I really don't think . . .'

'Your passage is HONEYMOON FRESH,' Christian says, extraordinarily loudly, startling the woman opposite me somewhat. 'Be grateful and stop being a ghastly feminist. Especially not in that dress. No one'll believe you. Now, champagne cocktail?'

'Yummy. But everyone is drinking white wine.'

'Fools!' he sighs, hailing a waiter with a languid wave of the hand and ordering us two cocktails each ('to save precious time').

It turns out, rather improbably, that Christian is Dunphy's best and oldest friend—or so he tells me—their friendship dating back to junior ballet school. Christian tells me he showed great promise himself—I'm inclined to believe him: he seems like the kind of man who gets what he wants—but eventually decided that dancing wasn't for him.

'Now,' Christian says. 'Eat your oysters like a good girl, and excuse me for a second.' He turns to the woman on his left, a faintly mustachioed sort of the type mentioned earlier. 'I'm Christian,' he says. 'Don't you always think oysters look *exactly* like ashtrays on which one has sneezed?'

I do as I'm told and eat up, in between making chit-chat with the man on my right, who is the dance critic for an Irish newspaper. I speak very slowly, not wanting to mimic his accent by mistake. In between talking and listening to him telling me all about Dunphy's talent, I glance over at our host. The girl, the blonde, is on his right, giggling and wriggling and showing too much cleavage. Every now and then, she turns her entire body to him and . . . well, you don't have to be an expert in body language to read the signs.

I feel a bit depressed, suddenly. I think I'm getting a mini-hangover from earlier.

'I'm back,' hisses Christian, just as I am wondering whether I should go home to Robert. 'Did you miss me? I've *abso-*

lutely given up with the creature on my left. I'm not designed to talk to people whose idea of style is a pair of *outsize wooden parrot earrings.*' He says the last words much as one might say 'faces smeared with excrement', and sniffs archly when I laugh—I really must introduce him to Kate. 'So, I'm all yours again. Aren't you glad?'

'Very.' Then, after a pause: 'Do you think your friend Sam's enjoying his evening? He looks happy.'

We look at Dunphy, who is laughing at something the blonde girl has said.

'Delirious,' says Christian. 'Wouldn't you be? Have you seen the papers?'

'The early editions? No.'

'Unanimous. They *love* him,' says Christian. 'And so they should.'

'Good,' I say, meaning it.

'And of course he's got his *friend* keeping him company,' Christian says.

'That's the main thing,' I say, feeling gloomy and piling my oyster shells into a little tower. 'That he should be happy. Not that I particularly care, obviously, barely knowing him. I'm talking more generally, really. About human beings. The greater good. One wishes for them to be happy. For mankind. It's the main thing.'

'You have very green eyes,' says Christian.

'Are we being metaphorical, by any chance?' I ask, amused.

'We might be. Do you know who his friend is?'

'Oh, for goodness' sake,' I say. 'Why should I care?'

'Why indeed?' says Christian. 'But I'll tell you anyway. It's Caitlin O'Riordan, now known as Fabergé.' Another laughter snort. 'And her brother, whom I gather you met, is called Feargus, now reinvented as Gus.'

I stare blankly at Christian.

'Darling,' he says. 'It's too funny. Do see the joke. The dear

O'Riordans are the children of Sam's mammy's neighbour back in Ireland. Sam's known them all his life. And Feargus, who has a nose for a wheeze, decided it was time he and his kid sister made it in London. He's been seeing the films and reading the books.'

'I still don't get it,' I say.

'Gus, as we must call him, decided that since it was so sexy to be Irish, he could do worse things than come over here and, well, score, really.' Christian is grinning. 'Make some money. Have a laugh. Be featured in *Tatler*. Hse's master-minded the whole thing. Although I do think Fabergé's a bit much as a name,' he says thoughtfully. 'I advised "Emerald", as in Cunard and Isle.'

'I see,' I say. 'Good for them. I bet they make it. She's certainly got the looks, though I'm not sure about him . . .'

'Oh, she was signed up by Models One in her second week here,' says Christian. 'My idea.'

'Right,' I say.

'And Sam's been such an angel to them,' Christian says. 'An angel of patience, considering they drive him mad. He's looked after them and made sure they weren't starving. He's found them a flat. He's asked them tonight . . . He's far too kind-hearted for one so handsome. Of course,' he adds, taking a drag of his cigarette, 'he thinks it's the best scam ever.'

'They make a very pretty couple,' I say.

'Darling! Gus is a horror!' says Christian.

'No, I meant, um, Fabergé and Dunphy.'

'My dear girl,' says Christian. 'They're not a couple. Whatever gave you that idea?'

I can't think of what to say. I can't think at all.

'Of course, she fancies him madly. Who wouldn't?' says Christian, giving me a sly look that ends in a wink. 'But Clara, she's fifteen! She's like his niece. No, he's looking after her as a favour to his mammy, that's all.'

'Christian,' I say. 'Would you like some more champagne?'

'Yes,' says Christian. 'I think we're going to be friends.'

Later, when we're having a nightcap in the bar before—Christian's idea—going dancing, he says, 'Tell me about your husband. Is he the swoonsome hunk who took you outside at the party, when you got too rat-arsed?'

'Yes,' I say, beaming from the compliment. 'His name's Robert.'

'And?'

I am always tempted to lie when people—strangers—ask me about Robert. Well, not lie outright, so much as embellish. He does this, I say, and this, and he looks like this, and we're so happy we're practically delirious. I've never got the hang of the English method when it comes to describing one's partner or children: it seems absolute belittling is *de rigueur*. 'My poor son, terribly plain, utterly friendless, and so spastically malcoordinated, bless him,' is the way one would describe an absurdly popular Adonis who happens to captain the first XI. 'My baby looks just like Winston Churchill—vast head, poor thing. Snorts like a pig and never sleeps. Awfully small for his age; autistic, I expect,' would be the correct way to talk about a perfect, angelic, beloved new-born. Similarly, I've noticed happily married women are keen to tell the world about 'poor old George, so fat, terrible gout in fact, frightful bore, no sex life to speak of,' with a proud gleam in their eye. As I say, I've never got the hang of it.

I've only known Christian for a couple of hours, but I have the feeling those sharp, dark eyes would see through any gilding of what is, after all, a perfectly reasonable lily. 'He edits a magazine,' I say. 'We have two children. We live in east London. I write, part-time. That's it, really.'

'Oh no, you don't,' says Christian. 'Don't be a tease. Spill. I demand full beanage.'

'Do you have a boyfriend?'

'Dozens,' Christian says with a dismissive wave of the hand. 'Carry on.'

'I get bored sometimes,' I blurt.

'We all get bored, darling. I, for instance, get so bored sometimes that I can barely breathe. Have another drink. Martini?'

'Please.' I nod. 'Very dry. It's not that kind of boredom, really,' I say guiltily, wondering why on earth I'm telling a stranger this.

'Ennui?'

'In a way, I suppose. I just have this funny notion that . . . well, that we ought to excite each other.'

'The *sauce!* Do you mean physically?'

'Partly. But also in general. You know — knots in the stomach, lying on the sofa having daydreams about kissing, looking forward to dates so much you get ready six hours ahead of time . . .'

'That's a crush, darling, not a marriage.'

'I know,' I sigh, feeling, unaccountably, utterly depressed. 'But that's what I want. I want to have a crush all the time.'

'It *does* exist, of course,' says Christian thoughtfully, patting my hand. 'But rarely.'

'I don't think it exists in real life,' I say. 'It always goes wrong. It always ends in . . . companionship. Comfort. Ease. I . . . I sometimes feel I'm living with my brother.'

'Yick, incest!' yells Christian. 'Or are we talking no hide-the-sausage?'

'No, no. The, er, sausage gets hidden. But most of the time — the un-sausagey hours, as it were — it feels fraternal.'

'Darling, most people would kill for fraternal. Do you fight?'

'Hardly ever.'

'Do you have affairs?' asks Christian, examining his fingernails. He says this during a longueur in the room's conversation, so that there is pin-drop silence and everyone hears.

'No,' I say, more crossly than I mean to. 'I don't. Now, when are we dancing?'

'Now would be good,' says Sam Dunphy, who has emerged from nowhere.

twenty-one

MY HEAD. *My head.* My brain has come loose and is crashing about like a mass of ball-bearings; it tilts every time I move it. Oh, my head. And my mouth. My mouth is lined with fur and guano. My throat has constricted, and I can't swallow, and feel sick when I do. Why did I smoke so much? My toes hurt from those bloody shoes, which were not dancing shoes, being a good size too small and having vertiginous heels.

It's 7.30. I got home at 3. Robert is still sleeping. He would not cha-cha-cha with me when I came in; he told me to be quiet and go to sleep. He said 'Shush' when I sang 'La Cucaracha'. He has stopped loving me, I think.

The boys are going to wake up any minute now. Why is there mud on my legs? Perhaps I fell over. Oh, God. Oh, God. I feel so sick. What am I going to do? We're going to Paris this evening. On the six o'clock flight. We'll get in in time for dinner. And drinks. Which I will sick up, because I am never going to drink alcohol again.

I wriggle down under the duvet. It's not all bad. At least I have a new best friend in Christian. Also, I think horrid Dunphy isn't horrid any more. I think he likes me a bit more now. And I've forgiven him. Yes, I have. He danced with me and Christian. He danced very well. As you would expect.

The rest is rather blurred. What happened then? Taxis, obviously. I don't remember saying goodbye to anyone. Do I? Thinking hurts my head. I am sick, sick, sick with guilt. Dunphy danced with me.

'Mummy is sick,' I croak at the boys as they come bounding in like a pair of mad, squealing Tiggers.

'I was sick one day,' says Jack. 'I cried. Bob the Builder had the sick on his hat.'

'Not sick like that, darling. I just mean I don't feel very well. Could you stop hopping for a second? You're making the bed shake.'

'Why are you sick, Mummy?' asks Charlie.

'Because I had too much wine, Charlie.'

'Wine! Yuck! It's made of people's feet, we learned it at school.'

I sigh and try, unsuccessfully, to sit up. 'Wine is not made from people's feet, Charlie. It is made from grapes.'

'No, people's feet,' says Charlie, looking solemn and rather disgusted by the idea — as well he might be. 'They stomp round and round a round wooden thing, a bawel, I think it's called, until their red foot juice comes.'

'Darling, I am going to be sick like Jack if you carry on. Those people are stomping on grapes. It's grape juice that comes out. And anyway, they don't make wine like that any more.'

'Ooh, I could crush a grape,' says Robert, opening one eye. 'Morning, boys. How are you feeling, best beloved?'

'Poorly,' I say. 'Very poorly indeed. Poorly and sick and not wanting to think about people's revolting feet.'

'Good party?'

'I sang Barry Manilow songs and danced,' I say miserably.

Robert bursts out laughing. 'Lovely,' he says. 'That must have been nice. Your dulcet tones . . .'

'We can't all have been choirboys, Robert,' I say grumpily. 'I know I have a horrible voice. It's not my fault.'

'Did their ears bleed?'

'No, they did not. Their ears twitched with joy.'

'You look a bit rough,' Robert continues. 'Your eyes are all rabbity and red.'

'I slept in my lenses,' I say, pushing Jack, who is miming rabbithood, off my stomach.

'I hate fizzy,' Jack says, apropos of nothing.

'Mummy loves fizzy wine,' Robert says unhelpfully.

'Mummy is teetotal,' I say. 'And Daddy's going to give you your breakfast today.'

'How?' says Robert, who is really getting very much on my nerves.

'By pouring some cereal into two bowls, adding milk and making toast, if you're up to it,' I say. 'And glasses of juice wouldn't go amiss.'

'But I never give them their breakfast,' says Robert. 'It's the weekend. I'm tired.'

'Go away, all of you. You are a *pathetic* human being,' I tell Robert. 'All men give their children breakfast sometimes. And I have a hangover. Which doesn't happen very often. Do help.'

'Hardly my fault you got drunk,' says Robert. Why is he being so churlish? 'I hardly stood there and forced you.'

'Robert. Please. Give them their breakfast.'

'God's sake,' huffs Robert, getting out of bed and stomping across the room to his dressing gown. 'My wife's an alkie. It's not very feminine, you know, Clara, getting drunk like that all over London, with strangers. It's hardly attractive.'

'Go away, Robert,' I say. And, eventually, he does.

And then, of course, Kate rings.

'Why are you sounding like that?' she demands. 'Have you got the flu? I do keep telling you to take echinacea. It strengthens the immune system. Yours is very weak, from overeating and lack of exercise. I haven't had a cold for two years now.'

'I have a hangover, Kate.'

'A hangover?' ('*A handbag?*') 'How revolting. Why on earth have you got a hangover?'

'Because I got drunk.'

'Clara! You've really got to take your life in hand. You eat too much, you get drunk . . . you're going to come unstuck. Do you have any nux vom?'

'What?'

'Don't say "what", say "excuse me". Nux vomica. Homoeopathic remedy for dipsomaniacs. It might help. Why were you drunk?'

'I went to a party.'

'I go to parties all the time and *I* don't get drunk,' Kate says. 'Drunk women, darling—nothing more unattractive, like tramp ladies who smell of urine. Poor Robert. Where was he?'

'I don't smell of urine, Kate. Robert was there, for a bit. But then I went dancing.'

'Who on earth with?'

'My new friend Christian, whom you'd love, by the way. I'm going to introduce you next week.'

'For God's sake, Clara. What are you doing going dancing in the middle of the night with strange men? He could have murdered you.' She shudders audibly. 'Or worse.'

'What's worse than being murdered?'

'Rape, Clara,' says Kate sternly. 'I really don't think you should be roaming the streets of London with rapists. You're in deep trouble. Meet me for lunch.'

'I can't, Kate. We're going to Paris and I need to pack.'

'I'm sending someone over with nux vom,' she says. 'I'll call you later to see how you are. God, you're selfish,' she adds, suddenly incensed as well as horrified. 'I was phoning to tell you Max and I have set a date.'

'Good, I'm glad. He's nice.'

'Nice? Nice? Is that all you can say?'

'Oh, Kate, please, not now.'

'Lear was right,' Kate says.

'Who's Lear?'

'KING Lear,' Kate yells. 'Christ, listen to you. I spent a fortune on your education and you're unfamiliar with even the basics.'

'It's just you said "Lear" as if you were talking about a close friend. You could have a friend called Leah, for all I know.'

'Lear *is* a close friend,' says Kate, furiously. 'Lear and I are twin souls.'

'"How sharper than a serpent's tooth . . ."' I say, making a monumental effort to keep hold of my temper.

'"To have a thankless child!" — yes, Clara. *Sharper.* Goodbye.'

I eventually manage to stagger out of bed — the whole room seems to be tilting to one side — and into a soothing, cleansing bath, which I have to leave early because Charlie and Jack sound like they're murdering each other downstairs; their screams carry all the way up two floors. I wrap a towel around me and race down, to find that Jack is lying on the kitchen floor, screaming and bleeding from his mouth.

'Oh, my God,' I cry. 'Charlie, what happened?'

'We were just fighting,' says Charlie in a small voice. He has gone white, like a little ghost. 'And I pushed him by mistake and he fell, and then blood came.'

'It hurts,' Jack sobs, spraying my face with blood. I open his mouth with my fingers and feel around. No broken teeth. His tongue's okay. He must have bitten his lip, hard.

I rock Jack in my arms and kiss him. 'You're going to be fine, darling,' I say, over and over. After a few minutes, Jack starts calming down. 'Charlie is a poo and I hate him,' he wails.

'I hate *you*,' says Charlie.

'*Do* you?' asks Jack in a perfectly normal voice, with no tears. He is apparently galvanized with fascination at the notion of Charlie's hatred, tipping his head to one side, his ailment temporarily forgotten.

'A bit,' says Charlie. 'Sometimes.'

'I *love* you sometimes,' says Jack, making a sad little face and twirling his hair in the way he did when he was a baby. 'But not when you make me fall. It hurts me so so much.'

'Mummy?' says Charlie in a small voice. 'Jack is quite sweet sometimes, isn't he?' He walks over to his brother and strokes his hair solemnly, whispering, 'Sorry.'

'You're both quite sweet sometimes,' I say, feeling choked. 'And I love you. Where's Daddy, by the way?'

'Upstairs, listening to his music.' Charlie shrugs. 'Come on, Jack. You can be Friar Tuck, if you like.'

'It's like being a single parent,' I tell Amber on the phone half an hour and two Nurofen later. 'No, really. I might as well be absolutely on my own, because that's what it's like. He's given them breakfast three times in his life. He's never, ever, not once, got up in the night, even when Jack was born and I was up every hour and nearly lost my *mind* through tiredness. And then he just buggers off and listens to *The Pearl Fishers* on his fucking earphones when he's bored of them. I mean, they could have had a really terrible, ambulancey accident. He'd never have heard. I was only trying to have a bloody bath in peace.'

'*You* would, though, Clara,' says Amber. 'You'd have heard.'

'That's my point exactly. Only I would hear. I might as well be by myself,' I repeat. 'I mean, he loves them, obviously, but really—I've never come across anyone so unwilling to help with them.'

'It's funny,' says Amber. 'He seems such a new man.'

'Well, he is, I suppose, in some respects. He's in touch with his feminine side in some ways, like clothes. But not in others, like bunging a fucking chicken into the oven every now and then. And he was nice last night, when I was drunk—he walked me round and gave me Evian. But you know, any friend would do that, wouldn't they? You'd do it.'

'Of course I would,' says Amber. 'I have.'

'So have I.' I sigh. 'It's like living with a friend, Amber. Is that really what we want?'

'Well, a friend you have sex with,' Amber says.

'Let's not even go there, Amber. Not now. And even if you did have sex, it wouldn't necessarily make it all okay,' I say. 'It doesn't mend it. You have sex like you brush your teeth. It's nice, it's fine, but it's hardly . . .'

'What?' says Amber. 'Spit it out.'

'Well,' I say. 'I'm probably not thinking straight because I think I have alcoholic poisoning. But it's not my idea of marriage. It's not my idea of teamwork. It's not my idea of sharing.'

'Oh dear,' says Amber, in a small voice.

'It's my idea of the perfect flat share,' I say. 'If we were flatmates we'd be in clover. But he's my husband.'

'Yes,' says Amber. 'And the father of your children. And you know, Clara, better than most, what happens when parents split up.'

'Oh, I wasn't talking about splitting up . . .' I gasp, appalled.

'Yes, you were.'

'I wasn't.'

'You were,' Amber insists. 'You know you were.'

There is a pause. It is quite long.

'Yes, I suppose I was,' I say.

I feel like I've pulled my finger out of the hole in the dam. Everything is coming pouring out. I might drown. We might all drown.

'We're leaving in a minute,' I say. 'I'll phone you from there.'

'Have a nice time,' says Amber. 'He does love you, you know.'

'I know.' I hang up and drag our huge suitcase—far larger than the weekend requires: Robert likes to be prepared for every sartorial eventuality—down into the hall.

'Ready?' says Robert. 'Let's go.'

The hotel is one of those places you drool about if you find yourself leafing through *Condé Nast Traveller* at the hairdresser's: old-fashioned enough to have elegant old ladies taking tea in the fountained, chandeliered marble lobby, but friendly enough for one not to feel like something the cat's dragged in. There's a hotel in London I sometimes go to to interview people, a temple of minimalism, where I feel like I'm making a mess, like I'm *soiling,* just by standing at reception. This hotel is not like that. It's splendid, opulent: a French Claridge's. It is delightful, and Robert and I beam at each other all the way up to our room.

The bellboy turns the key into the lock and motions us through. 'Christ!' I gasp. 'It's like a palace.'

'It's the honeymoon suite, Madame,' says the bellboy. 'This is your drawing room'—he gestures towards two vast, overstuffed brocade sofas, an elegant, spindly-legged bureau, a drinks cabinet, a giant state-of-the-art widescreen television, an Aubusson rug, and so on. 'And through here,' he says, leading us on, 'is the bedroom. Music, here,' he says. 'Champagne in here, chilled. The bathroom'—he beckons again—'is over here.' The bathroom is a huge 1930s-style affair, all marble and yellow lighting, with towels the size of bedsheets and toiletries from Floris. The bath is very deep. 'Jacuzzi,' he says, 'if you press this button.'

'Thank you,' says Robert, pressing a note into his hand. 'Merci.'

'Let me know if you need help with anything else,' says the bellboy in his precise English. 'Will you be dining in the restaurant tonight?'

'Yes,' says Robert. 'Clara? Yes, I think so. Nine o'clock, please.'

'Very good,' says the bellboy. 'Enjoy your stay. And congratulations!'

'He thinks we're married!' I say, sitting down on the bed.

'We are,' says Robert.

'I mean freshly married. He thinks it's our honeymoon.'

'Good,' says Robert. 'We'll get better service.'

'I'm going to unpack and have a bath,' I say. 'I feel all planey. How long until dinner?'

'About an hour. I'll go after you.'

He goes into the living room and pushes buttons. 'Music?' he shouts. 'There are a load of CDs. What do you fancy?'

'You choose, Robert. Something nice to have a bath to. But not too loud—I've got to call home.'

'Why?'

'To check on the boys,' I say, stifling a sigh of exasperation. 'And on your mother.' Robert's mother is looking after the boys—a treat to which they have looked forward all week.

'Can't you call tomorrow?'

'No. I want to call them now.'

'Okay,' says Robert, in a tight little voice. 'But we're away on our own, Clara. I thought this was about us.' He says the last two words in an American accent, to signify the fact that he gets the joke. But he's pissed off.

'It *is* about us,' I say primly. 'And so are our children.'

'Call, then,' says Robert. 'Tell me when you've finished.'

'Don't you want to talk to them?'

'Not really,' says Robert. 'We only left them five hours ago.'

'That's not the point,' I say. 'Oh, never mind.'

*

I undress, lock the door and have a divinely long soak, which washes away all traces of my hangover. I wash my hair and wrap it up in a towel. I'm standing in front of the mirror, examining my face, when the door handle turns.

'It's locked,' I shout.

'Well, open it,' says Robert.

'I'm in the bath,' I lie.

'Get out, then. I've brought you a glass of champagne.' I wrap myself in a towel, pad over to the door and open it. 'You can get back in,' Robert says.

'No, it's okay.'

'I have seen you naked before, you know.' Robert smiles.

'Yes, I know. But I've washed now.'

'Have some champagne.'

'In a while, Robert. I don't want another hangover.'

Robert sits on the loo seat and sips thoughtfully at his. 'Tell me more about last night,' he says.

'Oh, there's nothing much to say,' I say, feeling weary and applying moisturizer. 'I really liked this man called Christian. Do you remember, very camp, in the pink shawl?'

'Oh yes,' Robert says. 'Well groomed.'

'Quite. I was sitting next to him, and he made me laugh and laugh. We drank lots of cocktails, and then we sang, and then we went dancing.'

'Where?'

'A place called Mimi's, in a railway arch under a bridge somewhere. We did the mambo.'

'I didn't know you could.'

'I learned.' I grin, wondering what on earth I must have looked like. 'It was such fun.'

'Clearly,' says Robert impassively. 'Where was Sam Dunphy?'

'He was there.'

'He fancies you,' says Robert, creeping up behind me. 'I could tell from the way he was looking at you. And you fancy him.'

'He does not!' I yelp. 'He barely tolerates me. Well, no—I think he possibly slightly likes me. But that's all. As a friend. And I do not fancy him.'

'Yes,' says Robert, looking at me in the mirror. 'You do.'

'I do not,' I repeat. 'I just had a fun evening. No one asked me about primary schools or property prices or whether I preferred Tesco's to Sainsbury's. That's all.'

'Hmm,' says Robert, smiling, unconvinced. 'You protest too much.'

'Oh, shoo,' I say, perturbed. 'Let me get ready in peace.'

'Chin-chin,' says Robert, raising his glass. For a man who's just accused his wife of fancying someone, he looks remarkably cheery.

We have a drink in the bar before dinner. Robert orders me a bloody Mary. He's changed into a dark suit. He looks so at ease, Robert, in any given environment. East London last night, a five-star hotel now. He never sticks out, or looks square, or louche, or grotty. He never looks like he doesn't belong. He always knows what to do; how to behave.

We holidayed as children in a selection of Europe and North America's more fabulous hotels, so I'm hardly feeling like the oiky country mouse either. But, unlike Robert, I don't look the part. I look like someone who's only pretending, who's dressing up for a game. I look like someone who's only afforded service because of the company she's in. I look, really, like what I am: like the kind of person who's going to go home and change into comfy fleecy tracky bots. He doesn't.

We're shown into the dining room, which is as pretty and ornate—gilt, curls, a palpable opulence—as any I've seen. A bottle of champagne arrives with the manager's compliments, for the sexy young honeymooners.

'It's nice to be back here. It's a corny thing to say, but I really do love Paris, don't you, Robert? There's something so enchanting about it.'

'Remember our honeymoon?' Robert says, raising his glass to me for the second time this evening. 'Cheers. To Paris.'

'We were so young,' I say absent-mindedly. 'I mean, relatively speaking — people marry later these days. We were . . .'

'Twenty-four, five,' says Robert. 'Hardly spring chickens.'

'Oh, I don't know. I had no grey hairs. And I remember being rather overcome. You know, swanning around that posh hotel with the people with Vuitton luggage and big hair and me in my stilettos and little Lycra dresses . . .'

'And scarlet lipstick.' Robert smiles a sad kind of smile.

'Yes, and earrings as big as the Eiffel Tower. I looked like I belonged with the prozzies on the rue St Denis.'

'You looked great,' Robert says sombrely. 'We had fun.'

'God, didn't we?' I lapse into silence for a while. 'Funny how we'd never been back, until now.'

'Hmm,' says Robert. 'I didn't want to book us back into the Georges V.'

'Oh, no, absolutely,' I agree, nodding very quickly, because — hello — I am feeling very slightly tearful. He can think what he likes, but we were *young*. Young, dumb and full of hope.

'How's your hangover?' asks Robert. 'Will you drink some wine?'

'Absolutely,' I nod. 'Red. Especially,' I add, smiling and trying to lighten the mood, 'if you're going to insist on your *marital rights*.'

'You prefer to be drunk?' asks Robert. He doesn't look up. He is playing with breadcrumbs, brushing them one way, and then another, and lining them up, while perusing the wine list.

'Of course not,' I laugh. 'I was joking. Well, a bit. It's odd, you know, when you haven't done it for a while . . .'

'Hardly a very long while,' says Robert, still absorbed in the *carte des vins*. 'A few weeks.'

'Three months, actually.'

Robert says nothing.

'I wasn't in the bath,' I say.

'When?'

'Earlier. I wasn't in the bath. I didn't want you to come into the bathroom. So I said I was in the bath. Which wasn't true.'

'Why didn't you want me to come in?'

'Because I'm covered in boils,' I joke feebly, not entirely liking the direction I can't help steering the conversation towards.

'Why didn't you want me to come in?' Robert repeats.

'I didn't want you to think I looked fat, or plain, or . . . or homely,' I say sheepishly, folding a corner of my napkin into tiny little squares.

'I don't think that.'

I down the rest of my champagne in one.

'You were surprised, last night, weren't you?' I say. 'That I looked nice. That I looked — sexy.' I'm embarrassed to have said it, and cover up. 'Very sexy. Sexy laydee. Ha ha, Robert. That I looked *hot.*'

Robert doesn't smile and doesn't help me out. He pauses and then he says, 'Yes.'

'It's hard work, you know. It takes hours. I'd like to look like that all the time too, but I can't. Time . . .'

'I know. You have no time,' he says, sounding exceptionally bored.

This is not right. He isn't looking at me. I know what he is supposed to say. Perhaps I could say it for him. He could say, 'But I don't care, darling. You're always beautiful, to me. I love your face, you see, and I love you. I love the you in your face.' He could quote Yeats and tell me he'll love me, and my face, and my body, when I am old, and grey, and full of sleep. He could say — I'd say it, the other way round — that when you see someone you love, crying and sweating and shaking, looking very plain indeed, about to be wheeled into a theatre to give birth to your child — to your lovely child, that you made out of love—then nothing matters afterwards any more. No plainness. No lack of make-up. No looking sexy all the time. He made me a mother and I will always be grateful; he could murder me now, and I'd still say thank you for that. But then he took something away from me: his desire; my old self. My old self died when Charlie's wet, soft head appeared. I don't mind; I never did. But Robert would like it back. And it's too late. And it shouldn't matter, but it does.

'Robert?' I ask, and in the very act of asking find myself humiliated beyond humiliation. 'Robert, why don't you want to sleep with me?'

'Clara. For God's sake.' Robert lowers his voice to a sibilant hiss. 'It's been a few weeks, that's all.'

'Three months. It's never been three months before. A term. Quarter of a year.'

'Sometimes it has.'

'No, it hasn't.'

Robert changes tack. 'I hardly notice you bursting with enthusiasm,' he says.

'I'm scared of rejection.'

Robert bursts out laughing. 'Ohhhh,' he says, in a cod-American, self-help accent. 'Poor baby. Have you got in touch with your inner child recently, Clara? Really!' He laughs again. 'Scared of rejection! You *bite,* Clara. You're not scared. Of rejection, or anything else.' He actually looks up at me and beams, as if I'd made a really especially terrific joke.

'I wasn't joking,' I say. 'I am scared of rejection. Everyone is. I'd rather you didn't sleep with me than that I tried to make you and you turned me down.'

'You're not everyone,' he says, choosing to miss the point. 'You're a'—he winces at the word, but seems incapable of thinking up another one—'survivor.'

'For God's sake, Robert.' My temper rears up. 'No one wakes up in the morning out of choice thinking, Hello sky, hello trees, today I'm going to be a fucking *survivor.* Today

I'm going to pretend I'm all alone in the world, because that's the kind of terrific, fun challenge I enjoy. I am not a survivor, Robert, not by choice, and it is really completely moronic of you—after eight years! Eight YEARS!—to think I am. What kind of creature do you have me for?'

'A tough one,' says Robert hopefully.

'Toughened glass,' I say. 'Not shatter-proof.'

We take silent bites of our starters—something simple and aesthetically pleasing for him: a potato and truffle salad; something messy and all over the place for me: linguine with chunks of lobster, which match my burning face and smear my cheeks.

'It's what I like about you,' says Robert quietly.

'What is?'

'That you're tough. That you're not whingey. That you get on with it.'

'It's what you like about me?'

'Yes.'

'It's what you like?'

'Clara, please.'

'Well, you like the wrong thing. I don't want you to like me for that. You like me because I don't cry, basically,' I laugh, as one fat tear starts rolling down my cheek. 'Big mistake, Robert. You'd better stop liking me.'

'I'll never stop liking you, no matter . . . Don't cry, Clara.' He leans over and wipes my tear—why can't I muster up more? Torrents would be nice—with his scratchy linen napkin. I notice the cloth has mopped up some pasta sauce, as well as my tear. I was crying with a lobstery face. 'Please don't be sad,' he says.

'I am sad,' I say. 'And I am tired.'

'We could go up . . .'

'No! I mean I am tired of pretending that everything's okay. That this is what happens when you have been married for a time. That everyone goes through it. That it's okay and

193

normal and completely fucking *fine* for your husband not to want you. That it's fine, fine, fine for your husband to think you're *tough* and don't need any sleep or any help or God forbid any *support*. That it's *normal* for you to put me down . . .'

'I don't put you down.'

'Big Pig. Shops that do size 18. Pretending me telling you about my day makes you fall asleep. Letting the boys hurt themselves because you're listening to *opera*. Because *you're* tired. Ha! I could go on. That it's perfectly fucking *ordinary* never to talk about anything that matters. Like our children. Like choosing schools. Like the way you think it's funny not to know Charlie's teacher's *name*. Like why you wouldn't come to Somerset with me. Like . . .'

'I tease you less than you tease me, Clara.'

'I'm not cruel, Robert. Not to you.'

Robert puts his head in his hands as the waiter clears our starter away.

'It is normal,' says Robert. 'It's called marriage. We get on, don't we? We like each other. We potter along.'

'Spare me,' I shout. 'Spare me. I'm thirty-three. And so are you. I don't want to fucking *potter*. I don't want my children to have a mother who *potters* all by herself.'

'It's what people do,' says Robert quietly.

My fury melts away. 'I know,' I say. 'What's wrong with me?'

'You're selfish, Clara, and so am I.'

'Am I?' I wonder out loud. 'Am I that bad? Am I really freakishly, uniquely selfish?'

'Yes,' says Robert, giving me a terse smile. 'But you're not as bad as me.'

'I don't think I'm that bad,' I say, every iota of self-depre-cation deserting me. 'I don't think I'm that much of a mon-ster. I could do it, Robert. I could go on, and on, and on, for decades—till death us do part. I could do it, if I didn't feel so

. . . so by myself. So lonely. And,' I add, catching his expression, 'I know that sounds feeble, and wet, and repulsive. And self-indulgent. But I'm on my own, Robert, with you. All by myself, with you. You know that poem?'

'Christ. What poem?' Robert frowns. 'Do you really have to quote something at me now?'

I ignore him. 'I sleep with thee and wake with thee, And yet thou art not there; I fill my arms with thoughts of thee—and press the common air.' I take a sip of my wine. 'John Clare. I'm interpreting it wrong. But it's what I feel like.'

'I'm sorry,' says Robert. 'I'm sorry if you feel like that.'

'So am I,' I say. 'And I'm sorry you'd never noticed.'

'I hadn't,' says Robert. 'I just thought you had quite a nice time.'

'I did. I do.' Oh, never mind. I can't be bothered with this, I think to myself. I can do without the melodrama. I can do without feeling scared. Whatever. Never mind. It'll be okay. I say, 'Never mind, Robert. Let's just leave it. You know now, at any rate. Let's be glad you know and let's have a lovely weekend.'

'Okay,' says Robert, exhaling loudly. 'What shall we do tomorrow?'

'I don't know. Go to the Louvre? Go shopping? Go for lunch? Go to the flea markets?'

'I need to go to Versailles,' says Robert.

'Do you? Why?'

'To see about using a bit of it as a location for a fashion shoot,' says Robert, looking at his nails. 'I've been thinking about it for a while.'

'But it'll take hours. It'll take up the whole afternoon, Robert, and it's our last day. And we spent two days there the last time we were here . . . I'd rather go shopping,' I say.

'So would I, really, but this needs to be done. Why don't we split up?'

'Think of the children,' I say, flippant to the last.

Robert doesn't laugh. 'I don't know how,' he says bitterly. 'I meant tomorrow afternoon. Why don't I go to Versailles after an early lunch—go at 2, say—and meet you somewhere for tea? What's that pretty tea-room called, on the rue de Rivoli?'

'Angélina's. They make the best hot chocolate.'

'Yes, Angélina's. Why don't I meet you there at 5?'

'Hmm,' I say reluctantly. 'If you really have to go. It's only three hours, though, I suppose. And you get bored in make-up shops,' I add, brightening up. 'And in Prisunic.'

'I've never understood your fascination for stationery,' Robert says drily. 'I can think of better things to go into ecstasies over than exercise books.'

'It's partly the smell of clean paper,' I laugh, and so does he. 'And the feel of the pages. And the lovely colours, and lovely French pens.'

'Well,' says Robert, 'you can have a paper-fest, and I'll nip off, and we can go for tea and maybe early supper—the flight isn't till 10.'

'Okay,' I say, cheered by the thought of all those lined *cahiers* and notepaper and folders and biros. 'That's what we'll do.'

'Pudding,' says Robert.

'Sweetheart,' I say.

We both snigger amicably.

'No,' I say. 'Not for me. I'm tired. Maybe just coffee.'

'But you hate coffee,' says Robert.

And I don't say, Yes, but I'm scared of sharing a bed with you and I don't want to go up yet. I say, 'There's always a first time.'

twenty-two

I HAVE ANOTHER BATH, back in our extravagantly lovely, sexily luxurious suite. I read my book in the scented water; a nice book, in which nice people are happy pottering and forgive small affairs and big misdemeanours.

When I come out, an hour or so later, not wearing the black lace slip I had anticipated but rather an old pair of pyjama bottoms and a very loose T-shirt — it's not especially flattering, no — Robert is flicking between CNN and MTV, as men of his age tend to do. Am I young or old? they ask themselves with each press of the button. Am I still fun, or the kind of person who writes letters to newspapers? I want to be both, oh please let me be both. Flick, flick. Woah, baby. Flick. Oh good, the FTSE.

Nothing happens. I get into bed, removing the single, foil-wrapped Godiva chocolate that's been left on my pillow. I turn off my bedside lamp and wriggle down. I close my eyes. I am wide awake.

'Are you feeling better, Clara?' asks Robert, not taking his eyes off Brittney Spears' gyrations.

'Yes, thank you,' I say politely.

What would happen, now, if he got frisky? Would it help? No, to be perfectly frank with you, it wouldn't. There is such a thing as the kind of sex that heals all wounds, the kind of sex that repairs, the kind of sex that so floods you with intimacy that it forgives. But that's not the kind of sex we have. Which isn't a complaint as much as a statement of fact. We have the kind of sex that makes you laugh. Giggly, chummy sex. Pal sex. Well, that's not strictly true. At the moment, of course, we have no sex.

Later, much later, when I am still awake, though silent and closed-eyed, Robert finally puts his light out. He lies there stiffly — no, not stiffly in that way — and arranges his limbs into neat shapes. He smells of Extract of Limes and soap. His hand reaches out and strokes my hair. And then he sighs. Oh, such a sigh.

Things are always better in the morning. Always. Everything's worse at night: blacker, sharper, more final, more hysterical. And although I don't quite wake up filled with delirious, Pollyanna-esque joy, I get quite close. No hangover for starters. A morning's strolling and an afternoon's shopping; lunch at La Coupole. It could be worse, couldn't it? Christ, it could be worse. Everything could be worse, all the time. And that is the moral of the story. That is the thing to remember.

By breakfast time, I'm rather embarrassed by the previous evening's little outburst. Not so ashamed that I'd actually apologize, I decide on reflection — it's a close call — but ashamed all the same. I must have inherited my melodramatic streak from Kate. I can't believe I cried like that, like an imbecile, with lobster on my face. There was no need, I tell myself sternly, to nag and bitch and whinge. What did I think I was doing? What did I think was going to happen?

Anything, anything for an easy life.

Robert, on the other hand, isn't especially talkative this morning. He flicks through French *Vogue* at breakfast, gazing up at me silently every now and then. Perhaps he's comparing me to the models, I think, as I bite defiantly into an especially, reassuringly delicious brioche. Never mind. Never mind anything. I smile at his head; he looks up and smiles back. It's a funny sort of smile: wistful.

We wander around St Germain for a couple of hours, looking at paintings and overpriced antiques. We stop for coffee once or twice. We don't hold hands, I don't even hold his arm, but the pavements are very narrow. I make him go to a toy shop called, unattractively, the Blue Dwarf, and we buy little presents for the boys. I don't say anything annoying when Robert says, 'What does Jack like?'

Lunch is very civilized and almost calorie-free: ice-cold white wine and oysters, and a bracing sorbet for pudding. I feel rather Parisienne, with my little lunch-time regime. Robert reads a copy of *Glamour* which he has bizarrely brought with him all the way from London. I didn't realize he read all the French mags as well as the British ones.

He eventually tears himself away from the page. 'Where are you going?' he asks, with Gallic politesse.

'I'm just going to sort of roam about,' I reply. 'I haven't made a very detailed plan. Make-up and paper are what I'm really after, and maybe clothes.'

'Buy clothes,' says Robert. 'You have piles of make-up and piles of paper.'

'Maybe. I don't know if I can be arsed to try stuff on.'

'It's hardly exhausting. Here,' he says, peeling off a number of large notes from a fat wad of French francs, 'buy yourself a present, from me.'

'How sweet!' I cry. 'How kind, Robert. Thank you. I will.' I blow him a kiss. The elderly man at the table opposite, lunching alone, notices, and smiles at me. I smile back. My husband even gives me money for presents: a new blessing.

'Who are you smiling at?' asks Robert.

'That sweet old man, over there,' I say, 'behind you. He smiled when I blew you a kiss.'

'He probably saw me giving you the money,' Robert says.

'He probably thinks you're a prostitute.' It is his turn to smile.

No, I don't find it very funny either.

He goes off, rather regally, in one of the hotel's chauffeured cars. He is rather regally dressed to impress the no doubt über-snobs who run Versailles. He waves to me regally. Someone is going to lose their head, I think, bonkersly. Also: he might have offered me a lift.

I shop. I shop, and shop, and shop. I sniff and stroke to my heart's content in La Papeterie, my favourite stationers ever. I buy scent, something very grand and very old and Not Available in London, from the Guerlain boutique (I agree with Kate: modern scents all smell of plastic, or worse). I buy little snowshakers containing the Eiffel Tower for the boys. ('Do they need two presents?' 'Yes, Robert.' See? I even talk to him in my head. Because we are married!) I buy make-up, and have some of it applied at the Galeries Lafayette's Chanel counter: dark dark eyes, red red lips. I feel Frencher and Frencher, with my carmine mouth and empty stomach. I spy high, high, ludicrous, pink snakeskin shoes at Christian Loboutin, with a feather trim ('He thought you were a prostitute') and as I sit, trying them on, I think, for a second, of Dunphy's party. These aren't dancing shoes either, is what I think, and then I think: we danced very close. And then I buy the shoes.

More? Okay. I also buy a lighter with ladybirds on it; a plain black dress with a very low neck (*'Mon Dieu, comme c'est cher.' 'Oui, Madame. Mais c'est d'une beauté!'*); a silk lantern painted with almond blossom; a small, very sweet-faced stone tortoise; six scented candles (tuberose); Tintin socks for the boys ('Three presents?'); Fauchon biscuits for Robert's mother; a packet of Gauloises Blondes for me; a felt cloche hat (mistake); a second-hand volume of Maupassant short stories. I am laden with bags. I shop, and shop, and shop. Yes, I know it's nearly all for me.

And then it's 4.55 and I hail a cab to Angélina's. In the taxi, I put on the cloche hat, which is both unseasonal and not especially becoming, in the certain knowledge that it will make Robert laugh.

It's a long, narrow, crowded room, Angélina's, and not brightly lit—kind to the faces that have tea there regularly, I suppose; kind to ladies who are fading. I zigzag down the room, bashing my bags against the little gilt chairs, feeling like someone from the 1920s—except, of course, for my figure—in my new hat and new lipstick. It's a nice feeling, in a comical kind of way.

Robert is already there.

He doesn't laugh at my hat.

He doesn't smile, or say hello.

He says, 'Clara. Sit down.'

I say, 'I wasn't planning on standing throughout.'

'Listen,' he says, which is when I notice that he looks like he's about to vomit.

'Robert! Why are you ignoring my hat?' I sit down. 'Isn't it funny? Sort of funny, but nice? Look.' I turn my head, so he can see the hat in profile. 'I had my make-up done, Robert. I bought tons of things. I hope you don't mind. I wonder why Bic lighters are so sweet in France—look, ladybirds—and so dull in England. I bought the boys some things too . . .'

The ladybird lighter sits between us.

'Listen,' Robert repeats.

'What?' I say. 'What?'

'I have got a new job,' Robert says. 'Here. In Paris. I have just signed the contract. It becomes effective next Monday.'

I am stunned. My mouth opens, like a fish's, and shuts again. Then I say, 'What job?'

'Editing men's *Vogue*,' Robert says. 'It's called *Vogue Hommes.*'

'It's hardly going to be called *Vogue Chiens.* I'll have a hot chocolate and a *religieuse,*' I say to the waitress. In French, obviously. Thank God I speak it.

'Thank God I speak French,' I say.

Robert says nothing. *Robert ne dit rien.*

I reach for my cigarettes, and for my ladybird lighter, and as I fumble I become incredibly cross.

'You might have told me!' I say. 'You might have *said.*'

'Nothing was certain, until now.'

'You might have discussed it with me all the same. Christ. Fuck. I mean, where are we going to live? Where am I going to work? More to the point, where are the boys going to go to school? Oh, there's that English school, isn't there? But what if they're full? Oh, Robert, *really,* for God's sake. And what about our house in London? I suppose we'll rent it out?' My head is spinning. A voice says: Well, here's some excitement; be glad. And then another voice, a very tiny one, hisses, Oi, fuckwit, he wanted to come to Paris for a job interview. Not a sexy weekend with you, Miss Deluded. For work. See?

But I don't see.

And so I am very, very surprised when Robert says, 'No.'

I say, 'No? No renting? But I love our house. I don't want to sell it.'

Robert says, 'I am moving by myself. They've got me a flat. I am coming to live in Paris without you.'

And I still don't get it. I say, 'But why?' Ha! I actually say, 'But why?', all puzzled.

'Because I'm leaving,' says Robert. 'I'm leaving, Clara.'

Nothing goes black. Nothing spins. I don't feel dizzy, or bilious, or sick. I don't want to cry, yet, or shout. I say, quite quietly, 'But I thought we pottered along.'

'It's not what I want either,' says Robert. 'Pottering.'

'Do you love me? Or rather, when did you stop?'

'Of course I love you,' Robert sighs.

'Like a pet,' I say. 'You love me like a pet.'

'Yes,' says Robert, not unkindly. 'I suppose I do.'

'And it's not enough?'

'Not after last night. It made my mind up. It confirmed everything I've been thinking for months. Years, if I'm honest. Well, a couple.'

'I was hysterical,' I say hysterically, for which I could slap myself. 'Don't leave me because I was hysterical.'

'You weren't. You were right. I don't care about you enough. Not in the way you want.' He licks some crème patissière off his index finger.

'I don't want you to leave me,' I say.

'I'm sorry,' says Robert. And he gives a little comedy shrug.

'My babies,' I say. 'You're leaving your children.' I start crying now, properly. 'You're leaving your children,' I repeat. 'Like a *cunt*.'

Robert pushes his hands together, as if he were praying. Perhaps he is. What do I know?

'I know, Clara,' Robert says. 'But I'll see them every week-end. It's only a train ride away. They'll barely notice.'

Actually, this is true. But it doesn't help.

'You are a fucking *pig*, Robert,' I say. 'You are a fucking pig of *fuck*. Your head is so far up your arse you don't know you're born.'

Robert lights a cigarette. 'Oink,' he says, sadly.

Obviously, I try and leave the tea-room as swiftly and imperiously as possible, but am hampered by my large number of bags. As dramatic exits go, it's flawed.

My husband is leaving me. My husband of eight years. My shifty, secretive, sneaky husband is leaving me. I wonder whether he's having an affair. I will set fire to his clothes. I will ruin his life.

I am sobbing, and sobbing, and producing extraordinary quantities of mucus. I sob on the honeymoon bed; I howl on the loo. I feel ashamed, embarrassed, humiliated. My husband doesn't love me—doesn't even *fancy* me—and he's dumped me. What a cunt. What a cunt.

'You mustn't worry about money,' says Robert, a couple of hours later. He has let himself in and is taking off his suit jacket. 'Or the house. We'll put it in your name.'

'I wasn't worried about fucking *money*.'

'What, then?'

'Me. I was worried about me.'

'*Quelle surprise,*' says Robert.

Which I don't think is a particularly helpful remark. I mean, it is my life that seems to be collapsing around me. If I'm not allowed to wallow hippopotamically in self-pity at this precise moment, then I would like to know why. I should wallow more, in fact. I would be quite within my rights (marital) to slash my wrists in a warm bath, or pop my head into an oven for a while, if there were one, which, this not being a self-catering apartment, there isn't. All things considered, I don't think this river-of-mucus effect is *de trop* in any way. I think it's pretty self-contained, in the circs.

'Why?' I ask Robert, blowing my nose and, for once, not caring that I am incapable of doing so without sounding like a bassoon player. 'Why do you keep telling me how selfish I am?'

'You *are* selfish,' says Robert.

'In what ways, exactly? I mean, right now I am worried about a) the boys, b) my emotional well-being, c) what people are going to say—'

'Don't be so provincial,' says Robert. 'Who cares what people are going to say?'

'I do, arsehole,' I shout. 'I'm the one who's going to have to tell everyone—you, of course, being so fucking wet that you conveniently find yourself in another country.' Robert winces. 'I'm the one who's going to have to put up with the pitying looks and the speculation.' I'd stood up and started pacing, but the very thought of the forthcoming flood of pity —I really find pity exceptionally hard to take—makes me sit down again. 'I'm the one of whom people are going to say, "Well, of course, I've been thinking there was something wrong for a while now." I'm the one people are going to *feel sorry for,* and they'll say wanky things to me like "Be strong" . . . But that's okay, I suppose,' I sneer, 'because I am in fact so strong. Because I'm such a *survivor.* Because,' I sob, 'I never cry.'

'Clara, do stop,' Robert says gently. 'You'll be perfectly fine. And so will the boys.'

'It's like a bad dream, or a bad film. "Boys, Daddy and I love each other very much, but we can't be together any more." It's mad. They've never even heard us fighting. They'll think it's a joke. And so will our friends. They'll think I'm one of those women who can't function without a crisis—that I'm one of those sad bints who invent dramas out of nothing so they can feel their life is exciting and worth living.'

'You, of all people, should be able to work out a way of telling them. Ask Kate for advice, why don't you? And the thing is, Clara, that I never see the boys during the week anyway!'

'Unusually, for a father.'

'No. Quite normally.'

'*Very* unusually indeed, unless you're a night watchman. Most men manage a quick kiss before breakfast. Most men actually quite like the idea of coming home a bit early to give their children their bath once in a blue moon.'

'I'm not most men,' Robert says, which would be insufferable were it not for the heartbroken expression on his otherwise calm, white face. 'The point is, they only ever see me at weekends as it is, and that's not going to change.'

'They'll know you're not physically in the house, which is very unsettling, and which anyone could see if they weren't a self-obsessed arse. They're happy now because they may not *see* you, but they *know* you are there and that makes them feel safe. And now they won't feel safe any more. And I tried so hard'—the tears are coming again, oddly copiously—'to make them feel *safe*. That was all I ever wanted for them. I didn't care about anything else, about school reports or . . . or anything. *I wanted them to feel safe.* I wanted them to feel things were constant and unchanging and *solid*. Solid, Robert. And you'—I turn, screaming in rather a mad way, and stick my face right into his—'have fucked it up. You have fucked up the only thing I wanted for them.'

'I never made them feel safe,' says Robert quietly. 'Not them, not you.'

'They're little boys, Robert,' I shout. 'They're not aware of nuances. They felt safe because they had a mummy and a daddy and a nice house and some hamsters.'

'You're simplifying everything,' Robert sighs, walking off to find our suitcase. 'You make them feel safe. And you're not leaving.'

'As if I could! It's such a fucking luxury, Robert. And only you have it.'

'As if you'd want to, Clara, in a million years.'

I am lying down on the bed as Robert moves from the wardrobe to the suitcase, packing. He is packing very neatly. He is not chucking things in, but folding, smoothing, rolling up, inserting shoes into shoe-bags—he's like some American millionaire's Mexican maid, looking annoyed and swearing in Spanish because there's no monogrammed tissue paper to separate the layers of clothes.

I feel so sorry for myself that I think I might die. There is a terrible pain at the front of my head. I am curled on the bed like a creepy giant foetus, not actually rocking back and forth, but close. Robert is silent.

And then, suddenly, implausibly, I don't feel like I might die at all.

Yes, I know I'm supposed to be distraught for a good few weeks—months? years?—more, and lose a pleasing amount of weight as a result of being tormented, rendered sleepless, hungerless, *broken,* by agonies of pain. I'm supposed to find myself during these months or years, as if I'd been mislaid. I'm supposed to realize the importance of female friendship, and think all men are shits until, one golden dawn, I meet some sensitive little flower with a manly chest who proves to me that maybe, just maybe, there are exceptions. I'm supposed to join a gym. I'm supposed to buy a *dog.*

Well, I'm sorry, but I don't think so. There are, after all, limits.

I don't mean that, from lying there looking foetal and drowning in snot, I suddenly leap up, sing a song, dance a jig and race a lap of honour around the room. But a little light goes on. It says: oh, *do* stop whingeing. This is what you wanted. Okay, maybe you could have done without the humiliation angle — I agree, that sucks. But this is the natural culmination of everything, and the humiliation is the price you pay for trying to pretend. So stop pretending; don't pretend it came out of the blue, the idea of separating. Because you know perfectly well it didn't. You know perfectly well — yes, you do, liar — that it had occurred to you too. So come on, get up. Wash your face. Kate's voice pipes in at this stage: 'Darling, grim, I do see, but there's never any need to look *quite* so plain.' It's going to be okay. Of course it is. How could it not be? No one's died. It's going to be fine. Things could be worse, remember? Things could always be worse.

Robert has commandeered the suitcase. It is to be his suitcase, it turns out. We are a two-suitcase family. He was doing *his* packing; and then he ran down to the street to buy a new suitcase, an empty, brand-new suitcase, for me. And I packed it. He's not coming back to London with me — he 'can't face it, not right now'. He's booked himself into a smaller, cheaper hotel for a few nights. His apartment will be ready in a few days; I will send his things on. He has the *Vogue Hommes* Fed Ex number written neatly on a piece of Smythson card in his top pocket and he hands it to me. He will see us soon; not next weekend—he starts work the following Monday—but the weekend after that. He will phone tonight and speak to the boys.

The smell of airports always nauseates me slightly—diesel and plastic and rubber—but there's a smell of baking at Orly, a croissant smell, at 8.30 P.M. We sit and have coffee. I'm hungry.

'I'm sorry, you know,' says Robert. 'I'm so really and truly sorry.'

'Was there anybody else?'

'No, Clara. There was only ever you,' Robert says, and I believe him. The crotches of his suits are safe from my scissors. 'But it wasn't working any more, Clara, was it?'

'I don't know. No. I don't suppose it was. But I don't know what we're comparing ourselves against.'

'I want to be happy,' says Robert. 'And I want you to be happy, all the time.'

'Buy me a croissant, then,' I say, and Robert smiles the biggest smile of the last two days and does. He buys me two: one plain, one almond, wrapped in a napkin for the plane.

We say goodbye by Customs.

'I'm sorry,' Robert says again.

'Me too,' I say. 'For . . . whatever it was. For everything. Or nothing.' I laugh nervously—heeheehee, like in a comic.

'Don't be sorry,' says Robert. 'And kiss the boys for me,' he whispers, 'on their soft little heads.' He strokes my cheek with his hand and hugs me very tightly. 'Goodbye, Clara.'

'Goodbye, Robert.'

I've never seen my husband cry before. There's always a first time. And a last, I reflect, as he turns and walks away, and waves, and waves again, his fingers uncurling palely, slowly, strengthlessly. He does not turn around.

epilogue

Three months later

'WHY AM I DRESSED LIKE A GIRL?' asks Charlie.

'You're not dressed like a girl, darling. You're dressed like a pageboy. It's different. It's very special.'

'I'm full of flowers,' says Charlie, not entirely convinced. 'Flowers are girly.'

'Not always, Charlie,' I say. 'Anyway, it could be worse. You could be covered in Barbie-patterned pink fabric.'

'Aargh!' shouts Charlie, dizzy with horror.

'I look so so smart,' states Jack. 'I look so so smart. I love flowers. I love sniffin'.'

'Sniffing, Jack. Not sniffin'. You both look extremely smart,' I agree.

Kate has, wisely, desisted from picking the dress-the-children-as-dwarfs option so often favoured at weddings, when the bride appears followed by a retinue of sinister Oompa-Loompas in replica miniature-adult suits, like micro-publicans in burgundy nylon. The boys are wearing cream silk waistcoats, hand-embroidered with flowers, floppy, untailored silk jackets and loose matching trousers. (Jack nearly peed laughing when Max, Kate's intended, referred to these as 'pants'. Less impressively, so did I.)

'Come on,' I say. 'We're going to be late. Does anyone need to go to the loo?'

'No,' they both shout.

'Sure?'

'No,' says Jack. 'I am thinking.'

'Shoes on,' I say to Charlie.

'I've thought,' says Jack. 'I am going for a wee-wee. I will do the wee-wee standing up,' he announces, much as one might announce sawing a person in half for one's next trick.

'Hurry up,' I tell him, impressed by this new development. 'We're cutting it fine.'

'Is he meeting us at the church?' says Charlie.

'Yes, darling, he is.'

'Yay!' says Charlie. 'Can I sit next to him?'

'Perhaps,' I say. 'We'll see.'

Jack comes haring out of the downstairs loo. He likes peeing with the door open and so has overheard.

'Did you shake-shake?' asks Charlie concernedly. 'Remember, Jack, you have to shake afterwards.'

'I shaked,' says Jack. 'Mummy? I want to sit next to him,' he yelps, sounding grief-stricken. 'I want to sit on him. On the lap of him.'

'We'll work something out,' I say. 'Don't worry.' Then: 'Let's go,' pushing the children out of the door.

There's somebody else's confetti on the steps of Chelsea town hall. The steps are pastel with it: tiny dots of baby pink, powder blue, chick yellow. We race up the stairs and follow the Weddings sign to the registrar's office.

They're all there, waiting outside. Flo sweeps Charlie into her arms. 'I'm going to *shower* this boy with kisses,' she says, to his embarrassment and delight. Evie scoops Jack up and whoops her congratulations when he says, 'Hello, Auntie Evie. I do standing-up wee-wees.'

Max is here, and Tom, and Max's children, judging by

their nice teeth—a man and a woman, both looking alike—blond and wheaten—being friendly and introducing themselves to everyone. There are fifteen of us, all in all, including friends and witnesses.

Robert rushes in a few seconds later.

'Daddy!' the boys scream, flinging themselves around his neck.

'Hello, my darlings,' says Robert, squeezing them tight. 'I've missed you. I've got presents for you.' He looks up. 'Hello, Clara.'

'Hello, Robert,' I say, kissing him hello. 'How's tricks?'

'Not wildly different from the way they were when we spoke yesterday,' he grins. 'But great.' He stands up, one child on each arm, nearly collapsing under the weight. 'I still love the work, which is good, and I still love Paris.'

'We love it too, don't we, boys?'

'*Oui! Oui!*' the children squeal, and then collapse into a predictable heap of giggles.

Robert's company pays for us to take the Eurostar to Paris twice a month for the weekend, with Robert coming to London the other two weeks. Sometimes I don't go, but send Helena, our longed-for, lovely au pair instead. Helena has changed my life. And I know the boys love her, because they tell me so.

'I did a standing-up wee-wee!' Jack tells Robert, bursting with pride.

'And did you remember to shake-shake?' asks Robert, showing no sign of his customary fastidiousness.

'Robert!' I say, astonished. 'How do you know about shake-shakes?'

'I do wee-wees too, you know,' he laughs.

'I used to wonder what you did in the bathroom,' I tell him, smiling at the recollection. It feels a million years old.

'I shook-shook,' says Robert. 'And I'm teaching Jack to shake too.' He kisses Jack and ruffles Charlie's hair. 'They're really the sweetest boys,' he says. 'You've done a very good job, Clara. I'd never really noticed before.'

I smile at him. 'Thanks.'

Kate looks amazing. She is wearing a long, scarlet, sculpted column of a dress. There is a garland of wild roses in her glossed, shining hair. She walks, very slowly, towards us, holding her head very high, and comes to a stop by the children. She reminds me, not for the first time, of Audrey Hepburn in a couture gown.

'Good morning. What do you think?' she asks.

'You look *beautiful,*' says Jack. 'Like the queen.'

'The queen?' says Kate. 'I am not a German midget, darling,' she tells Jack, 'with a housewife's face. Am I?'

'No,' says Jack. 'I meant the queen in a story. The Snow one.'

'Much better,' she smiles, kissing his head.

'You look divine, Kate,' says Flo.

'I'm so proud of you, Kate,' says Evie, who is, I can tell, not going to be able to contain her wedding tears for very much longer.

'Wow!' says Robert. 'That's the best wedding outfit I've ever seen.'

'Hello, Robert darling, deserter of daughters,' says Kate. 'Do you think? I thought oyster, or maybe greige, but so gloomy, those colours—better suited to carpets, I think. In boarding houses. Run by women with very large breasts and *unsupportive bras.* Still,' she says, looking around her and beaming megawatt smiles at her friends and relatives, 'I didn't want to go too Whore of Babylon either. But I think the final result is rather chic, don't you?'

'Absolutely,' says Robert. 'It's divinely chic.'

'Yes,' says Kate. 'I utterly agree. Now, where is my groom?'

'Here,' says Max, who has appeared from nowhere in an impeccably crisp morning suit. He embraces her. 'You're a vision, Kate,' he says, with tears in his eyes. 'And I love you.'

Kate leans her Nefertiti-shaped head on his shoulder. 'Don't be *intimate* in front of the children,' she says, but very kindly, as she slips her hand into his.

Evie has started weeping, and I must say I'm feeling a little moist-eyed myself.

The ceremony over—no, Robert and I didn't catch each other's eye and shudder, quickly, with regret—we pile into waiting taxis, thoughtfully preordered by Max, and race to the church for the service of blessing. Two hundred guests will already be seated inside. I know from earlier that the red of the peonies with which Evie, Flo and I decorated the church will be glowing pinkly in the mid-morning sun. We walk down the path, a higgledy mass of hats and heels and flying hair.

Sam Dunphy is leaning against a tree, morning-suited, smoking a cigarette. The children spy him first, and race, arms outheld. By the time I reach him, they are holding on to his legs and begging him to hop.

'Oh, please hop,' says Jack. 'Please hop with us.'

'Oh yes,' says Charlie, *'please.* No one ever hops with us,' he adds, making a tragic face. 'Not a soul hops.'

Dunphy grins, and hops a couple of elegant hops to their excited screams. 'Hello, Clara,' he says, when we are close enough. 'And Robert. Hello.'

'Hello,' I say, and stroke his arm with one finger in greeting.

'Hello again. Nice suit,' says Robert, shaking hands.

'These are my sisters, Evie and Flo,' I say.

'Ooh,' says Evie. 'Clara, you total sauce. Oh, er, hello.'

'Evie!' says Flo. 'For God's sake. Hello. She has no manners, poor thing. I'm Florence. Conceived there, you know. Very romantic place. Made the parents *madly frisky.'*

'Really,' says Dunphy, grinning easily. 'It's great to meet you both. And where's Kate?'

'She's in the last car, she'll be along in a minute.'

'Evie,' says Flo, 'and Robert, and Mr Dunphy, why don't you all go in? Me and Clara need to discuss *arrangements*.'

'Oh no, no, we don't,' I say, knowing what's coming up.

'Yes,' says Flo, shooing them away. 'We do.'

They wander off down the path, Robert and Dunphy chatting animatedly.

Flo grabs me by the arm. 'Clara,' she says, not unlike Kate. 'Facts. Information. Goss. Tell. Spill every bean.'

'There isn't much to tell,' I say feebly, wishing Kate would hurry up.

'Kate said he was heaven, and he is,' says Flo.

'Hmm.'

'What are you doing introducing people to Kate at this early stage? Are you passionately in love?' She pauses for breath and gasps theatrically. 'I've just thought, Clara! Oh, *God*. You might be on the rebound. Oh, no.'

'I didn't introduce him. I introduced his friend Christian a couple of months ago. He just sort of *appeared* for coffee. And I am not rebounding, thank you.'

'The one she calls "Christian-My-Brother"?' says Flo.

'That's the one.' I laugh. '"Christian-My-Twin". I knew they'd get on.'

'And?'

'And what?'

Flo sighs. 'If you're not rebounding, are you, as I said, passionately in love? Is it madly sexy all the time and do you have to say, "Easy, tiger," because he's always going grr grr with, you know, sexiness?'

'Maybe,' I say. 'And maybe not.'

Flo sighs.

'Don't sigh, Flo. I don't need anyone to go grrr grr. I have my life back. I wake up and I want to laugh. And that's why I'm happy. And now we have to go in.'

'How glamorous,' says Flo, completely ignoring me. 'You could get divorced and married in the same day.'

'I could not!' I say. 'We haven't even slept together.'

'No!' says Flo, goggle-eyed. 'The sweetness! Like old people in films.'

I suppress the urge to giggle. 'I like him, Flo. He's my friend. He's the children's friend. Kate asked him today. And that's all.'

'The romance!' says Flo dreamily.

'Don't jump the gun, Florence, and stop talking in exclamations.'

'What about darling Robert?' says Flo.

'Darling Robert is blissfully happy. And he says he likes Dunphy. And I don't see any reason not to believe him.'

Kate's cream-coloured Bentley pulls up outside.

'Madly late,' she shouts. 'But *sweet* Father Bernard won't mind. Is everyone inside?'

'Yes,' I say. 'We'll go in now.'

'Is your boyfriend here?' asks Kate, stroking the nape of my neck like she did when I was a child.

I sigh. 'He's not . . .' I start saying.

Kate gives me a look.

'Perhaps,' I say, kissing her cheek for luck and taking her hand. 'Now let's get you married.'

'Fourth time lucky,' says Flo.

Which is, of course, always a possibility.